BROCKLEFORD FESTIVAL

The first of the Brockleford Chronicles

Helen Weygang

For Keiron and Judith (wherever you are) who gave me the whole daft idea in the first place

<u>Author's note</u>

This story is set in the summer of 1994 when the next Olympics would be in 1996 in Atlanta and athletes had to earn a livig, when the Royal Ulster Constabulary (RUC) was still the police force for Northern Ireland, when hardly anybody had a mobile phone and the internet was beyond the imagination of most people. A time of quiet naivety and long, hot days.

CHAPTERS

1. In which a young man caught in the rain moves in with a shy girl from Devon

2. In which an ageing composer meets a new muse

3. In which an accusation is made

4. In which a concert is attended

5. In which tea and cakes are served at a garden party

6. In which the weather turns unbearably hot but nobody goes swimming

7. In which the Festival is almost halted by a scandal

8. In which a book is finally launched and a fence pole is thrown

9. In which a cello sonata is ultimately performed on a trombone

10. In which the first touches of autumn turn minds to thoughts of farewell

CHAPTER ONE

In which a young man caught in the rain moves in with a shy girl from Devon.

Stella McGinty felt rather sorry for the young man who had just sat down at the other side of her desk. She guessed that when his red hair wasn't rain sodden and tied back with an elastic band it was quite magnificent, and when his dark blue eyes were laughing he was exceedingly handsome. In the meantime there he sat; rain-soaked, unsmiling and, frankly, somewhat miserable.

"Liam isn't it?" she offered briskly.

The young man blushed scarlet. "Yes. Liam McGuinness."

"Ah, another Mc. Is your family from Scotland?"

"Northern Ireland."

"Oh." Stella didn't like it when she got her regional accents wrong and the embarrassment sharpened her tone more than she had intended. "And what makes you want to come and work for a one-eyed music festival?"

This was safer ground for the wretched Liam. "I've played the cello since I was little and I've just finished a temporary job helping out with the admin of the local youth orchestra."

"In Ireland?"

"In Catford."

"I think you might find Brockleford a little quiet and parochial after Catford. I'm looking for two office juniors to help out just for this summer as this is rather a special year. It's not what you might call a dazzling career move."

Liam had already worked out that much but his need for escape was desperate. "The job would be good experience for me as I'm hoping to be able to train as an arts administrator eventually." His brain couldn't believe his tongue was telling such lies. He didn't have a clue what he wanted to do with his life.

Stella McGinty didn't remember such declarations about the future appearing on Liam McGuinness's application form. But then, life had been pretty hectic and she couldn't remember all of the candidates. A quick glance down at her desk did not reveal the requisite application. She was going to have to improvise. "How old are you, Liam?"

"Twenty three."

"And you graduated in?"

"Music. With honours."

"From?"

Liam wondered briefly whether Stella McGinty had read his form. She must have done, he assumed, she had called him for interview after all. But if he wanted the job he was going to have to humour her. "Jesus College, Cambridge. Sports scholarship."

"Cricket?" Stella hazarded desperately, trying to salvage some dignity

"Javelin."

"Oh." Stella allowed herself a brief, delicious image of this barbaric young man, red hair flying in the Irish wind, hurling a spear at advancing hordes of marauders. "And you want a career in arts administration?"

"Yes." Liam replied decisively but not quite quickly enough. There was a glitter of amusement in the eyes of Stella McGinty.

"This is a tiny festival in the wilds of the West Country; it is not Harrogate or Aldeburgh. We are fortunate, I suppose, in that we do have Ted Ellerby's name on the headed paper and this is very much his festival. You know his music well, do you?"

Edward Ellerby, Sir, CBE, OM; an ageing bastion in the world of composition and feared among young counter-tenors. "I know some of it. His fifth symphony for instance. I, er, sang in a performance recently."

Warning bells clanged in Stella's brain. She abandoned all pretence of nonchalance and dug out the application form from among the general detritus on her desk. Here it was. Liam McGuinness. Sings alto and plays the cello. Stella had taken to the rather shy young man with his red hair halfway down his back, and his huge, terrified eyes. She could not know whether he was reluctant to talk about his singing or whether he had heard the rumour about Ted and counter-tenors but either way that slight pause in his answer bothered her. A bit of gentle fishing was called for. "Are you married, Liam?"

There was a tinge of panic behind the puzzlement in his eyes. "No."

"Girlfriend?"

"Not any more."

"Boyfriend?"

It was at that moment Liam McGuinness knew the rumours about Sir Edward Ellerby and counter-tenors were probably true and he guessed it might be prudent to declare his sexual orientations right from the start. "I had a girlfriend from the day I went to Jesus until the day we left. She went back to Lewisham, I got the job in Catford and went to look her up but she'd moved away with no forwarding address."

Stella recognised a broken heart when one didn't introduce itself – she had had plenty of practice hiding one herself in the past. "Sorry." To her immense relief, her office door was flung open and her secretary tore in puffing slightly. "Ah, Sigourney, this is Liam, he's applied for one of the summer jobs."

Sigourney tossed back her bobbed dark hair and bestowed a dazzlingly false smile on the awestruck bumpkin. "So pleased to meet you! Do call me Sigs, everyone else does. So tell me, sweetie, why should we give you this job?"

Liam gulped and physically recoiled from the tall, elegant woman who swept round the room before settling herself imposingly in the second chair behind Stella McGinty's desk.

"Sorry I'm a bit late, Stella, dreadful queue in the bakery and I'm quite out of bread at home." She picked up Liam's application form, scanned it quickly then fixed her gaze on the suffering applicant. "Well?"

"Because I'd be good at it?" he offered desperately and glanced towards the door. Even as he looked at it, the treacherous piece of wood gently swung shut and the latch clicked. He had never been too sure about aggressive women.

"He's rather sweet isn't he?" Sigs proclaimed to the room in general. "Are you musical?"

"He's an alto," Stella told her and a meaningful look was exchanged. "Wants a career in arts administration," she added and smiled rather enigmatically.

"Oh hell, let's hire him," Sigs declared.

"Good idea. When can you start?"

Liam thought this was completely mad. Stella McGinty was the Director of the festival, Sigourney Hawkes was, he had gleaned from the literature they had sent him, her secretary. Still, it didn't matter to him who made the decision so long as it was the right one for him. "Soon as you like. I finished with Catford orchestra last week."

"Monday?" Sigs checked with Stella and the latter nodded. "Nine thirty. See you then. Show in the next one on your way out. I'll drop you a note about finding digs and such. Bye, Liam. See you on Monday."

Two women watched as the young man rose six foot four tall and walked so athletically from the room.

Sigs pulled an approving face at Stella. "That'll set the cat among the pigeons."

"You mean it'll upset the cat who's already got the monopoly in pigeons?"

"Quite. I think we're on the same wavelength with that one. Bit of all right, isn't he? Gorgeous bum."

Liam closed the door behind him and thought that perhaps he had dreamed the whole scenario. He noticed the brown-haired girl sitting bunched up on one of the uncomfortable chairs in the outer office.

"You the next one in?"

"I imagine so, if you're the last one out. Is it my turn?"

Liam nodded. He thought she looked rather frail and defenceless and thought a light conversation might help. "They're a funny pair, but I think they're harmless. Do you know anywhere to get some lunch round here?"

"No, sorry, I'm not local."

Liam had always had a weakness for large, green eyes that looked as though tears were about to fall. "Tell you what, I'll wait here for you and we'll go and find somewhere when you're done."

"Thank you. I must admit I wouldn't mind the company. What's your name?"

"Liam McGuinness."

"Nice name. I'm Julie Hutchinson." She smiled awkwardly, "which is really rather a boring name. Where in Ireland are you from?"

"County Derry."

"I'm from Devon."

Liam was about to try to get the chat moving by saying he didn't know a thing about Devon but Julie seemed disinclined to linger. She offered another shy, sad smile, and then bravely opened the office door.

*　　　*　　　*

When Stella McGinty next saw Liam she knew she had been quite right. His red hair, unleashed and curling all over the place was definitely magnificent and there were already some nudges and mutterings between the girls in the outer office. Enjoying every moment, but just a little bit disappointed that the resident musicologist was not back from holiday until that evening, Stella abruptly summoned Liam to her room.

"Good morning, I hope your digs are quite satisfactory."

"I haven't been in them yet. Drove up from London this morning. But I did contact the landladies as you suggested so all I've got to do is call in for the key sometime."

"You can do that right now. You're scheduled to help them all morning going through the photographs. I told you when I invited you to interview that this year sees the twenty-fifth anniversary of the revised version of Ted's second opera, didn't I? Well, we're a bit behind with the commemorative volume so it's all hands to the pump to get the pictures together. I'll get one of the girls to show you the way. Debbie!" Stella roared across the outer office. "Take Liam to the archive. Now. And don't stop off at the bakery like you usually do. Show him the village while you're about it. You're not expected until ten."

Debbie turned out to be very thin, very blonde and rather stupid. She smiled encouragingly at Liam and hadn't even escorted him from the building before she asked, "Have you got a girlfriend?"

For a brief second Liam contemplated telling a bald-faced lie. But then again, he was only in Brockleford for a few months so it really didn't matter. "Not at the moment."

"Oh good." Debbie hesitated. "Do you want to go along the high street past the shops all the way or do you want to go across the green and that way? We have to go along the high street for a bit anyway, it's just that Stella did say to show you the village."

Liam, who had been brought up with several sisters, had a rough idea what it would be like going past shops with a woman like Debbie. "Can we go across the green?"

"OK," Debbie replied without offence. She turned down the side of the festival offices and set off with sure steps along a narrow passageway that widened out to run between two rows of picturesque cottages. She vaguely waved an expressive arm at the tiny dwellings. "Brockleford's ever so pretty really. I've lived here all my life. Of course, this is the posh bit. I can't afford to live here and lots of the people are really old. Retired spies and such. But most of them are ever so nice. Where do you live?"

"Labrador Cottage," Liam supplied as he walked beside Debbie past windows lower than the level of his eyes.

"Oh, Lotty and Dotty's spare house. You are lucky. Is it nice inside?"

"Haven't been in it yet."

"Oh. I'll point it out to you as we pass." Robbed of conversation in Liam's presence, Debbie walked on in silence and hoped they wouldn't meet her boyfriend. He would never understand that she was walking secluded alleyways with this very attractive redhead because her boss had told her to. The two popped out of the passageway and the village green opened out in front of them. Liam looked at the church beside the triangular green and noted the painted cottages and the neat gardens.

"That's Labrador cottage." Debbie announced, obviously proud of her knowledge. "The pink one."

Liam couldn't fail to notice the cottage at one end of the terraced row opposite the church as it had a cast iron two-dimensional Labrador screwed above the front door, forever pointing out across the fields beyond the cottage, and the name painted in three inch high letters on the garden gate. He thought how incongruous it looked painted pink at the end of a row of cream cottages. With dread visions of profusions of chintz and other country cottage delights he asked his guide, "Any idea what it's like inside?"

"Don't know. I've never been in it. All battered old furniture I should imagine if it's anything like Lotty and Dotty's own house."

Chintz was mentally replaced with melamine and chipboard but Liam had promised the Misses de Grys he would be renting their cottage and had even sent off a cheque for a month's deposit in advance. Sigs had made it sound quite nice, too. He supposed seekers of sanctuary couldn't be too fussy about their eventual destinations. He looked away from the cottage and realised Debbie hadn't stopped walking.

Debbie marched straight across the green, not bothering to skirt the cricket pitch as Liam did, then shot into another narrow passageway. The flagstones of this alley were shaded by the church and the moss was still a little slippery after all the recent rain. Liam steadied himself with a hand on the church wall but the flints were sharp and cold to his touch. Brockleford, it seemed, looked very pretty but was singularly hostile to the unwary.

"Is that your real hair?" Debbie asked next as she skipped down a flight of steps at the end of the alley.

Liam's size ten feet had more of a problem with the narrow steps and he was thankful to arrive at the bottom without twisting an ankle. "Yes."

"It's lovely. Do you mind if I touch it?"

The refusal hadn't got from his brain to his lips before Debbie had run her slender fingers through the tempestuous curls and nearly wrenched half his hair out by the roots as it was so knotted.

"Dear me," she giggled. "Can I lend you my hairbrush?" She wasn't the slightest bit put off by his lack of reply. Most good looking men, she had found out, were incredibly sulky. It never occurred to her that they were, perhaps, sometimes rather shy.

This alley led into the high street. Liam knew it was the high street because Debbie's rate of walking slowed dramatically and there were shops on both sides of the road. He thought it might be useful to see what retail outlets were on offer.

"When's early closing day?" he asked his guide who had been sorely distracted by some jewel-coloured sweaters in the window of the ladies' outfitters.

"Wednesday. And market day's on Thursday." Debbie caught a glimpse of the two of them side by side reflected in a shop window. 'If only,' she thought, and allowed herself a hedonistic image of Liam McGuinness, red hair all over the place, prostrate on her bed. "Most of the shops are here and everything," she explained kindly, dutifully fulfilling the role of guide as she perceived it. "The bakery's ever so good. I go in there nearly every day for something." The expected expression of surprise and compliment on her slender figure never came. "I like the needlework shop too," she added in case the taciturn Liam McGuinness thought she was rather greedy.

Liam felt obliged to make an effort as all this dawdling through shops was evoking some memories he would rather forget. "Do you sew?"

"Knit mostly." To prove her point and to show how flattered she was that he was taking an interest, Debbie paused to look in the window of the needlecraft shop, quite unaware that her companion was not very happy about this. She thought she'd better not push her luck by going in for that pink cotton. Stella wouldn't be too pleased if she went back to the office clutching a bag of yarn. She tore herself away from temptation. "There's another small grocery just up there beyond the florist and there's a good fish shop back towards the offices that's a chippie in the evenings. There's a supermarket out of the village a bit and a brilliant Chinese but you'll need a car to get there. Have you got a car?"

"Yes." Liam replied politely, glad his guide was setting off again even though Debbie's local knowledge was useful.

"What sort?"

"A green one," he offered, guessing his companion wasn't too bothered about technicalities.

"That's nice, I like green, and it must suit your hair." Debbie looked at the clock on the market cross and forgot it was ten minutes fast. "Help! We're going to be late. Come on." She grabbed Liam's wrist as though he had been a truculent child but he didn't let her hang onto it for long. Debbie said not another word for the rest of their walk.

The high street petered out into a country lane. At the speed derestriction signs Debbie turned left along a cart track which had a vicious blackthorn hedge on one side, protecting an obviously private golf course. Way above the fairways and the bunkers the exclusive club house stood with its lounge windows facing the town and the morning sun reflected off the panes like the unseeing eyes of a jealous god.

"Here we are!" Debbie announced rather too brightly.

Liam looked up at the tiny leaded windows and thatched roof of Last Chance Cottage and wished for a more propitious name.

"I'm sure either Dotty or Lotty will show you the way back." Debbie banged on the door with her fist then almost ran away and didn't look back.

Liam guessed she was a bit upset that he hadn't let her tow him along the street like an idiot. He took a deep breath and listened to the shrieking in the cottage. It was all a far cry from Catford.

"No! Get back! It's only someone at the door! Stay! Sit! I said SIT! Oh, flaming Norah! Dotty, get the door will you?!"

"Can't, sorry, got fox poo all up my wellies after Lady finished rolling in it. Can't be anyone important. You go."

"I can't. Billy just won't let go of my cardigan."

"Oh, hell." Footsteps shuffled closer to the door. "Who is it?" bawled a hostile voice.

"Liam McGuinness. Stella McGinty sent me along to help with the photographs."

"Oh, lor'! Sorry, dear, quite forgot. Do come on in, excuse the smell of foxes but Lady's been rolling in it all over the golf course."

The blue-painted door was flung open and Liam nearly gagged on the stench of fox but guessed it would be polite to step into the house anyway. He ducked under the roof beam and just about managed to stand upright in the tiny hall. "Hullo. Sorry, is this a bad time?"

"Not at all. Just let me get out of my wellies and we can get on. Do go on into the music room."

Liam followed the direction of the vaguely waving arm and located a room at the back of the house where the sunlight danced on a baby grand piano. In the conservatory beyond, a black Labrador basked near the windows among a sea of half-dead geraniums and fledgling tomato plants with her back to a tiny garden that seemed to be all apple trees and bare earth.

"Hullo!" cried a voice behind him and Liam turned to confront a rather short but wide lady who held out some keys on one finger. "Labrador cottage keys before I forget. I've shut Billy away in the car so you'll be quite safe. The photos are all in the attic so come along and you and I can get stuck in. I'm sure Dotty will make us some coffee in a minute just as soon as she's hosed down her wellies."

Liam knew that if he didn't ask he would hate himself for ever. "Doesn't Billy mind?"

"Good heavens, no. Billy's our Jack Russell. Bit old and cantankerous now, like his owners. Doesn't go much for men. That great lump over there is Lady; she'd lick you to death soon as look at you. Right, up to the attic with you. Got any dogs?"

"My family have a couple."

"Really? What breed?"

"Water spaniels."

"Oh, they can be a bit smelly, can't they? Still, I suppose it would be that or setters judging by your accent. Northern Ireland?"

Liam didn't like the accusation in her voice. "County Derry. Little hamlet at the foot of the Sperrin mountains."

"Sounds quite charming." There was an awkward pause and Lotty de Grys was afraid she had put her foot in something. To her relief this rather frightening young man seemed pleasantly shy after all. She was never too sure about men who had such long hair. Always made them look a bit ruffianly somehow. She decided against demanding an autobiography just yet; Liam McGuinness had his secrets by the look of him. "Attic," she reminded them both a little more kindly.

Liam followed the bustling posterior up a narrow flight of stairs barely wider than his shoulders and into a large room with a sloping roof and dormer windows which peered myopically out from the thatch. Everywhere there were papers.

Papers in proper files, papers in produce boxes, papers in carrier bags and papers just in heaps. Scattered on this ocean of papers were the flotsam of photographs. Black and white prints jostled with colour prints and sheets and sheets of slides.

"Welcome to the Ted Ellerby archive." Liam's guide said proudly. "Now sit yourself down and I'll explain it all to you."

There was nowhere to sit. Liam looked around wildly for an instant then realised he had no option but to copy his hostess. He shoved his hair back over his shoulders and sat crossed-legged on the bit of threadbare carpet exposed like an uninhabited island in the middle of a raging sea.

*   *   *

By half past five on that Monday afternoon, Julie Hutchinson was ready to cry. She had spent the whole day filing little bits of paper away, most of them in triplicate if not sextuplicate. Nearly all of them undated which made it doubly hard to file them chronologically as she had been instructed to do. As if that hadn't been enough, there had been all the chatter in the office. The only names she had heard all day were those of Ted Ellerby, Liam McGuinness and Nick Greenwood. One she had been brought up to revere, one had once sat shyly beside her in the village pub over a bowl of scampi and the third she had never heard of until that morning. Nick Greenwood, from what she could gather, was the only unattached man in the village under the age of fifty. Conductor of anything amateur from the choirs and orchestras to ladies' affections. He seemed to have dated most of the female population of Brockleford under the age of thirty five except for Sigourney Hawkes who was surprisingly dismissive of the festival's musicologist.

Sigs had been to the bakery and bought doughnuts for everyone, obviously in the hope it would loosen the new girl's tongue, but Julie guarded her secrets closely. They weren't going to learn from her anything about the suspected infidelity of her boyfriend in the Amy, her parents' recent divorce, or any of the other neuroses that still kept her awake at night. She guessed they would dismiss her as a sulky bitch but she really didn't care. All she wanted to do was get away from the whole awful mess for a few months.

She was glad to get back to Labrador Cottage which she had rented for the summer. It was a pity it was all pink paint outside and rosebud-sprigged wallpaper inside but she guessed she could live with that for a while. The front garden was a mixture of quarry tiles and herbs and seemed to be pretending that it was somewhere in the Mediterranean rather than facing a very English church across a village green that still had its aged horse chestnut trees. An irritating spurt of water dribbled down the chops of an oxidised lion's face splattered crookedly into the yellow brick wall at one side of the garden and Julie made a mental note to find the switch that would turn it off. She was momentarily curious about the green Saab outside but guessed it belonged to one of the more affluent residents. All she wanted at that moment was to have a bath, wash her hair and then see about a bite to eat before settling down with the radio and her cross-stitch. She was startled, and not best pleased, to fall over a cello case in the hall. The sound of her hitting a wall brought a familiar face out of the living room.

"Oh, hullo. What are you doing here?" she asked politely and made a point of putting the key in her pocket.

"I could ask you the same," the Irish tones challenged.

"I've rented the cottage from Miss de Grys for the summer."

"Well now, there's a funny thing. So have I. I wondered whose stuff that was in the front bedroom. So, Miss Hutchinson, shall we share?"

Julie really couldn't see why Liam was so amused. "Those stupid, stupid old women! I bet they let it to me and then forgot and let it to you as well. I can't stay here, I mean, what will the neighbours think?"

"The neighbours don't know us from an alien from Mars. There are two bedrooms and a bathroom, all with locks on the doors. Besides which I have neither the mental nor physical energy to find somewhere else to live. But I think it might be a good idea to tell our landladies that we are not paying two lots of rent."

Julie wasn't too sure but she had had a long day too. "Well, all right. What do you want me to cook for supper?"

"Now why should you be getting all sexist about this? I'll go throw some more potatoes in the pot and we can eat in about half an hour if you want to have a bath or something."

If Julie had known Liam better, she would have flung her arms around his neck and wept tears of gratitude on his shoulder. "That would be lovely. Thank you."

"Go have that tub. You're not a veggie, are you?"

"Not quite." Julie escaped to the bedroom at the front of the house and checked the bolt on the door.

*   *   *

They eventually found the switch that turned off the incontinent lion and they brushed the dead woodlice and leaves off the rather rickety bench under the living room window so they could sit side by side and look out across the green. The village was quiet, drowsing under the first stars of the warm May evening. There was a dog barking somewhere but the two siting in the Mediterranean garden hardly heard it. They hadn't conversed much over their meal. Liam had been somewhat taken aback to find out Julie had quite a sharp tongue in her head when she chose to use it. She had been quite shy and uptight when they had shared the scampi in the pub.

Julie thought Liam was a bit whimsical but that suited her mood. He certainly wasn't the flamboyant Romeo his looks suggested and she began to think that maybe it would be alright to share a house with him for a few months. She gathered from the little he had said that he had spent a rather boring day in the attic of the Misses de Grys and she wondered if they had told him about the social scene.

"Have you been invited to play in the local orchestra?" she asked and Liam jumped. He had been miles away and the sound of her voice startled him.

"Haven't been invited to do anything," he replied and didn't mean to sound so grumpy.

Julie loved to play music but didn't want to go by herself. "Tuesday evenings, apparently. I said I'd maybe go along. Why don't you come too?"

Liam wished she would leave him alone. "What do you play?"

"Oboe. I've been invited to sing in the church choir too. Apparently they're short of altos. Do you sing?"

Liam looked across the green to the forbidding church and remembered the times he would have been terrified of the priest back home castrating him if he stepped through such pagan portals. It was too complicated to explain that he really didn't want to get involved in whatever social life Brockleford had to offer. All he wanted was a sanctuary. No choirs, no orchestras and no entanglements with the opposite sex. "Not in churches."

"We could try the orchestra?"

Liam knew it had been a bad idea to bring the cello, but there hadn't been anywhere else to leave it short of shipping it back to Ireland. "Maybe."

"Good evening!" cried a voice at the gate. A portly young gentleman, nearer to forty than thirty, pushed open the garden gate and strode in, holding out a greeting hand as he came. "Nick Greenwood. Just thought I'd drop by and welcome you as I'm passing on my way to take choir practice. Stella tells me I've got a couple of altos with you two so come along." He looked Julie up and down, paid particular attention to her upper anatomy and her wrists and then smiled charmingly. "Or would you rather get settled in your first night here? I must say that nobody warned me you two are an item."

"We're not," Liam pointed out, having none of Julie's intuition.

"Really?" came the approving purr. "I suppose those idiot old women told you both that you could rent the cottage. They did that once before as I remember and it finished up with the police getting involved. Anyway, do at least come and listen. We're working on Hayden's *Maria Theresa* for a concert in the festival. Either of you know it? Of course, Ted keeps promising us a special commission but there's no sign of that yet. Have you met Ted? Charming chap. He's away in Germany at the moment."

Julie had the feeling she had offended Liam somehow and got rashly to her feet. "I'll come if you like. I love the *Maria Theresa*. Not promising to sing this time though."

Liam almost had to put his hand on his upper lip to stop it curling. Right goody-two-shoes this Julie Hutchinson looked like being.

"Can I persuade you along too?" Nick asked the other man and looked disapprovingly at the breadth of his shoulders and the length of his legs.

Liam couldn't think of a plausible excuse quickly enough so he just shook his head and smiled apologetically.

It never occurred to Julie that Liam wanted to be left alone. She thought he was just being bashful and needed a bit of prompting. "I'm sure Liam would like to play in the orchestra. He's a cellist."

"Really? Now that is interesting. If there's one thing this place hasn't got it's a half-decent cellist. See you tomorrow then, Liam."

Liam watched them go. Proper little traitress that Julie had turned out to be. He was going to have to watch his step with her after all. Nick and Julie walked side by side across the green with Nick still pontificating about something. And they hadn't even asked if he was a good cellist. Just assumed. As people always did. Liam went disgustedly back inside the cottage and, as there was nothing else to do, went to find his running shoes.

*   *   *

Dotty and Lotty were tussling with Billy and Lady on their early morning walk the next day when a half-familiar figure pounded past them across the golf course.

"Good heavens!" Lotty exclaimed, "I do believe that's young Liam. My, he must be fit. Must be what comes of having water spaniels. Nice lad, but he doesn't say very much."

Dotty finally worked out the direction in which Lady had left her pointing. "Someone's upset him. You can always tell the sort. Had hundreds of heart-broken teenagers in my classes over the years."

Lotty's pupils had been about ten years younger than those of her sister, but even infants had had their problems. "Could well be. Oh no! Billy's seen that cat again. Billy! Come here! Come here when you're called!"

Stella McGinty was just bringing in the milk when the sound of running footsteps made her look up from her doorstep. Liam McGuinness was approaching her front gate at such a speed she guessed he must be pretty fit but she was no respecter of training routines. She knotted her dressing gown sash a little more tightly and physically halted the young man as he drew level with her privet hedge.

"How did you get on with those two yesterday?"

Liam's eyes lost their dreaming look and he focussed on her with almost a scowl. "Oh, OK. I've got some pictures to bring in later."

"Good-oh. Ted's back from Germany today so I'll take you and Julie along to be introduced. Did you say you've got a car?"

"Yes."

"Right, you can take me and Sigs to the publishers later this morning." She could no longer ignore the fact he was sweating profusely even if he was barely panting. "Been for a jog?"

"Training run. Five miles."

"Oh. Every day?"

"Twice a day. Longer at weekends. Couldn't bring the javelin with me but I can do the more general training."

"You're serious about this javelin thing then?"

"I should get back in the British team next year but this year I need to earn money."

Stella was impressed. "Well, good luck to you. Sorry, I thought you'd just been jogging round the block. Won't stop you again. See you later."

Liam was thankful to have escaped without the interrogation which he was sure Stella McGinty was more than capable of. He got a bit lost somewhere in the various alleyways but the tower of the church guided him back to the green and to Labrador Cottage. Julie was dozing at the kitchen table, her nose nearly in her bowl of cornflakes as she sliced a banana on top of them.

"Been jogging?" she asked. "Want some coffee?"

"I'll do myself some tea in a minute. Don't worry about me."

After a shower, Liam felt half human again and he trotted down the stairs with his hair dripping water all down the back of his shirt. Julie was eating the cornflakes but clearly the crunching of the flakes was causing her some discomfort.

"How was the choir?" Liam asked politely as he made himself some blackcurrant tea.

"Dire. Full of geriatric old ladies wobbling somewhere off the top of the stave and a few old men who were more mezzo than tenor. They've got a bass who's not too bad. I think Nick said he's the postman, or milkman, or something. I'm sorry, I think I've just eaten your banana."

Liam was beginning to wonder if Julie wasn't well. "Doesn't matter. I've got some apples somewhere."

"Sorry, I'm not very good in the mornings. I'd better go for a wash."

Liam watched her trail from the kitchen and had to remind himself sternly that this sleepy kitten was the same tigress who had more or less promised he would go and play in the orchestra. He hardened his heart against her and started looking for the apples.

* * *

It was a silent walk from Labrador Cottage to the offices of the Brockleford Festival that morning. Liam didn't like to push Julie to talk and she was grateful for the peace. Neither of them felt inclined to navigate the alleyways so they took the direct, if slightly longer, route along the green then down the length of Oxford Road where the offices were situated.

Julie wandered dispiritedly over to the heap of papers waiting to be filed while Liam hovered uncertainly near Sigs' desk with a bundle of photographs in his hand.

Sigs snatched the photographs without interrupting her telephone conversation and Liam wasn't sure whether he had been dismissed or not. Sigs was smiling into the receiver, but there was something reminiscent of the fabled smile of the crocodile in the way her lips were drawn back. Her next words worried the young man standing rather foolishly beside her desk.

"Yes, Lotty sweetie, he's right here now…Of course I'll tell him." Relief soon followed. "Yes, I do understand about Billy and the delivery man…Of course we won't expect to see you this morning…Yes, dear, I hope you get your cooker too. 'Bye Lotty."

Sigs threw the receiver back on to the telephone and awarded Liam a flash of her teeth. "Liam, you are a star! There is no other word for you. You've so bowled over Lotty and Dotty they want you back at the cottage today to help them with their sorting out."

Liam felt a bit cheated that he was to be fobbed off with the company of the two batty old women again.

Sigs saw the look of disappointment on Liam's face and felt a twinge of sympathy. She thought it might be kinder to make excuses. "Nick's writing programme notes today which always puts him in a foul mood and besides which Debbie's been spreading the most awful gossip about how his date last night ran out on him. So all in all things won't be too pleasant round here."

Liam was thinking of a morose young woman eating his banana and hoped Nick hadn't overstepped the bounds of decency with Julie. "And who was the date?" he thought to check before he appointed himself champion of his fellow tenant.

"Oh, goodness knows. Some silly tart he picked up somewhere. Not too fussy, our Nicholas. Oh, before you go, do pop along to see Phyllis, she was yelling for your P45 all of yesterday. You do have a P45, don't you? Turn right out of here and go to the end of the corridor. You can't miss her."

31

Liam knew this time he had been dismissed. He paused for a word with Julie at the filing cabinet but didn't know where to start. A gentle enquiry seemed a good opening gambit.

"You all right with that lot?"

"Yes, fine." Julie looked up at him and smiled wryly. "You heard about me and Nick then?"

"Something along the lines of 'he offered, you refused'?"

"Something like. I'll buy you a banana from the shop over the road at lunchtime."

"I don't begrudge you a banana, honest."

"I insist. Did Sigs tell you to go and see Phyllis? I got cornered by her yesterday. She's very nice. Apparently she's the doctor's wife."

Bolstered a little by Julie's reassurances, Liam set off along the corridor. The offices of the festival were in what had once been the first floor of an old coaching inn and Liam's footsteps were muffled on the faded elegance of the carpet. He found Phyllis' office by the sound of the adding machine whirring but even though the door was open he thought it best to knock.

"Come in!" barked a rather hoarse voice. Phyllis Bond turned off her personal fan and looked despairingly at the young man in her doorway. She thought he looked a slob with that mane of red hair half way down his back and it wouldn't have surprised her in the least to see he had rings in his ears and a stud in his nose. Such seemed to be the predilections among the young. She looked as best she could but apart from a slightly frayed leather bracelet on his left wrist he appeared to be wearing no ornamentation, not even a watch she noted sadly.

There was something not quite respectable about a man who didn't wear a watch. His jeans and sweatshirt bordered on shabby and he really didn't look the kind of young man she would want to meet in an alley on a dark night. "Ah, so you're Liam McGuinness. Got your P45?"

Liam thought the room was rather cool for Phyllis to be fanning herself but he had been brought up to be polite so he didn't say anything as he handed across the dog-eared piece of paper from the back pocket of his jeans.

"Dear me, what have you done with this?" Phyllis took the paper gingerly in her long fingers and glanced at it. "London Borough of Lewisham. Funny, Stella told me you're Irish. What were you doing in Lewisham?"

"Just a temporary job."

Phyllis had never cared much for the Belfast accent. She found it slightly less comprehensible than the Glasgow and even that often required the services of a translator. She didn't have the energy that morning to try and have a conversation. "Well, nice to have met you. I gather you're at Last Chance Cottage again today." Phyllis looked beyond the ragamuffin in her doorway and her face broke into a beam. "Morning, Nick. How was the holiday? Did you get back in time for choir practice?"

Liam left them to it. It would appear Mrs Bond may not choose to have time to gossip with the new boy but she certainly had her favourites. He wasn't normally given to eavesdropping but Nick's well-educated tones carried easily along the corridor.

"Oh God, you should have heard them. I invited that Julie Hutchinson along to make up the altos. She was dreadful. Then when I offered to buy her a drink in the pub afterwards she ran out on me. Never seen anything like it."

"You off to Lotty's then?" Stella asked Liam as she passed him in the corridor on his way to the stairs.

"Yes."

"Well, good luck. Look out for Billy. Been to see Phyllis yet?"

"Just now."

"Good lad." Stella watched the young man walk away from her and admired that tail of red hair. "Damn!" she muttered half aloud. "Blasted publishers today." She saw Julie was hard at work with about ten years' worth of filing but passed no comments. She was rather surprised to have Sigs shoot into her office hard on her heels and close the door.

"Heard the latest?" Sigs asked eagerly.

"Probably not."

"Dotty and Lotty have double-booked Labrador Cottage again. Liam and Julie are sharing it. Think anything will come of it?"

Stella still remembered what had happened last time but this was a much more inviting prospect. She thought for a few moments. "Doubt it. Couple of shy rabbits like that? It'll be August before they say 'Good morning' to each other."

"Bet you a tenner?"

"Done."

CHAPTER TWO

In which an ageing composer meets a new muse

Liam was better prepared for his second day at the Edward Ellerby archive. He had put on old clothes so it didn't matter that he had to sit on the floor and he had already learned that there was no logic to the filing system in that attic. Lotty set him to work taking bits of paper out of the carrier bags and transferring them to produce boxes each proudly labelled with the name of a Ted Ellerby composition. The work wasn't hard and he had plenty of time to think about the chain of events that had brought him to Brockleford. If he focussed his eyes on the horizon he could just make out the mountains of Wales. It had been a long time since he had been near any mountains and he wasn't sure he was glad to be so close to them even if it was for only a few months.

Lotty de Grys was somewhat taken aback when her helper turned up in clothes not even fit for the charity shop. She was not a great believer in putting on one's best dress to crawl around the floor, but she thought he might have done a bit better than old jeans and a scruffy sweatshirt that had a mended tear in the left sleeve. She couldn't fault his work. He was certainly diligent and quick when it came to putting those cuttings and programmes in the right boxes and she began to dare to go back ro her dreams of a catalogue as the two worked in silence.

Dotty brought them up some coffee in the middle of the morning. "Have you explained to Liam about the catalogue?" she asked her sister.

"Not yet. He's only just about learned where the pieces of paper go," Lotty responded rather tartly, not yet willing to share her ambition.

"We're going to catalogue all these," Dotty told Liam proudly. "Lotty's bought hundreds of those little cards so it'll be just like a proper library."

"The idea is to compile as complete an index of performances as we can," Lotty supplemented realising she had no option but to elucidate before her woolly sister got it all back to front somehow. "Maybe you'd like to help us out with it? I don't suppose you know what Stella's got lined up for you at the office?"

Liam could think of nothing worse than having to write out thousands of index cards and thought the sisters would do better to invest in a computer and a database which so far as he could tell was the way things were going. At least they had been in Lewisham. Still, it was only for a few months. "Be glad to help," was the best he could manage. "Would you like to ask Stella?"

"I'll have a word when I go in tomorrow," Lotty promised, not failing to note the dread expression on Liam's face, but not sure if it was thoughts of a card index or of asking Stella that had caused it.

"I thought I'd make some bread this morning," Dotty offered vaguely going off at her own peculiar tangent as was her wont.

"Is that a good idea?" her sister enquired mildly, resolving to resume the matter of the catalogue when Dotty had gone again. "The new cooker's due today."

"Yes, I know, dear, but at least if I get the bread going then there'll be something to put in it when it comes. Would you like a loaf, Liam dear?"

"I don't want to put you to any trouble," Liam tried hopefully, dreading something more akin to a house brick than the staff of life.

"No trouble at all," Dotty assured him. "Would you like it with sun-dried tomatoes, black olives or walnuts? The nuts are off our own tree. I always use organic flour. Or you could just have a plain one. Wholemeal or granary?"

"Tomatoes sounds great, thank you." Liam guessed Dotty knew he hadn't been expecting such a choice and he could have sworn she was chuckling with triumph as she went back down the stairs and started banging utensils in the kitchen.

"Lady, no! Leave the flour alone! Oh, Lady, now look what you've done. Go on, out in the garden, the pair of you!"

Liam closed his ears to the noises downstairs and went back to the press cuttings. "Lived here long?" he asked politely as a break seemed to have been declared but he refused the biscuit that Lotty offered.

"Ten years. Of course, we've been coming to the festival since it started. We were both a lot younger then and still teaching but it was a lovely break for us in the summer. It never occurred to us that we would retire anywhere other than here. And we just couldn't believe our luck when Ted asked us to run the archive." She smiled fondly at the memory. "I'm afraid Dotty and I both rather shamelessly set out caps at Ted in those days. Well, he was rather handsome. Still is, come to that. He started the festival when he moved here about forty years ago. Of course, the cynics say he only started it as that was the only way he could get his music played. He was a bomber pilot during the war, you know."

Liam wondered how come Lotty didn't know about Sir Edward's reputation with countertenors, then realised she probably did but still hadn't given up hope. "I'm ashamed to say I know very little about him. Personally, that is. I know some of his music."

"Yes, well, I suppose we should expect no more in one of your age. He shared a house with George Smith-Turner in those days. You've heard of George, of course?"

"Best English countertenor ever."

Lotty's face glowed with approval. "Absolutely. Gossip said there was more than friendship in it, but I never believed it. They met in the RAF. George was Ted's rear gunner. People have said Ted's got a thing about countertenors but I think he still misses George. He died soon after we moved here so that must be ten years ago now. Ted still lives in the old manor house between the new houses and the village. Look out for it next time you're passing, it's just a bit further down Oxford Road from the Festival. Drink up your coffee before you slop it all over the archive. Are you sure you don't want a fig roll? Dotty makes the most delicious fig rolls you can imagine."

There was a pause and Liam guessed he was expected to speak. "I have to watch what I eat. I'm in training," he added rather lamely as Lotty raised one eyebrow.

Lotty shot him a disbelieving glance. "Really? Well, I'm sure one fig roll won't kill you. Go on, or Dotty will be very upset."

Liam ate the biscuit rather than upset Dotty and it certainly lived up to expectations. He wished he could cope better with bossy old women as Lotty foisted a second fig roll onto him and he meekly drank the coffee. He didn't even like coffee.

"There you see, you're still alive. Now where was I? Oh yes, Ted and George."

Liam couldn't quite force his mind to absorb the chatter but it helped to while away the morning. A particularly intense, but rather repetitious, description of the first performance of *Maytime Wedding* which had been so disastrous Edward Ellerby had felt obliged to rewrite almost from scratch, was interrupted by someone banging on the front door.

"Oh, blast, bother, sod and damnation!" Lotty exclaimed. "I hope that's the cooker. Dotty, can you get that?"

"On my way!" There came the most appalling clatter of a baking tin being dropped on the kitchen floor and Liam had a sudden image of Dotty wiping floury hands all down her dark red cardigan just before she opened the door.

"Oh, hullo, Stella."

"I've bagged Liam and his car to take Sigs and me to the publishers. Is he available?"

"Should think so. Liam! Stella wants you."

Liam was quite reluctant to leave Lotty and her chatter after all. "Sorry, looks like I've got to go."

"Don't worry about it. See you when you get back."

Liam tried to ignore the fact he had a mild headache as he dutifully went down the stairs to find Stella and Sigs were crowding out the tiny hall while a frustrated Billy launched assaults on the kitchen door.

"Quick round trip to the publisher," Stella reminded him. "Shouldn't be long. Where are you parked?"

"Back outside Labrador Cottage."

"Come along then, best not dawdle."

*   *   *   *

The two women looked attentively at the cars parked outside the row of cottages facing the church. They knew the Land Rover belonged to the doctor who must be visiting Mrs Sewell who had just had her sixth. The other vehicles were strangers, most probably the transporters of tourists who always so adored this tiny village set at one end of a slightly larger town. Stella and Sigs were both trying to guess. Sigs favoured the rather garish black and yellow 2CV, although Stella inclined more towards the battered red Fiesta. The two exchanged a look of disbelief when Liam took a key from his pocket, pressed the button on the fob and a very smart dark green Saab unset its alarms and unlocked its doors.

"Is that your car?" Sigs asked first.

"Yes."

"Catford must have paid you better wages than we are," Sigs remarked drily. "Or has Daddy got money?"

"I won it."

"Well, congratulations," Stella replied a shade enviously. "Wish I could win something like that."

Sigs tried to work out how she could get Liam to lend her his car for a day or so. "Did you have to do one of those witty tie-break things? I can never make them short enough."

"Something like that." There was no way Liam was going to admit the truth but the two ladies were sharp.

"Left hand drive," Stella noticed immediately. "Won it abroad, did you?"

"In Sweden."

"Registered in Northern Ireland though. Very swish. The publishers are going to think we've won the Pools. Come along then, Sigs, let's sit in the back."

Liam tried to listen to the two women as well as look for a manor house as he drove. The old cottages of the original village gave way to various estates, the architecture of each was the epitome of the decade in which it had been built. They swept past the last of the mock-country designs of the eighties and were out in the rolling countryside. It was useless to try to pick up the chat. The occasional glance in the mirror showed him no more than exchange of papers so he had to hope that these two, as others had assumed, believed he had won the car in an athletics competition. A secretive smile crossed his face as he switched on the CD player and some gentle bluegrass filled the conditioned air.

"Pick up the A road towards Chester at the next roundabout," Stella instructed without commenting on the choice of music. "It's not too far along."

The odometer told Liam he had travelled fifteen miles along the A road before Stella shrieked, "Turn left! This is it. Bother, I always miss that gateway."

The name of Flint Farm impinged on Liam's mind as he swung the car abruptly up the drive. He would have been quite happy just to sit in the car and wait for the women but they insisted he came inside too. So had had to listen while Stella ranted and screamed that the font size was wrong, that the captions were missing and that the index was a disaster zone. Sigs sat elegantly on a swivel chair and swivelled until her face turned green.

"Useless bunch of incompetents!" Stella thundered. "Give me those proofs. I suppose I'll just have to waste another night of my life checking them over again. Really, I don't know why I waste my time with you amateurs. Come along you two. And don't drive so fast, young Liam, you're not on a race track." She thrust the sheaf of paper into his arms just before they all got back into the car. "Here you are. Little job for you and Julie since you're living together. I'll give her the master copy and the two of you can check it through tonight. I'm quite sure Labrador Cottage doesn't run to a television."

Liam wanted to remonstrate about the phrase "living together" but Stella didn't give him a chance.

"Come on then, don't just stand there with those puppy-dog eyes. I've got work to do even if you are spending your days chatting with Lotty at the festival's expense."

Back they went, along the A road, past the eighties, the seventies and the sixties and then back to the original village.

"Stop!" Stella commanded and Liam obediently floored the brake. "There's Ted's car. Up the drive you go. No time like the present."

Liam had barely absorbed the image of an imposing grey stone building before he had to concentrate on avoiding the cats and chickens that were running all over the drive.

"Dear Ted," Stella sighed sarcastically. "Will insist on living in a madhouse. I hope to goodness he gets all the menagerie shut away before the house opens for the festival. The man is losing it. I'd swear he is. Still, he is over seventy so what else can you expect?"

Ted Ellerby had been startled by the screech of tyres outside his gate and he lethargically looked round from unloading the boot of his car. Probably another tourist coming to gawp he said to himself and wished he had the energy to put the car in the garage. A dark green Saab stopped momentarily and then came in through the gateway. He recognised Stella McGinty in what he thought was the driver's seat which baffled him as he knew she had been banned for a year after the last Christmas party. Then he noticed it was a left-hand drive but he didn't recognise the driver. Rather a good-looking fellow he thought to himself and with any luck not just a jobbing taxi driver. He abandoned his unloading.

"Stella," he greeted the lady who had just got out of the green car. "Lovely to see you." A meaningless air kiss was exchanged. "Going to introduce me?"

"This is Liam McGuinness. He's working here for the summer. Said I'd bring him along to meet you."

Ted ignored her and took the hand of Liam McGuinness. He noticed that this redhead had neither the usual brown nor pale blue eyes but a strange, almost indigo glare. "Where are you from, Liam?"

"County Derry." Liam knew for certain then that the rumours were true. He recovered his hand and shoved both his hands in the pockets of his jeans.

Ted had always adored Ireland. "Lovely part of the world. Are you from Derry itself?"

"No. Small hamlet near the Sperrin mountains."

"How glorious. Not much music going on there though, I shouldn't think."

"Not a lot, no."

"Are you musical at all? I presume you must be or you wouldn't want to work for a music festival."

"I play the cello." Liam thought it best to tread warily even though this elderly gentleman seemed harmless enough on first acquaintance. He wished he was the sort who could be more witty and entertaining when in the presence of the illustrious.

Stella was feeling spiteful after the way Ted had cut her dead in his eagerness to be introduced. "Rubbish. You told me yourself you'd sung Ted's fifth symphony."

"Really?" the composer sighed. "How did you find that top G?" He tucked what was not meant to be a paternal hand through Liam's elbow. "But do come along in and have some coffee all of you, and maybe I can persuade Liam to sing for me."

Coffee was served in the drawing room by a diminutive, bespectacled housekeeper. Liam couldn't help but admire the room with its French windows looking out over the fields away from the newer houses of Brockleford. He didn't dare say anything when his second cup of coffee of the day was handed to him without anyone asking him if he actually wanted it.

He hoped that the idea of him singing would be forgotten but Ted Ellerby barely waited for his guests to drink the rather weak instant coffee.

"Right then, young Liam, what are you going to sing for us? I'll play the piano for you."

Liam knew the company was expecting some Handel or, even better, one of Ellerby's own works so he cussedly declared, "*Golden Days.*"

"Ah, shades of Mario Lanza. What key?"

"G major."

"Fine, fire away. No, don't sit on the sofa like that. Come and stand over here by the piano."

It seemed the indomitable Ted Ellerby knew his lights as well as his classics. Liam stood awkwardly by the grand piano beside the windows where he could look out at the fields. He wished he had chosen another song. He'd used this one to court his lady love, and his voice cracked on the highest notes as he remembered.

Ted Ellerby thought he had been transported back several decades to when his beloved George would stand beside him, one hand on his shoulder, and would pour out notes like a nightingale. Liam McGuinness certainly lacked the polish of George Smith-Turner, but he had a pure voice, suffering somewhat from indifferent, if not downright bad, training and his breath control was certainly open to criticism. Rather than get carried away with emotion in front of those two silly women who would have spread the gossip all over the village, Ted Ellerby sniffed.

"Yes, well. Get yourself some decent lessons and you won't be too bad. Try these for size." He casually handed across a manuscript book that lay on top of the piano. It had always been his intention that George should sing those songs but George had keeled over and died in the middle of a recital and Ted had never even had the chance to show him those tender settings of Anglo-Saxon love poems.

Liam took the manuscript without realising what he held in his hands. "What language is this?"

"Anglo-Saxon. Do your best, lad."

Liam groaned under his breath and was glad his sight-reading was good.

Stella McGinty nearly leapt to her feet and snatched the book from the innocent grasp of the young man who tried so hard to get his stubborn Irish tongue round the vowels and consonants of Anglo-Saxon. She knew all of Ted Ellerby's songs and this wasn't part of the standard repertoire. She looked across at Sigs who was furtively finishing off the chocolate chip biscuits and not even aware of what was happening.

"Ted," Stella began when Liam had got to the end of the first song. "What are those?"

"Just some old things I dashed off for poor George. He never got to see them. I think I'd quite like Liam to have then instead. He has a feel for the music. Liam, lad, I'll speak to Anna for you and see if she'll come out of retirement and give you a few lessons. Well done, lad. Care to stay for lunch?"

"He can't," Stella chipped in. "He's expected back by Lotty and Dotty any minute now. I'm sure you can invite him back another time."

Ted Ellerby was too old and too famous to put up with such high-handedness from an administrator. "Miss McGinty, you do not tell me how to run my life, you do not tell me who I may or may not invite for lunch and you most emphatically do not bring delightful counter-tenors along here then take them away from me. Liam, you have a tongue in your head, do you wish to stay for lunch or don't you?"

Liam thought guiltily of the fig rolls and chocolate chip he had already eaten in excess of his strict diet. "I'm sorry, today's not a good day. Maybe some other time?"

"Thursday. I'll invite Anna along as well and I'll get this song cycle finished by then. Been kicking around on top of the piano since George died, be good to get it done. And if you can't afford Anna's fees I'll pay them for you"

Liam was overwhelmed by the generosity. "That's very good of you. Thank you."

"Don't thank me yet. I'll call in the dues when you're so far in my debt you won't be able to say 'no'."

Stella bounced to her feet. "Come along, Liam. Sigs, stop eating all of Ted's biscuits. Thank you for the coffee, Ted."

Ted Ellerby followed his visitors to the front door but detained Liam with a hand on his arm. "I meant what I said," he rumbled ominously. "Every word."

Liam thought he ought to get a few things straight before Ted Ellerby got the wrong idea. "You're very generous, Sir Edward, but I've never been in anyone's debt. If I can't afford the lessons then I won't have them and if there's a price for singing your songs then I won't sing them."

"How old are you, Liam?"

"Twenty three."

"I am fifty years older than you. You are a fit and healthy young man and I am a doddering old fool who has trouble getting in and out of the bath. Tell me honestly, do you think I'm going to wrestle you to the ground and tear the trousers off you with my teeth?"

Liam couldn't meet the amused brown eyes of his challenger. "I suppose not."

"Good. Now get along with you and I'll see you on Thursday." He sent Liam on his way with a friendly smack on the behind and his eyes were clouded with memories as he watched the young man walk towards his car. He turned back to the drawing room and to the manuscript that had waited over ten years to be finished.

* * *

"I gather you were a bit of hit with Edward Ellerby," Julie remarked to Liam over Tuesday tea of scrambled eggs on toast. "What's he really like?"

"Just a sad old man. I felt a bit sorry for him to be truthful."

"Are you going for your run before or after orchestra?"

"I don't really want..." Liam began lamely.

Julie steeled herself to be honest. "Look, I ran out on Nick last night and he's done nothing but badger me all day in the office. I don't want to go across on my own but not to go would be even worse. Anyway, if the orchestra's as bad as the choir we'll only be going once and we ought to show willing."

"Why? We're here for a few months to help out with the festival. Come September we'll both be looking for jobs again."

"That's as may be, but if you want to get a half-decent reference out of this lot, you'd better play the game."

Liam looked down at his plate of food. "I never was much good at playing games," he said bitterly.

Something of an enigma this Liam McGuinness, Julie thought to herself. She like enigmas. There hadn't yet been one in her life she hadn't solved. "Want to talk about it?"

"No. Thank you. Want to talk about you?"

"Touché!" she acknowledged. "Let's make a pact. Friends for the summer? No entanglements, no messy relationships, just friends such as we used to have when we were children?"

"Done," he agreed and offered his hand.

*   *   *

"You came then," Nick hailed Julie cheerfully when she walked into the church that evening.

"Certainly did. And brought along that new cellist for you too."

"Well done, Jules."

Julie repressed her temper. "Please don't call me that."

"I was only being friendly," Nick persisted glibly. "Hullo, Liam, glad you could make it. Go and find yourselves some places, folks."

Julie had been expecting another geriatric shambles like the choir and she watched as the disorganised rabble eventually sorted itself out into a small orchestra that even ran to brass and percussion players. She looked round as she warmed up her oboe and saw Debbie grinning at her from the third desk of the second violins. Liam made the third cellist so he was stuck at the back looking a bit lost and forlorn somehow.

Nick rapped his baton on his stand and the musicians obediently quietened. "Good evening, folks. Just like to welcome Julie and Liam to the fold. Right, let's run through the Berwald."

Liam hated Berwald but he had already learned that he was a particular favourite of Ted Ellerby, who considered himself something of a scholar on the quiet. He was impressed by the standard of the orchestra even if some of the players were obviously past retirement age. He looked round the ranks as best he could and noticed Lotty de Grys playing the trombone while her sister merrily bashed approximately the right percussion instrument at almost the right time.

"Stop!" Nick yelled "Dotty, what are you doing? What the hell have you tuned the timps to?"

Dotty raised her glasses and peered at the music on the stand in front of her. "Sorry, Nick. I was playing the Schubert."

The orchestra set off again for a few bars before their temperamental conductor stopped them again. This time the second violins came in for a scathing blast from his tongue. A bit later on it was the horns, then the flutes and finally the violas. After that a tea break was declared and Julie thankfully put down her oboe and went to seek out Liam.

"Not as bad as I'd thought," she muttered to Liam. "How are the cellos?"

Liam shrugged. "OK, I suppose. God, I'm out of practice."

"Hullo, Liam," Lotty cried and rushed across nearly spilling her tea in her enthusiasm. "Hullo, you must be Julie. How are you settling in to the cottage? I'm awfully sorry about the mix-up. I gave Liam one deposit back. Has he told you?"

"Yes, we shared it out over tea."

"Good-oh. Must say it makes a jolly change to see some new faces in this band."

"I didn't expect you to play the trombone," Julie put in not knowing, as Liam did, that Lotty didn't need responses to conversation.

"That's because when I was very young and foolish I played in a swing band, among other things. Saxophone if I could but I got more work with the trombone. Then I got to be sensible and went in for teaching instead. You'll see, one day you'll become sensible too. Now do run along and get your tea the pair of you." Lotty watched the two cross the hall to the trestle table and mused sadly that it was hard to imagine they had ever been anything but sensible.

"Ever felt like a twelve year old?" Liam muttered to Julie. "And if Nick invites you down the pub tonight just make sure you tell him we've got some proof-reading to do."

Yes, boss," Julie grinned.

They met up with Debbie at the table. She was deliberating which biscuit to take and didn't notice them at first.

"Hi-i!" she shrieked, pronouncing the normally brief greeting in the curiously duo-syllabic way peculiar to festival staff. "Nobody told me you two are an item."

"We're not," they said in unison.

"Oh good. Liam, do you know anything about cars? Sigs said you drive a really nifty Swedish number and mine's been making a horrible noise."

"Not much. Can just about change a wheel in a crisis."

"Oh, that's a shame. Well, would you mind coming and listening to it?"

"What, now?"

"If you're not doing anything else," she sighed and batted her eyelashes at him.

"What do you know about cars?" he asked Julie.

"Less than you. But I'll come and have a listen too if you like." A funny feeling told her he did like.

"Julie!" Nick hailed her. "Don't run off. I want a word with you about the second movement."

Julie watched Liam and Debbie leave the hall together and wished she was going with them. She really didn't want to have to talk about the second movement with anyone. And she just knew what was going to come after the discussion on dynamics. The confident smile and the smooth, "What are you doing after the rehearsal?"

She had thought he might change his opening line for a second attempt but this time genuine salvation was at hand. "Proof-reading with Liam. Stella wants us to go through the second draft of the commemorative volume."

"Oh, knickers to Stella. Leave McGuinness to do the reading and come for a drink."

"I can't, I promised Liam."

"Look, just what the hell is that guy to you anyway? You said yourself you'd never even met him until you interviewed for the job and now you act like the pair of you are married."

"He asked me first," she said stubbornly.

"Right. OK. Now I'm asking you first. How about tomorrow?"

Julie was trapped. She knew malicious gossip would spread if she accepted but even worse rumours could fly if she declined. She wished Liam would come back but her champion had obviously been delayed by Debbie. "Can I see how the proof-reading is going?"

"No you can't. Look, one drink. It's not like I'm asking you to leap into bed with me."

Julie shuddered at the thought of it. "I'll think about it," she said and hated herself for not being more decisive. She escaped into the cool May evening and leaned on the first tombstone she came across.

Debbie's giggle wafted to her ears. "Oh dear, silly me."

There was a long silence and Julie didn't even like to conjecture. A car bonnet slammed and footsteps swished through the long grass towards her.

"You all right?" anxious Irish tones enquired.

"Fine. I just got propositioned."

"You and me both. Silly cow had put some water in her windscreen washer and left the cap off. No wonder the car was rattling."

"Liam?" wailed Debbie. "Where are you?"

"Oh, bloody hell," he muttered under his breath. "What is it with everyone in this place?"

Debbie retraced her steps from her car to the church door , annoyed her little ploy hadn't kept the delectable Liam with her for longer. She would have done something to the spark plugs except she wasn't quite sure what a spark plug looked like, and it sounded rather terminal somehow. She was even more put out to see Liam and Julie leaning on the same tombstone. Feeling spurned and unloved, she stomped off to rejoin the rehearsal where she spitefully told Nick that the second oboe and the back desk of the cellos were getting rather intimate outside.

Nick Greenwood didn't like to think another man was going to get to Julie Hutchinson before he did. It wasn't that he found her incredibly irresistible, he was just not in the habit of being beaten to any woman. He leaned out of the church door and bawled into the gathering darkness, "Get back inside you two, we've got some Schubert to play."

*   *   *

Julie waited until she was sure Liam had gone out for his early morning run before she even got out of bed the next morning. They had both seen the looks they got when they went back into the church and from the catty smirk on Debbie's face the gossip was well and truly flying. Julie had been half afraid Liam would think it was a huge joke but he hadn't looked very pleased either. Nick had sulked all the rest of the rehearsal, which, she felt, should have left her feeling flattered. Instead she was plain furious and it made it worse to know the rumours would be all round that incestuous office by the time she got in to work.

She washed quickly and had just found her own supply of bananas when Liam came back in.

"Goodness, have you run five miles already?" Then she noticed his face looked pinched and he was hobbling rather than walking with one hand on his left thigh. "What have you done?"

He crashed down onto one of the chairs at the kitchen table. "I haven't got a clue. I'd not even got to the end of the road when it suddenly hurt like hell. Must have pulled a muscle."

"Too much sitting on attic floors. Should I call the doctor?"

"No, I'm sure it's not that bad." Liam tried to get to his feet, yelped a bit and sat down again.

"I'll call the doctor."

*   *   *

"You owe me a tenner," Sigs told her boss as soon as Stella came into the office.

Stella didn't believe it. "You mean Liam and Julie?"

"Most certainly do. Phyllis was just saying Fred's had to go to Labrador Cottage to tend to Liam already."

"Hush," Phyllis cautioned as Julie came in. She got off Sigs' desk and tried to look innocent.

"How's the patient?" Nick asked and couldn't repress a grin.

"Resting."

"God, you must be a goer," he remarked lewdly. "One second it's snogging in the churchyard and next he's laid up with groin strain."

Julie's face went scarlet but she held her ground. "No he isn't. He's pulled a muscle."

Debbie sidled up to her. "But where is the muscle in question and how did he pull it?"

"He was out for his run and, oh, I don't know. I didn't ask."

Sigs beamed at the suffering Julie. "Nasty strain from what Phyllis has said."

Julie bit back her retort about the Hippocratic Oath of doctors. "He's been told to rest for a few days, that's all."

"Well I want those proofs back by tomorrow," Stella told her. "Have you finished them yet?"

"We've done the first four chapters."

"Then I suggest you get back home and do the rest of them. Go on. We can't hold up the book launch just because the office temp has twisted his ankle."

Julie went back to Labrador Cottage where Liam, well dosed with painkillers, was resting on the sofa. "Don't ever catch anything embarrassing," she told him. "Dr Bond is part of the gossip conspiracy."

"Had a feeling he was. We been fired?"

"'Working from home', as they say. Got to get the proofs finished. Coffee?"

"Lemon tea, please. I'd offer to help but those drugs are taking a long time to work."

"You stop where you are. Do you want to read or check?"

"I'll read, your writing's neater than mine."

*   *   *

By half past twelve the first six chapters were done and there were only another two to go. Liam's throat was sore from all the reading and neither he nor Julie was sorry to be interrupted by the banging of the door knocker. The accompanying barking told them what was going on.

"I'll go," Julie said rather unnecessarily.

Lady bounced down the hall and into the living room where she would have leaped on Liam except she had learned the command of "stay!".

Dotty wandered in to the room behind her dog. "Hullo, Liam, I heard you're not well. Not something you ate, I hope?"

"Pulled a muscle."

"Oh dear. Will it stop you throwing your javelins all over the place?"

"Just for a few days."

"Oh, I am sorry. Look, I've brought some lunch for you. Julie, dear, have you moved the saucepans? Which reminds me, although I don't know why it should, Ted sends his regards."

"You mean the gossip has got as far as Ted Ellerby?" Julie asked.

"Of course. He popped round to the cottage earlier this morning and asked where you were. He was most upset to hear you're not well. Asked me to give you this and says he'll write a nice little cello piece for you to play with the orchestra. It's a bit of a miracle really, he hasn't written a note since George died."

Liam recognised the manuscript book he was given. Anglo-Saxon love songs. That was about the last thing he needed.

Dotty was half way out to the kitchen. "Oh, and he says if you're not mobile by tomorrow he'll bring Anna round here for lunch. Have you met Anna? She was in all his operas when the festival started. Lovely old thing but a bit mad."

There came a terrible clatter of a saucepan being dropped and Julie and Lady shot out to the kitchen to see what had been spilled on the floor.

* * *

The Mediterranean garden was a haven that evening. Julie thought she had never lived in such a perfect place before. The scent of herbs rose underfoot, a gentle breeze was rustling the horse chestnut trees on the green and she believed she would get used to lemon tea if she drank it often enough.

"What a day," she sighed and stretched out her legs.

The idyll was shattered by the discordant clanging of church bells.

Liam steadied his breathing. "What on earth is that?"

Julie was surprised that he should be so nervous. "Bell ringing practice most likely. They always used to ring them on Wednesdays back home. You all right? You seem very jumpy."

"It's my nerves," he told her and smiled bravely.

Julie remembered this young man came from one of the trouble spots of the world. She didn't feel up to an intense discussion that evening and dared not put a hand, no matter how sisterly and consoling, anywhere about his person. A change of conversation was the best she could offer. "Do you think Ted's really going to write a cello piece?"

"Probably." Liam let the sound of the bells merge into the twilight. One day, he hoped, he would learn to relax. "You sure you want to get the lunch ready tomorrow?"

"To meet Ted Ellerby I will cheerfully cook some lunch. How does bread and cheese sound? I can dash to the supermarket in the morning and lay in some supplies."

Liam glanced at her profile as she sat so rigidly beside him. "You, as Sigs would say, are a star," he told her and leaned towards her to kiss her cheek.

Julie flushed and moved a bit further away from him on the bench. "Don't."

"Sorry."

CHAPTER THREE

In which an accusation is made

Julie wished there was a dining room at Labrador Cottage. It didn't seem quite right somehow, making someone as illustrious as Edward Ellerby eat in the kitchen. She looked at the young man hovering rather nervously by the door. "How's the leg today?"

"Bit better."

"You do look all screwed up. I'm sure it won't be that bad."

"It could be even worse. I could make a right fool of myself in front of Edward Ellerby and Anna Forrester. I mean, I never hoped to be good enough to earn a living by singing so why am I doing this?"

"Well Sir Edward must think you've got some talent or he wouldn't be bothering with you."

Liam knew Julie would be shocked if he confessed his innermost fear that all Sir Edward wanted out of him was a hard session between the sheets and wouldn't care if he sang like a crow. "Maybe you're right."

The thundering of the door knocker announced the arrival of the lunch guests.

"I'll go," Liam said wanly. "Head straight for the sympathy vote."

Julie half smiled with pity to see the tall and athletic Liam hopping along the hall to the door. He was obviously terrified of not singing well enough to impress Sir Edward Ellerby and she wondered how she could ever have thought he was a hooligan just because his hair was so long.

Ted Ellerby was glad he had brought someone with him or he thought he would probably have cried to see the proud Liam McGuinness hobbling along and obviously in pain.

"Liam, how are you? This is Anna Forrester, you may have heard of her."

"Indeed I have," he admitted and offered Anna his hand.

She accepted the hand briefly. "If you ever want get anywhere in the singing world you'll lose that accent. Charming and your birthright it may be, but you won't get anywhere while you sound like a Sinn Fein activist. Even if you are one."

Liam, lost for an answer, stood back to let the visitors into the hall. "Hope you don't mind eating in the kitchen but it's the only room really."

"Don't mind at all," Ted assured him. "Got a piano?"

"No, sorry."

Anna frowned at Ted. "It doesn't matter. I'll need to hear no more than three notes to know if he's worth working on."

"So few?" Liam asked and let his breath out.

"In theory. In fact I'll want a couple of scales at least. Is this your wife?"

"Ah, no. This is Julie Hutchinson. We, um, share the house. Julie, Ted Ellerby and Anna Forrester."

Anna Forrester was not inclined to social chit chat although she had the courtesy to shake hands with Julie. "Liam, front room I think. We'll leave these two to chat. When will you be serving luncheon, Julie?"

"When you like. It's only salad. And Liam and I are finishing the proof-reading at home today so we don't have to be back in the office."

Anna glanced at her elegant watch. "One o'clock then. That gives us half an hour. I won't charge for this session as I'm doing it as a favour for Ted."

Julie looked from the closed door to a smiling Ted. "Well. She's not what I expected at all."

"She never is."

Julie realised the eminent Sir Edward was still standing just inside her kitchen door. "Sorry, do sit down. Would you like a drink of something?"

"No, thank you. I'll wait until lunch. Sit yourself down, Julie, stop getting so agitated."

His smile was warm and charming and Julie almost forget he was rich and famous and in her kitchen. "Well, she seems such a bully and poor Liam's not very fit at the moment."

"It's the old adage of the bark and the bite."

Julie was not consoled. She hadn't heard Liam sing before except for a few snatches of Abba in the bath and she was pleasantly surprised to hear the pure, clear tones of the counter-tenor. Scale after scale after scale. Then some exercises. Anna had discreetly closed the doors so her remarks were muffled but the two in the kitchen could hear that the voice was definitely improving.

"He's not bad, is he?" Julie remarked at five to one.

"He has a lovely voice. George could sing like a nightingale, a voice of honey. Liam, on the other hand, has a voice like cut diamonds. Can't you hear the purity in it? It's like crystal fragmenting into rainbows."

Julie thought that was going a bit over the top but she supposed creative geniuses had to be allowed their superlatives. "I'll warm up the bread for lunch."

"Is it one of Dotty's loaves?"

"Yes, it was meant to have tomatoes in it."

"But instead has green olives. Yes, I know. I sometimes think she's colour blind. Still it's wonderful bread." Ted turned to face the two who came into the kitchen. "Well, Anna?"

"He sings like a choirboy from the Balls Pond Road. I can get him started, refine his technique a bit, get his breath control problems sorted out, but I can't coach him as far as he needs to go. You know who would be good for him? Enrico Thingy out in Milan. When he's mastered the basics."

"I do believe you're right. Well, Liam, fancy spending the winter in Milan?"

Liam hadn't forgotten the promise of dues being called in. "No, not particularly, but thank you for asking. I was hoping I'd be wintering in Australia with the British athletics team but that's looking less and less likely now I've done my leg in."

"Liam, you have reached one of those points in your life where you have to make a choice," Ted explained as though to a child. "Anna is offering to teach you and recommend you to this chap in Milan who could probably help you to become established as one of the better alto singers in this world. You, on the other hand, seem to want to devote your life to chucking bits of metal at line judges. A career which, I hardly need to point out, won't sustain you much beyond your thirtieth birthday. I mean, just how good are you with a javelin anyway?"

Julie wasn't expecting to see a sparkle of anger in Liam's eyes.

"I currently hold the Commonwealth record. I've won gold at the Commonwealth, and silver at the European and World championships. I missed out on the last Olympics because I had ... I just missed out on them, OK? And I've been promising myself a trip to the Olympics since I was about six years old and first threw a poker across the living room at home. So I hope you'll understand that I'm finding it kind of hard to get excited at the thought of singing in Italy when I'd rather be in Atlanta in two years' time."

Ted Ellerby was too old to be afraid of temper. "Yet, here you are, working for a music festival with your javelin, where? Not in Brockleford, that's for sure."

Liam flushed and bit at his lip, "My trainer advised me to take some time off. So I'm taking it."

There was a silence in the kitchen. Clearly Liam McGuinness had his problems but they were not open to discussion.

*   *   *

It was cooler that night so the two in the Mediterranean garden had to put their coats on to sit out there but they wouldn't have sat anywhere else. As was becoming their custom, they sat side by side on the bench, drinking lemon tea and having long bouts of silence between sporadic conversation.

"Made a bit of a fool of myself, didn't I?" Liam remarked vaguely after one silence.

Julie had been thinking along similar lines and was glad he had mentioned it first. "Not at all. I'm sorry, I suppose none of us really took your javelin-throwing seriously enough. I mean it does seem a bit odd that you're working here for four months instead of doing competitions and things."

Liam bowed his head so his hair fell forward to hide his face. "I haven't thrown competitively for nearly a year. I've done two competitions since the girlfriend dumped me, one of which was the Olympic selection trials for Barcelona. In that one I got foot-faulted on every throw. Then they told me to try for a competition in Sweden because they really wanted me in the team and didn't like to judge me on one bad show. So I did even worse and fell flat on my face."

The enigma was becoming soluble and it all made horrible sense. "I'm sorry. It's rotten when the one you love kicks you in the teeth, isn't it." He had bared his soul to her, she could do no less for him. "I was engaged until about a month ago. Paul's in the Army. Then he wrote me a letter. At least I think he did. Unfortunately he must have sent it to the wrong person because I got the one he'd written to Cynthia saying rude things about me."

Liam didn't say a word. Just put his arm across her shoulders and this time she shuffled towards him.

*   *   *

It was Saturday and two shy people stood side by side in the kitchen of Labrador Cottage and looked at the washing machine. Even worse was the knowledge that the lady next door with all the children could look out of her upstairs window and see exactly what would be drying on the line in the back courtyard.

Julie gathered her courage. "It seems daft to do two loads and we both, well, wear underwear. Don't you? I mean, everybody does. And as you'd better not bend your leg too much then I'll do it. Go and get your stuff."

"I couldn't impose," he tried.

It was sad to hear the sounds of County Londonderry leaving his voice. "I insist. Go on."

"Do you really want to?"

Julie wasn't going to admit to the embarrassment. "I can't get used to you not sounding so Irish," she tried, going off on a different tack to avoid the issue.

"Nor can I but I'm sure Anna's right and she is going to coach me half price for the summer."

"Can't you be Irish among friends even?"

He raised one eyebrow. "And are you my friend then, Julie Hutchinson?" he enquired in a thick brogue.

"I hope so. I'm sorry I was a bit of a rat about the orchestra."

Something crackly was pushed through the letterbox of Labrador Cottage then what sounded like a complete collection of national telephone directories thundered onto the mat.

"Fan mail!" Julie declared and escaped from a conversation that was threatening to get awkward at any moment. She scooped up the heap and her spirits fell even though she wasn't expecting anything. Two gardening magazines and some doggy literature addressed to Dotty and Lotty. The crackling had been made by a small Jiffy bag that had gone from Paris to County Londonderry to Brockleford and was addressed in a feminine hand to Mr L D McGuinness.

"One for you," she announced, "and some stuff for Lotty and Dotty which I can walk across later. From a lady in Paris who doesn't know where you live."

"Paris?"

Julie was worried by the expression on his face as he looked at the writing. "I'll go and get the washing together."

"Thanks. I've left a heap on the floor somewhere. Sorry. Wasn't expecting you to do it."

Julie took as long as she dared over the washing-collecting but they hadn't accumulated very much between them and she loitered a while on the upstairs landing not liking to intrude. She liked it even less when she heard the front door bang open and shut, the beep of the Saab's alarm and then the roar of two and a half litres of Swedish engine setting off through the village like a rocket.

She looked out of the front bedroom window but the Saab was already gone from view. A feeling in her stomach told her that Liam McGuinness was still a hot-headed Irishman in spite of his Cambridge education. There was nothing she could do. If he had flounced into the garden she might have tried a bit of diplomacy but he could be half way across Wales in an hour. Back to the kitchen she went and paused. It was all there on the table. The Jiffy bag, a scrap of pale mauve paper and the most exquisite diamond ring she had ever seen in her life.

"I'm not going to be nosy," she said out loud. The washing went in the machine and was presently churning round. "On the other hand, if he didn't want me to see it, he'd have taken it away. No, he left in a temper. I'm sure it's not meant for my eyes." She made herself some coffee, sat at the table and tried not to read the note upside down. It was no good. Option B was the more appealing. He must have meant her to read it. Guiltily she picked up the paper.

L,

Was clearing out some old junk while unpacking here. Meant to give this back ages ago. M

Julie gasped at the bald effrontery of the note. Next she picked up the ring and looked at it. A Lilliputian diamond set in what looked like silver filigree work. Bit small for her finger but very pretty. She jumped as the door knocker rapped, the ring shot over her knuckle and she was stuck with it. A duster had to serve as a disguise in a crisis and she went to the door hoping it wasn't going to be a policeman asking her if she knew someone who drove a dark green Saab.

Lady and Billy leaped over the doorstep and went racing all over the cottage at once.

"Hullo, dear," Lotty greeted her. "Just thought we'd come to check up on the patient."

Just for a split second Julie wondered if these two ladies would have come rushing round if she had been the one with the ailment. But they were, after all, her landladies so she had better be nice to them. "He's gone out. I've no idea how long for. Do you want to come in for coffee? I've just made some."

It was impossible to make coffee and keep a duster round one's left hand unobtrusive.

"Have you hurt your hand?" Dotty enquired sympathetically, privately thinking these two young people did seem very accident prone.

"Cut my finger. Not badly," Julie offered desperately.

Lotty sighed fondly at yet another wayward child. "Go and wash it at once. I'll finish off the coffee."

Julie thankfully went up the stairs, fished Lady's head out of the toilet bowl and sent the dog downstairs then shut the door and unwound the duster. She tried soap, she tried cold water, she tried brute force but nothing was going to shift that stubborn gem from her finger. Finally, in despair, she twisted the stone underneath, wrapped round a sticking plaster and went back to join her guests.

"How's the finger?" Lotty enquired.

"Fine, thank you. Is Lady supposed to drink out of toilets?"

"No, but she usually does. There wasn't any bleach in it was there?"

"No."

"Oh good. I think her sense of smell is going a bit in her old age."

As they somehow did, Lotty and Dotty got the conversation round to Ted Ellerby and Julie had a niggling headache as well as a sore finger when the growling of her stomach was counterpointed by the front door opening again.

"Visitors, Liam," she called in case he was still in a foul temper and about to start throwing things. "What on earth have you done?" she cried as soon as she saw him.

"My dear, have you had an accident with a lawn mower?" Lotty enquired.

"I went to get my hair cut and lost my nerve half way through."

"It looks dreadful," Dotty lamented. "You can't possibly go out like that. You must sue the hairdresser."

"It wasn't his fault. I changed my mind. It doesn't matter. It'll grow."

Nobody thought to enquire about his pulled muscle after that. The visitors declined lunch and departed for their own home with their magazines and their dogs, and the two tenants sat down to some bread and cheese.

"I've got some sewing scissors somewhere. Want me to tidy you up a bit?" Julie offered as Liam seemed to be quite over his temper now.

"How could she do it? Why throw it back at me again? I'd rather she'd kept the stupid ring. Where is it anyway? Julie? What have you done with it?"

"Would you be cross if I said I'd lost it?"

"Not at all. I don't want it, but I'd be curious to know how you managed it."

"What about if I said I tried it for size and it got stuck?"

"I'd let you keep it."

She held out her hand. "On my wedding finger?"

To her relief, Liam grinned hugely and for one delightfully terrifying moment she thought he was going to kiss her hand. But he didn't.

"Well, I'm sure that ought to teach you some sort of a lesson but I'm not sure what. I was just so mad at her it's a wonder I didn't run over anybody. At least I don't think I ran over anybody."

"Where did you go to get your hair cut?"

"I have no idea. It's a bit of a pity my temper ran out just after the bloke had started cutting. I'll take the ear ring out after lunch."

"But you don't... oh, my. You were in a temper. Show me?" Julie looked at the obviously sore left ear with a gold star-shaped stud in it. "Ouch. Suits you in a barbaric kind of way."

"I just get that mad. Does the hair look so ridiculous?"

"Frankly, yes. But my offer of tidying it up is still on."

Liam smiled wearily. "Thank you. And I meant what I said. You can keep the ring. On any finger you like. I'm past caring."

*   *   *

Julie went to church on Sunday morning. She went with a very sore finger but at least there wasn't a ring on it. It had been quite a battle with the ice cubes and the soap but two people had been tougher than any silver filigree. It was a pity, she mused, that Liam's dreadful haircut hadn't been so easily put right. She had done the best she could but he now had a madly curling fringe which didn't go at all with the thick mat of it still hanging down his back.

Normally she liked going to church but there was something about St Michael and All Angels which unsettled her. Something slightly hypocritical in the attitude of the congregation. She spared a moment to miss the cosy little church in Devon where those who worshipped could feel the presence of their forebears going back over hundreds of years. Brockleford church had barely celebrated its centenary. Which was a curious thing in a village where the bridge over the river had borne the weight of medieval pack horses. The vicar glared down at his flock from the pulpit and told them of the evils of wealth and material possession which left Julie feeling rather out of things.

She got back to Labrador Cottage dissatisfied in her soul to find Liam doing the ironing and making such a good job of her frilly-collared white blouse she didn't like to interrupt.

"Lunch won't be long," Liam informed her without losing his concentration on the job in hand. "How was the sermon? All hellfire and brimstone for people who read others' letters?"

"Something like that. I was thinking about that church. Why is it Victorian and everything else round here is much older?"

"Do you think I'm into local history now?" was the amused enquiry. "You could always ask Lotty and Dotty."

"True. But they haven't been here all that long."

"So you could ask the vicar."

"Suppose so." Julie busied herself with the table laying. "Don't you go to church?"

"Not any more."

She took the hint that the subject was closed. "How's the ear?"

"Still there. I can't decide whether to take it out or not. Might remind me to keep my temper in future." He sat the iron on its heel and handed across a crisp, white blouse. "Talking with Ted, and then that thing from Mandy, made me think a bit. Ted's right. I've got to make the choice. Either I'm going to go all out for the javelin throwing while I'm young enough or I'm going to pack it in and go for the singing."

Julie could feel he had used just the right amount of starch on her blouse. Was there nothing this man couldn't get right? "Lucky you to have such a choice to make."

There was an edge to her voice that made Liam think he needed to lighten this conversation. He was sure Julie would help him come to the right decision but there were things that needed to be got out of the way first. "Mean to tell me you haven't?"

"No," she said rather bitterly. "I got a very indifferent degree in business administration and marketing from a university that was a polytechnic only a few years ago and apart from that all I can do is type a little. My mother wants nothing more than for me to give up all my silly ideas about having a career, go home, get married and have lots of babies for her to cuddle."

Liam began to feel he was getting somewhere at last. "So she wasn't too pleased when the letter to Cynthia arrived?"

"I never told her. I sent a letter to Paul telling him what to do with himself, saw this job advertised in *Classical Music* and went for it. So far as my mother knows I'm still engaged to a colour sergeant in the Royal Artillery."

"Julie, you have dug one big hole for yourself."

She wouldn't look at him. "Maybe if I dig it deep enough it'll bury me," she snapped.

He held out his hand and knew not to intrude. "Give me back the blouse."

"Why?"

"You've just screwed the collar up again."

Julie meekly gave back the garment and wondered why she had told so much to this man who had shared her house for less than a week. It would have been so easy to take him into her confidence. Scream and shout until she cried and felt better. But Julie Hutchinson had locked up her emotions and kept a tight hold on the key.

"Have I got time to go to the supermarket and buy us some wine?" she asked calmly.

Liam shot her a hard look and knew the moment was gone. "Twenty minutes. Take the car. Keys are on the dresser."

*   *   *

"Saw you in the supermarket on Sunday," Debbie remarked casually to Julie first thing Monday morning. "Driving Liam's car."

Before any details could be demanded by the interrogator, Julie was saved by Stella's head popping out of her office door.

"Ah, Julie, come here a moment, please." Door shut again, Stella smiled sweetly. "Liam gone back to Lotty and Dotty?"

"Nine o'clock this morning."

"Good. How's his leg?"

Julie was starting to wonder why she was being asked about Liam all the time. "Much better," she offered hoping to move the conversation on to her role in the proceedings.

"Good. Right then. About the exhibition for the festival. As I'm sure you know, this is to all intents and purposes the twenty fifth anniversary of *Maytime Wedding* and while we can't run to staging the damn thing we can at least put on an exhibition in the church hall. How are you at exhibitions?"

"I did display work as part of my degree."

"Thought you said you had. Right then. Nick is writing the captions and I've got Lotty and Dotty sorting out ephemera no doubt with Liam's help. What I want you to do is get yourself along to the hall and draft me out a proposed floor plan. I picked up the key from the vicar this morning so you can pop it back through his letter box when you've done."

It didn't occur to Julie that such a job could take so long. By the time she had drawn up one plan, taken it back to the office and had it turned down by Stella, with some annoyingly justifiable reasons, she was getting a bit fractious. Thankful she hadn't returned the key yet, Julie went back to the church hall and had another go, wishing Stella had given her the whole story of available stands and tables in the first place. She thought she had done better the second time but Stella still wasn't impressed. The director and the summer help went over the plan until they were both sick of it but had finally agreed on the arrangement. Julie arrived back at Labrador Cottage in the evening hot, filthy dirty from crawling round the floor with a tape measure, and very bad-tempered. Liam wasn't in so she took a bath and washed her hair then charged out of the bathroom in her dressing gown and turban to collide with her fellow-lodger on the landing.

"You look like I want to feel," he told her. "Spent the whole day crawling round the floor of Lotty's loft. Fancy doing the tea tonight?"

"No problem."

Two weary people sat out on the bench in the Mediterranean garden that evening and didn't speak for a long while.

"How's the leg?"

"Aches a bit. Don't think I'll be doing the full training run for a while."

"But won't you need to get back into serious training soon?"

Liam sighed and looked away across the green. "Probably. Unless I go for the singing." He finally confessed what had been bothering him for half of the day. "Ted's asked me to live with him."

Julie was genuinely shocked. "What?! That sounds...." She didn't know how to finish the sentence.

"Indecent? That's what I thought too. I don't know. I think maybe he's just looking for a bit of company. Am I being naïve here?"

Julie was glad the evening gloom could hide her blushes. "Perhaps. What did you say?"

"I declined. Think he was a bit upset about it. It seemed rude somehow to say I didn't trust him to keep his hands to himself but that's what it all comes down to."

"So you're staying with me for a bit longer?"

"Yes. Do you mind?"

"Not at all." She caught the quizzical look in his eye as he turned towards her and she grinned. "There's a whole heap of washing up in there just begging to be done."

"You're a slave driver and no mistake. I'll wash if you wipe."

*   *   *

Ted Ellerby dropped in to the orchestral rehearsal the next evening. None of the musicians dared stop playing while Nick still waved his arms around so ferociously in front of them but attentions were sorely distracted. It was well known that Ted hadn't written a note since George died but, unless eyes bespectacled, lensed or unaided were all deceived, that was a manuscript book he had in his hands.

"Nick," Ted hailed him as Berwald eventually ground to an undignified halt. "Brought along something for you all to try."

Nick Greenwood turned and saw the manuscript book too. It was hard to keep his voice steady. "Evening, Ted. What have you got?"

"I've dashed off a cello sonata. I'm afraid the parts are a bit wonky but I think your band can cope with them. My hand's not as steady as it used to be."

Nick looked at his principal cellist. A pleasant but definitely past it ex-pro who had arthritic fingers and poor eyesight. "You think Roy is up to it?" he muttered when Ted arrived next to him.

"Roy? Good grief, you don't think this is for him, do you? No, I want young McGuinness to play it. Best cellist you've had in this band for a long time or so the Misses de Grys tell me."

Nick knew that was true, but he rather resented the arrival of the redheaded young man who was taking away the attentions of the ladies. "I can't give this to the new boy."

"Then I shall take it away again."

"Tea break!" Nick bawled at the musicians who didn't have one deaf ear among them. "Liam, a word."

Julie unashamedly tagged along at Liam's elbow.

Nick barely repressed his growl. "Seems Ted's written you a cello sonata. Care to have a look at it in case it's too difficult then I can give it to Roy to play."

Liam got the message and flushed as he took the sheets of paper from Ted. To his unspoken relief the Sonata didn't deserve the title as it was only two pages long but it had the right number of movements to it. Just very short ones. He dutifully looked at the frightening number of black dots on the page, showed it to Julie and gave Ted his nicest smile. "Way beyond my standard. You'd better let Roy play it."

Nick beamed and Ted howled. "Oh no, McGuinness. If you're not up to it yet then you jolly well take it away and practise it. I didn't do this for Roy to make a mess of it. I want you to play it, with this orchestra, in the festival. I've already told Stella to programme it as part of the orchestra's concert."

Nick cast covetous eyes at the sheets of paper in the composer's hand. The old duffer was nearly seventy four and not likely to be writing too much more. "Oh, for God's sake, play it, Liam. Julie, get him some tea and he can sit and run through it now."

Ted was triumphant. "Thank you, Nick. Come along, Liam. I'll take you through it. I'm sure you can manage it."

"May I see the score?" Nick asked politely. He grabbed the manuscript as though it was a bag of gold and greedily drank in the notes. A new Ted Ellerby composition. And he was going to conduct the premiere. This should get him out of the world of musicology and writing programme notes for less than talented amateurs.

"I thought I might conduct the first performance myself," Ted pointed out tartly and tried to get his work back.

Liam had caught the glare in the glacial grey eyes of Nick Greenwood and was feeling a bit put out at being so bullied. "Why not let Nick have a go? You can be promoted to adviser."

Ted recognised spite when he saw it and acknowledged silently that this Irishman was tougher inside than he pretended. "Oh, go on then. But I'll sit in and listen. Nick, you go and study the score. Now, where's that Julie got to? Ah, there she is. Julie, be a love and take the parts round to the band."

The players eagerly took their parts from Julie. There was a bit of a spat between the horn players as to who should be first and who second but most of them just looked at what they had been given. Julie handed out the percussion and trombone parts last.

"It's nice to see Ted writing again," Dotty sighed. "Oh my goodness, does he really think I can play this?"

A silence fell when a lone cello started to be played. It was unmistakeably an Ellerby work. All the little nuances were there but it was also, as the soloist had feared, way beyond his capabilities.

"Glad it's not me playing that," Roy muttered.

"No!" Ted shouted at the suffering Liam. "Take that bar again. That's a D sharp, not a natural."

The requisite note was sharpened but the whole thing fell apart again just a few notes later.

Ted Ellerby glowered. "You are an incompetent! From the top! And play it up to speed."

Nick, placated now he had the premiere assured, tried to intervene. "Go easy, Ted. He is sight-reading it."

"He calls himself a musician. He is a waster of my time. Let me hear the whole thing."

The orchestra abandoned their cups of tea and almost ran to their places. The babble of excitement died down when Nick raised his baton.

"Good luck, everyone," he prayed.

Ted Ellerby prowled along the perimeters of the orchestra and listened as the valiant band of musicians struggled through the fifteen minutes of music.

"Diabolical!" he shouted at the end. "I'll come back in two weeks and if I still can't recognise it I'm taking the damn thing away and burning it."

*   *   *

It was a sober twosome who sat on the seat in the Mediterranean garden and drank lemon tea that evening.

"Got it a bit wrong, didn't I?" Liam confessed. "I did upset him."

"Just a bit. I'd no idea he could get so mad."

Car headlights swept across the green and the two on the seat nearly bolted when Ted parked his Volvo outside the hedge of Labrador Cottage and almost kicked open the gate. The bench wasn't big enough for three so Liam chivalrously got up so the older man could sit down.

"I've come to apologise," Ted said gruffly. "I shouldn't have shouted at you all like I did."

Liam thought of the proud composer who had had famous orchestras clamouring for his work and renowned soloists had paid vast fortunes for commissions. Now all he could manage was a ferociously difficult cello sonata for a bunch of amateurs. "Fancy some lemon tea? There's maybe some left in the pot."

"Thank you. I don't deserve such kindness."

Liam left the two of them in the garden and Ted sighed deeply. "Was I very rude, Julie?"

"No, not really."

"Now you're humouring me. I was. Maybe I should take the music away and make it easier."

"No, I'm sure we'll all cope. It was just a bit of a shock."

"Maybe. I asked Liam to come and live with me. I think he thought I'd made an indecent proposal to him."

"He told me." Julie was quite shocked when the eminent Ted Ellerby sounded almost tearful.

"You're a good friend to him. He needs friends. And so do you."

Liam found the two of them sitting in silence and hoped they hadn't had a row.

"When are you seeing Anna again?" Ted asked as he took the mug of tea he was given and watched his host sit cross-legged on the quarry tiles, folding up those long limbs with an enviable suppleness.

"Tomorrow week."

"Good, good. She'll work you hard but it'll be good for you." Ted sipped at the tea and looked away across the green. "It's a nice place Brockleford. George loved to walk round the green in the dark. I always told him he was a fool and he'd get mugged at worst or tread in something unspeakable at the least. But he wouldn't listen. And what have you done to your hair?"

So they told him. All about Mandy and Paris and the stuck ring and somehow Paul and Cynthia came into it as well.

Ted fondly ruffled the messy red hair. "I like the ear ring on you. Goes with your natural air of savagery. So you both came to Brockleford to find a sanctuary? So did I but that was a long time ago. Maybe that's why most people come here. That young Sigourney had a ring on her finger when she first arrived but she doesn't now. And Stella McGinty, nice woman but unmarried. Is Brockleford the last refuge for all the hope-less people in the world? Maybe it is. I must go. I've enjoyed our little chat. Next time we must do it in more comfort. Why don't the two of you come to the Manor for the weekend?"

"Sounds nice," Julie admitted cautiously.

"Good. I'll take that as a yes. Might even get the old croquet set out. Either of you two play?" He laughed as two heads were shaken. "Shame on the pair of you. Well, goodnight. And thank you for the tea and forgiveness."

*　　*　　*

By Saturday evening, Julie's left ankle was bruised from a blow by a croquet ball and the two guests both knew they had eaten far too much. After supper Ted insisted on making Liam go through the cello sonata while Julie curled round in an armchair in the drawing room and tried to stay awake while missing her cross stitch. Liam, expecting something of the kind, hadn't taken his cello or the music but Ted had been one step ahead of him. Lying on its side next to the grand piano in the drawing room had been a requisite instrument and on the piano was a photocopy of the music.

"Didn't know you played," the innocent Julie remarked when she first saw the cello. It made a lot more sense for Ted Ellerby to have written a work for an instrument he already played rather than for the one favoured by a young man he had known for just a few days.

"I don't. Saw it in a Sotheby's sale catalogue and put in a telephone bid."

Julie looked at Liam and saw his face had paled. He had the expression of one who had just had a terrible thought and didn't like to speak it aloud. She noticed that he didn't assume he was meant to keep the cello. He said not a word of thanks at the time and barely glanced at the instrument on the floor. After supper he dutifully played it while Ted accompanied him on the piano but the cello had been unused too long and its sound was dull.

"Been neglected, poor thing," Ted mused. "You'd better take it home and knock some life back into it."

Julie wanted to smile at the look of panic on Liam's face but all his protests were brushed aside.

"I'm not giving it to you," Ted pointed out. "Just lending it. Now, be grateful and stop arguing."

It had been made quite plain to the guests that they were expected to spend the night at the Manor in spite of the fact it was walking distance from Labrador Cottage and it was nearly two in the morning before Ted finally gave in to his fatigue and despatched his guests to their rooms. Julie lay awake for a while, convinced that Liam would come seeking sanctuary on the couch in her bedroom but he didn't come so she hoped he was safely asleep in his bed. It wasn't so much what he had said as what he had left out that had made her realise what he feared most from Ted Ellerby.

Liam had been intending to see if there was a chair in Julie's room he could use but he was afraid she might get the wrong idea and make a scene. He crept miserably into the huge bed, tucked the bedclothes as tight round himself as he could and, in spite of everything, went straight to sleep. He was half woken a while later by what felt like someone getting into the bed but the movement was no more than a dream. It was the sound of rain that woke him fully and he realised it was daylight. A furtive glace over his shoulder revealed he was alone in the bed but there was a slight dent in the other pillow. He shuddered once, sent up a silent prayer of thanks, and bolted for a shower in the ensuite.

*   *   *

May passed unnoticed into June. Coats were still needed in the Mediterranean garden in the evenings but the two in Labrador Cottage spent less time out there. Liam felt obliged to work on the cello sonata and Julie was having to put in extra hours on the exhibition. Nick had given her the captions, Lotty and Dotty had bombarded her with photographs and other material and Stella had told her to stop grizzling (if not in so many words) and deal with the catalogue printers herself. So the shy

Julie Hutchinson had learned to deal with recalcitrant printers, she had honed her artistic skills and abandoned her favourite subjects of cartoon rabbits and squirrels for more adventurous designs and began to wish she had the nerve to ask for a pay rise.

Liam was kept busy rushing around the county in his car, fetching and carrying and helping Julie with the more manual aspects of her exhibition. If he was envious of her elevation he never said a word, but it made her feel rather uncomfortable.

Ted Ellerby attended the second rehearsal of his cello sonata, told the musicians that they would do and then didn't go near the church on a Tuesday evening again.

It was the middle of June before Liam and Julie made the time to sit on their favourite seat. They had even managed to do a bit of weeding between them, much to Dotty's delight and the garden was a peaceful haven after yet another busy day.

"I reckon they'll be asking you to stay on in the autumn," Liam remarked vaguely.

"Doubt it."

"You'll see. I'll bet you anything that they manage to find a bit in the budget for you and give you a grand title. Something like Publicity Manager."

"Hm. And you don't think they'll extend the compliment to you?"

"No. I am a thorn in Nick Greenwood's side. If it weren't for the fact Ted seems to have adopted me I'd have been fired long since."

"But you do your work. You work really hard."

"Look at the work they give me. There's nothing responsible, nothing that calls for one ounce of intelligence. In fact, it's pretty boring."

Julie couldn't deny it. There were feelings in the office. Vibes that she had picked up and she was certain Nick Greenwood was at the bottom of it. A jealous hatred of the young man who had stolen the hearts of the ladies without even trying. "So what will you do in the autumn?"

He shrugged. "Nothing to keep me here."

"Unless you live with Ted."

"And do what?" he snorted. "Can you imagine it? The least I could expect is to be branded a gold-digging gay. If I were a woman they'd call me a tart and a bimbo. But I don't think you can use such expressions about men."

"But you would know it wasn't true."

"I couldn't take it," he admitted flatly. "Everyone would say I got wherever I get on the back of Ted Ellerby. If you know what I'm getting at."

Julie felt her face go scarlet as she understood exactly what he meant. It was all getting far too complicated and involved and she had the most awful feeling she would only make it worse if she either offered to move in as well and thus save his reputation or confess how much she would miss him when he went. "Remember what we said at the beginning? No messy entanglements?"

"Yes."

"Then let's stick with that. I bet you a week of washing up that if we went and walked round the green, you'd walk into a tree first."

"That I wouldn't. I can see like an owl in the dark."

"Bet's on?"

"Bet's on."

If Debbie hadn't wanted to keep her telephone conversation secret, she wouldn't have been crossing the green to the public box that night. And if she hadn't been crossing the green, she wouldn't have seen the two figures giggling softly and shoving each other all over the place. She wiped her hand across her streaming eyes and had an idea.

*   *   *

It was Sigs' birthday on the fourteenth of June and she brought in a chocolate cake that she had made herself. Julie and Liam were both working in the office, one on her exhibition and the other sorting out tickets for the postal bookings which had opened that day. As it was someone's birthday, Phyllis emerged from her cocoon of files and calculators and joined the others in the main office for coffee break.

"Anyone heard from Debbie this morning?" Stella asked generally.

There were negative noises all around and Sigs added, "She phoned in sick yesterday so I suppose she's still not well."

The doctor's wife pricked up her ears. "Oh? Anything serious?"

"Tummy bug she said."

Phyllis sighed triumphantly. "There's something doing the rounds. Poor old Fred's been rushed off his feet at the surgery. I can't help wondering if Dotty's bread has anything to do with it. Her kitchen can't exactly be meeting EC standards of hygiene can it?"

The others, all of whom had succumbed to Dotty's bread at some time in their lives, thought that was a bit hard. But it was well known that if you spurned the bread the first time it was offered, as Phyllis had done all those years ago, you didn't get a second chance.

"I'm sure it was nothing serious," Sigs cut in before Phyllis got too personal. "She didn't sound too bad on the phone. Just a bit depressed but I gather she's had a row with her boyfriend recently."

There was a wise silence. It was sad that poor Debbie had to live in the more modern part of Brockleford. One of those ghastly houses, all slab sides and large windows. And she shared it with a man who wasn't her husband. Nobody had yet succeeded in finding out whether the gentleman in question had a wife somewhere else but Debbie was devoted to him. Even when he smacked her round the head she wouldn't have a word said against him. Stella and Sigs had both tried to make her understand that she shouldn't have to put up with such treatment but Debbie didn't seem to mind. More often she would come in to the office starry-eyed and full of details of her love life. She had only come in twice with a black eye and then she had said it was her fault because she was stupid.

"A permanent row or one of the usuals?" Stella asked.

Sigs shrugged as she cut up the cake. "Who can tell with Debbie? It's not the kind of relationship I'd choose. Right, gather round everyone."

Members of staff dutifully crowded round, serenaded Sigs with an inharmonious version of *Happy Birthday to You*, then Nick made sure he got the largest piece of cake.

Triumphant in his nutritional conquest, Nick smiled patronisingly at Liam. "How's the cello sonata coming along?"

"Not very well," was the honest admission. Liam was hoping to get away with not eating the cake but Sigs unsympathetically shoved a plate into his hand.

"Here you are. Eat it up. Got to get a bit of fat on you."

"I'm getting too fat now," he tried valiantly but as the only other man in the room was the decidedly overweight Nick, the rest jeered good-naturedly.

Nick was resentful of the other's broad-shouldered physique but lacked the enthusiasm to tone up his own muscles. He didn't need to improve anything anyway. He never had any problems. "Been doing lots of practice?" he pursued relentlessly hoping to gain a shameful admission of neglect.

"Played the thing so much I've memorised it." Liam knew he was being got at but couldn't work out why.

"Well ask Ted to make it easier next time you're together." Nick paused for dramatic effect. "He could alter the sonata a bit too."

Liam flushed at the insult and didn't know what to say.

Nick sniffed triumphantly and wondered what he'd look like with an ear ring. He had a sudden, dread thought that maybe McGuinness' silence was because it was true and he really had moved into the Ellerbian bed. He needed to get things sorted out. A bit of teasing was one thing but if that redhead had taken over from George the consequences didn't bear thinking about.

"Sorry, old chap. Bit close to the bone was I?"

Liam, to his relief, had made sense of the bitching. Nick was bothered that he, the interloper, could get very cosy with Ted and upset a lot of assumptions. He felt that at last the upper hand was his and it couldn't hurt to string Greenwood along for a while. "I'd better get back to my tickets."

He turned away from the chatter and the others let him go without a murmur of dissent. Nick Greenwood started to wonder, and the ranks closed again as though the tides had washed over a drowning man.

Julie looked towards Liam for a second as he sat at the desk, hair all flopped forwards as he sorted out the piles of applications. He didn't belong chained up at a desk. Liam McGuinness belonged out in the world, red hair flying in the wind as he waged his war on any enemy that chanced to come along. She glanced across and saw the look Nick Greenwood was giving the only other man in the office. There was something going on between those two and she didn't like it one little bit.

Stella McGinty had also seen the way the musicologist was glaring at the summer help. She let a decent interval elapse then went across to the young man who had not only got the applications all sorted out but had nearly finished working out how best to allocate the tickets.

Liam looked up as Stella perched on the edge of the desk. His heart sank as he waited for another rebuke or snide comment even though Stella had only ever been nice to him before.

"You all right?" Stella asked. "You're very quiet."

He shrugged. "I'm OK."

"You just wish Nick would stop needling you? I know. I can see it all over your face. Just ignore him. He's not worth getting yourself all worked up about. You're a bright lad, you've made a big hit with old Ted and, between you, me and the gatepost, a certain Greenwoodian nose is a little out of joint. How are the tickets going?"

Liam was almost consoled and he smiled. "Fine. Nearly sorted."

"Well done. Since you're so efficient you can deal with the student helpers as well. Ask Sigs for the list and to tell you what to do. She hates doing it. Lovely girl but her sense of logic is one out on its own. And don't let Nick bother you. All right?"

"OK."

Stella wasn't convinced she had managed to cheer him up at all but she couldn't spend all her time worrying about the summer help.

Julie had just finished checking through her exhibition lists for the last time before the catalogue was sent to the printer when Debbie came into the office. Julie put down her list and watched as the red-eyed and distraught Debbie wandered across to her own desk, slumped rather that sat in her chair and wept.

"Oh my word!" Sigs cried and rushed across the room with a box of tissues and a consoling arm across the shoulders. "Debbie, whatever is the matter?"

Stella came to her doorway to see what all the shrieking was about. "Everything all right, Sigs?"

"Not really. Debbie's in an awful state."

Debbie was terrified her nerve would fail her. She had been hoping her victim would be in the office but it wasn't going to be easy. "I'm expecting a baby," she gulped.

"But that's wonderful news," Sigs gushed and tried to sound sincere.

Debbie realised no one was going to ask the crucial question. They all assumed her boyfriend was the father, so she was going to have to do this unprompted. She got to her feet, took a deep breath and crossed the office. There was a shocked silence all round as she sat herself on Liam's lap, put her arms round his neck and kissed him soundly on the lips.

"You'll have to marry me now," she told him.

CHAPTER FOUR

In which a concert is attended

Stella McGinty looked at the young man standing mutinously just inside her office door and still pitied him. He didn't look guilty of the deed of which he was accused but there was a strange air of resignation about him which bothered her slightly.

"I'm sorry, Liam, but what can I do? She says you two had some fun outside in the church car park and you say you didn't. I've known Debbie for four years and you for about as many weeks and while I realise what you do with another consenting adult in your own time is your business, keeping order among the staff during office hours is mine."

"She's got me, hasn't she?" Liam admitted sadly, glad that Stella hadn't yelled at him. "Are you going to fire me?"

"I've got no grounds. If you're tough enough to face down all that's going to be thrown at you then I'm perfectly happy for you to stay. As I just said, your own time is your own and I'm not going to dictate moral behaviour to you, Debbie, or anyone else." Stella almost smiled to hear such words from her own lips. With her past history too.

Liam knew this audience at least was sympathetic whether it was all a ghastly mistake or whether he really had been sowing wild oats. "I can't believe I was such a naïve idiot as to go along with the broken down car story. Is anybody that stupid these days?"

"I think some of you retain a refreshing innocence. Let's get you out of the way for today at least. Go to the publishers with the revised proofs, stay there and check them over and don't come back until tomorrow. Take Julie with you."

Facts clicked in Liam's mind as he took the bundle of papers. "Julie was out in the churchyard too. Can't she back me up?"

"In the car park?"

"Well, no. I was just going back to the church when I saw her leaning on a gravestone and not looking too well."

"Have a word with her. In the meantime you keep your head down and keep away from Debbie."

Debbie was warming to her role. For one thing she had the sympathy vote. None of the others believed that a man like Liam McGuinness could keep his trousers on given half a chance. You only had to look at him. She dodged away from Sigs when Liam slipped out of Stella's office and arrested him in his tracks. There was something so sensuous about the feel of his hair on her hands and she thought that if she kissed him hard enough she'd get a reaction out of him eventually.

"When shall we go and see the vicar?" she asked wistfully. "It'll have to be soon or I'll never fit into my white dress."

She hadn't heard his brogue so strong for a long time. "You'll never get me in front of any vicar. The only man of God I respect is the Catholic priest and do you think I'd go against the teachings of the Holy Book and commit such a sin as you accuse me of?"

A difference of religion had never entered Debbie's head. She backed away from Liam and stared at him as though he was completely mad. "You're Catholic?"

"Christened, confirmed and confessed."

"Well he's bound to deny it then," Nick crowed. "Bloody hypocrites the lot of them. Come on, you had a shag. Admit it."

"Liam!" Stella roared from her doorway. "Publishers. Now. And take Julie with you."

Julie wasn't sorry to escape from the office. The affront to religion was almost too much for her even if the jibe had been aimed at another's faith. She held out her hand to Liam as the two set off on the walk to Labrador Cottage. "Give me the car keys."

"Why?"

"Because last time you were this mad you came back with half a haircut and a ring in your ear. I'll drive, you sit and simmer and maybe we'll get you back without you having your nose tattooed."

*　　*　　*

As soon as the door had closed behind the miscreant and his companion, all eyes turned to Debbie. Stella knew that if she called the girl in for a discreet chat the others would hear the story eventually so she went out to join them.

"Well, Debbie? Do you want to speak to me in private or don't you mind if you have an audience?"

Debbie loved having an audience. She sighed perfectly. "I knew he'd deny it, but what else can I do? He was so wonderful. Just him and me and the wind in the grass."

Chins were leaned on hands and eyes sharpened.

"I told him I thought there was something wrong with my car and would he mind having a look at it. Julie nearly came too but Nick wanted to talk to her about something. So it was just Liam and me. We didn't even wait until he'd found out what was wrong with the car."

Stella thought she ought to get something sorted out before it all got too out of hand and while there were witnesses present. "Hold on a minute, Debbie. Let's just get one thing clear. You did agree?"

"Oh, yes. I'm not saying he raped me. I mean he wouldn't would he? He's too nice. I thought he'd be really brutal what with him looking so rough but he was ever so gentle. Treated me like a real lady. Even apologised afterwards. And said thank you. But I hate it when men say thank you, makes me feel like a tart."

Stella and Sigs exchanged a look across Debbie's head. It all sounded too horribly probable.

* * *

"Well?" Julie asked as she drove past the supermarket in the 1970s part of Brockleford.

Liam didn't turn his gaze from the side window. "Well, what? Stella didn't believe me although she was good about it, bet your life none of the others does. She's got me trapped. I can't believe I fell for it."

"And it's because you did I believe you."

He looked at her then. "You do?"

"Of course. I have shared a house with you for best part of a month so I think I know what sort of things you're likely to get up to. Even when you're in a paddy. What are you going to do?"

"Did occur to me to take up Ted's offer of living with him and declaring myself a closet gay."

"I don't think anyone would believe that for one minute."

"Ted would like to."

"You are getting yourself into a right state."

"Well, wouldn't you if you thought you might have to marry Debbie?"

"Who says? I'll stand up in court and be your character witness. I'll say I've shared a house with you and you've never laid a finger on me."

There came a startled gulp from the passenger seat. "You don't think it might come to court, do you?"

Julie wasn't sure but she hated to see him in such a mess. "Not for one minute. Anyway all you've got to do is put her off until the baby is born then see what colour hair it's got. Let's face it, any child of yours wouldn't stand a chance."

"I could just marry her."

Julie worked it out. "Why? To spite Mandy? You might just as well marry Stella for all the happiness it would bring you."

He turned his head away again and the mane of hair hid his blushes. "I might find it funnier but, it's just that, what with being raised a strict Catholic and all that, I mean, I'm not sure I'd know what to do anyway."

At first Julie was shocked that he should have admitted such an intimate thing to her, then she took it as quite a compliment. "Well don't come to me for lessons, because I don't know either."

He almost laughed then and was glad he had told her. "Julie, we are two of a kind. Are there any others of us out there?"

"Doubt it, so we'd better stick together. Which turning do I want at the roundabout?"

* * *

Julie thought Liam was being a craven coward that evening at tea time when he refused to go to the orchestra rehearsal. She could understand that he didn't want to be in the same room as Debbie but she thought it wouldn't do his reputation any good to start sulking.

"Well, if you're not going, I'd better stay in and keep you company."

"You don't have to."

"Might be safer. If I go across and you don't and Debbie's there she's bright enough to work out that means you're here on your own."

Liam got the point. "True. Shall we go and pull up some of Dotty's weeds for her? I could do with some fresh air."

Weeding was a pleasant enough pastime for two people who had never had anything like their own garden before and had little to do except pull out a few horticultural invaders from between the quarry tiles.

"Must be nice to have a garden," Julie remarked idly as she admired a rather handsome dandelion.

"Too much like hard work for me. Nice if you were rich and could afford to pay someone else to do it for you. I like the idea of a garden to sit in but not one to weed."

"Call that weeding?" asked an amused voice.

Two would-be gardeners looked up to see Ted Ellerby leaning on the gate.

"Had a funny feeling you two wouldn't be at the rehearsal tonight. So, young Liam, you've been a bit of a bad lad from what I hear."

"I never touched her."

"No need to bite my head off, I'm on your side."

"You're about the only one who is," came the grumble.

"Go and make us some tea, you ratbag," Julie requested kindly.

Liam pulled a face but did as he was told.

"How's he taking it?" Ted asked as he came into the garden.

"Not very well." There was no way Julie was going to share the secret confided in the car. "He can't hide away for ever. Stella's being really nice and says she hasn't got any grounds to sack him but I think Nick might manage to persuade her otherwise before too much longer."

"Don't overestimate Greenwood's power in this place. It's not as great as he thinks it is. Shall we go inside?"

They sat round the kitchen table drinking lemon tea and eating chocolate digestives.

"Fact is, Liam," Ted began rather hesitantly, "last year some time the opera house in Santa Fe asked me if I'd like to attend their revival of *The Tavern*. At the time I said I didn't think I could cope with the journey but now I think maybe it might be a good idea to go. So that's all been arranged and I wondered if you'd like to come with me." He finished in a bit of a breathless flurry and hated himself for fearing rejection at his age. He gave the other man the kind of look that used to melt George's heart.

Liam got the message. He started and flushed, but he knew he had to make a stand once and for all. "I couldn't. I mean it's good of you to ask me, but I'm supposed to be working here."

Ted realised it was hopeless; what was he thinking of anyway? But he could still keep Liam as a friend. "I know. Now don't go flying into one of your Irish tempers but I thought it might do you some good to get away from the Debbie situation for a bit and I'm sure if I asked Stella nicely she'd give you a week off."

Julie could see Liam was horribly tempted now the flirting had stopped but he had a strong sense of honour.

"I can't. Really. Thanks anyway. I signed a contract to work here until the fifteenth of September and there was no provision for any weeks off. Besides which, and I don't know how to put this without sounding offensive, I think the interest you're showing in me is one reason people round here don't like me much."

Ted wasn't the slightest bit offended and he admired the other's honesty. "One reason? It's the only reason. Ever since I started making a name for myself I have been surrounded by the sycophants and the crawlers. Now you two are different. Whether you're shy, bloody-minded or just plain couldn't-care-less I've no idea but I like you two. You've cheered me up in my old age and I shall expect an invitation to your wedding and to have the firstborn named after me." He grinned again with a roguish charm. "Now I've sent the pair of you as red as beetroots. That's what I like about being old. You can be as rude as hell and people just think you're going gaga. All right, I shall excuse you Santa Fe. But I would like to invite the two of you to take a holiday with me when your contracts are up. I've got a dear friend who lives in Italy now and I know he'd love to have us stay in his villa for a month or so."

Ted Ellerby left Labrador Cottage like an septuagenarian whirlwind and the two residents leaned wearily against the front door when it closed behind him.

"Italy," Julie breathed. "For a few months? How on earth am I going to explain that to my mother?" She nudged Liam's arm. "You know you nearly pulled there, don't you?"

Liam's smile was wry. "Trust me, there is nothing that man could tempt me with that would make me sleep with him."

*   *   *

For nearly a week Debbie tried to get Liam to admit his folly and he made sure he was never left alone with her. The ticket sales and the student helpers were sorted out in record time that year and Stella McGinty began to wish she could afford to keep on both of the summer helpers. From the way Debbie was chattering on she wouldn't be coming back after she had had her baby and Stella felt a bit sorry for Debbie. The poor girl seemed to have a rather naïve idea that babies were all talcum powder and toothless smiles. Stella allowed herself the luxury of a little plotting. If Debbie went then that left one job vacancy but two eminently eligible summer helpers. She knew which one Nick would rather she kept on but Stella couldn't decide. Liam had a good sense of humour and went through his appointed tasks like a rocket. He had mastered the computer system faster than anyone else and altogether seemed the better option. But there was something about him that made her hesitate. Something a little restless. Liam McGuinness was just passing through on his way to somewhere. Julie, on the other hand, was quietly methodical. She didn't have flashes of brilliance but her exhibition designs were perfectly charming and at least as good as any professional could turn out. The Chairman had been nagging Stella to do more in the way of publicity and education and here Julie would be ideal.

Stella gave up battering her brains over the matter and went to see Phyllis. Gossip or not, Phyllis Bond could be relied on to be discreet when she had to be.

"Right, Phyllis, what are we going to go about Liam and Julie?"

Phyllis looked up from her ledgers and eventually focussed through the right bit of her new varifocal lenses. Blessed things, they weren't helping at all. "What about them?" she demanded, wondering if something had occurred when she wasn't listening and feeling slightly more piqued in case it had. Anyone other than Stella would have received the sharp side of her tongue. "Are they getting married or something?"

Stella recognised the signs and made sure the door was closed. "Not a good day?"

"Never is, these days. Such a pain, getting old. My eyes won't focus, more grey in my hair, chin starting to sag. Tell me it gets better?"

Stella looked at Phyllis, still an attractive woman in her middle years, and had to smile. She had been through it all about ten years ago but hadn't had so much to lose in the first place. "Trust me, it gets better. Now about these two. I'd guess the budget won't stretch to keeping them both on in the autumn?"

"Not unless you halve what is already a pitiful salary and share it between them. I presume you're working on the assumption that Debbie's leaving sometime? We can't keep her on and another one as well."

"I wish Ted would write us a few more blockbusters. The festival could really do with a thumping great premiere. Oh well, maybe next year."

"If we keep Liam on."

"Right. But I can't in all honesty justify it by saying he's the better worker. They're both good in their own way."

"You keep Liam on and I bet Nick will have quit by Christmas. Look, I'm sure he'll find something else to do. He's got brains under all that hair."

Stella was quite well aware that Nick was a favourite of Mrs Bond. "Can you see if we can shave a bit off our other budgets somewhere?"

Phyllis pulled a face. "You know how close we're sailing to the wind these days. Can't you butter up the Chairman a bit?"

"I've buttered until I'm blue in the face. There's just no money anywhere."

"I'll go through the figures again but I think you're going to have to resign yourself to losing one of them."

Stella sighed. "I know. Well, it's early days yet. We'll see how the pair of them shape up. They might solve the crisis themselves and neither of them might want to stay on."

Phyllis felt oddly cheated after her visitor had gone. It was just typical of Sigs' sense of humour to appoint a challenger. Still, as she had said, Liam McGuinness had brains and he wouldn't stay where he wasn't wanted.

*   *   *

June remained cold and wet and Julie couldn't help but notice that Liam had given up going for his twice-daily runs. Occasionally but less frequently she would hear rhythmic thumps from his room that implied some sort of exercise routine was being followed but more and more often she heard him practising his singing. She had to admit that Anna Forrester's reputedly brutal techniques were having quite an effect. It saddened her a little to think that Liam was giving up on his hopes of Olympic glory but if he had foot-faulted and then gone flat on his face she could understand that maybe his nerve had gone.

It was when the glossy leaflet came unsolicited through the letterbox that she knew she was right. She wandered along to the breakfast table and gave Liam his letter and the leaflet. She had lived with him long enough to know when his mother was writing him letters so she put the leaflet on the top.

"You might like to look at this before you get engrossed in the latest chapter of *War and Peace* from your mother."

Liam smiled fondly as he took the letter. "Dear old Ma. Never could write less than twenty pages. What's this then?"

"New sports centre opening up on the other side of town. Got to get you fit for Atlanta."

He put the leaflet on the table. "I was told to take time off so I'm taking it."

"For how long?"

"None of your business," he told her perfectly truthfully and stalked out of the kitchen taking his breakfast with him.

Julie hated him when he got in one of his huffy moods and, as she had found out, Liam McGuinness excelled in huffs. The best tactic, she had learned, was to let him get on with it.

* * *

Julie went to the sports centre the day it opened, signed up for a course of aerobics as living with an athlete had made her feel very unfit, and picked up an application form to use the multi-gym. She had made up her mind that a certain javelin thrower was not going to miss the Olympics and she was getting used to his huffs and his tempers by this time. She rather spitefully waited until it was coffee break in the office and there were several witnesses present.

"Thought you might like to sign up for the gym," she announced airily and plonked the form down on top of the pile of ticket applications in front of Liam. "As you're supposed to be in training."

Sigs didn't notice how Liam flushed. "Is this at the new centre?" she asked. "I must admit I had thought about signing up for some aerobics or something. I ought to try to get myself a bit fitter."

Julie panicked at the thought of Sigs being in the same aerobics class. She wasn't sure she could cope with the idea of Sigourney Hawkes in a leotard. And you could bet your life, she thought to herself, that it would be a fluorescent pink number and probably teamed with neon yellow leggings.

"Liam, angel, lend me that piece of paper. It's bound to have the telephone number on it."

He, not unthankful, handed over the form.

"Thank you, angel. Oh, by the way, I've got some concert tickets for you two."

From the way the smiles ran round the office, the two temporary staff guessed they were the victims of a plot

"What concert?" Liam asked suspiciously.

"Local youth orchestra does a bash in St Bartholomew's once a year and as the festival gives them some money they always send us a couple of comps. I'll give you the tickets in a mo."

"When is it?" Julie thought to ask while two desperate minds raced for excuses.

"Tonight, sweetie. I'm afraid you'll have to go, the little kiddies won't have anyone to give the bouquet to if you don't." She refrained from mentioning that if things didn't get any better the poor little darlings wouldn't get any money at all. It was such a pity Ted had stopped writing. A new Ellerby work would be just the thing to revive the festival. Sigs whisked back to her desk and everyone heard her triumphantly procure the last place in the seven thirty class on Thursdays.

Julie's heart crashed. She had got the second place in that very self-same class. Pink and yellow leotards went for the burn in her mind the rest of the day.

*   *   *

"We were set up!" Julie yelled from her bedroom as she heard Liam thud along the landing from the bathroom to his room.

"Dead right we were. What do you reckon is suitable retribution?"

"Slow roasting and boiling in oil are two options that come to mind."

"You're a vindictive woman, Julie Hutchinson. Remind me not to get in your bad books."

Julie looked out of her window, decided a coat might be a good idea, then went onto the landing. Liam's door was still firmly closed and there were some very funny puffing noises coming from his room.

"Are you all right in there?"

"You've shrunk these trousers in the wash. I'd swear you have."

The truth occurred to Julie. "You're putting on weight, fatso. Hurry up, or we'll be late."

There came some incoherent mumbling, a few rustles and thuds then Liam strode out of his room puling his jacket on over a sleeveless T-shirt as he came.

"You can't go out in those ratty old jeans."

"They're the only things I can sit down in. You're right, I've been eating too much. You look very smart."

"Thank you. I now feel overdressed."

"Never. I'm just a born slob. Sure you want to walk?"

Julie nodded. "It's a nice evening and you need to lose some weight."

"if you make one more remark about weight...."

"What?" she challenged, no longer afraid of that sparkle in his eye.

"I'll think of something."

*   *   *

The concert wasn't as bad as they had feared. For those more accustomed to the strains of the Amsterdam Concertgebouw or the London Symphony Orchestra it was a little raw and discordant but for a bunch of kids in the middle of nowhere it was a good show. The habitual thanks were given to the Brockleford Festival for its sponsorship but Julie could not be persuaded on to the stage so Liam had to go and collect the bouquet on behalf of the sponsors which raised a few eyebrows. But he managed a perfectly charming, if very short, acceptance speech which surprised Julie and made her even more thankful she hadn't been the one to go up on stage.

"So what's up with you?" Liam asked as the two set off back to the old part of Brockleford.

Julie felt a bit of a fool now it was all over "I just couldn't face the thought of everyone looking at me."

"Idiot," he remarked fondly and gave her the flowers. "Here, I'm not carrying these around like a big jessie."

She took the flowers but decided against remarking it had been a long time since a man had given her some blooms. She had almost forgotten what it was like to walk beside a young man and to hold flowers in her arms. Not so long ago she had thought the memories would never fade and now it was as though she was recalling a dream.

"Field path?" Liam asked,

Julie nodded mutely. She felt oddly like crying but didn't know why. There had been no affection whatsoever in the way she had been handed the flowers but just for a second she had felt his hand, surprisingly cool, beneath hers.

They left the churchyard by a gate and set off along the edge of a field. The river Brockle gurgled alongside but they walked past the footbridge that would have taken them over the river to join the road back to the village.

Julie walked slowly, her arms full of flowers and was finally at peace with the world. "I could get to like living here. It's so quiet and, I don't know, like nothing ever changes here."

"What was that Ted said?" Liam queried. "Is Brockleford the last refuge for all the hope-less people in the world?"

"Cynic." Julie, her eyes on the flowers, tripped over something on the ground and would have gone sprawling if Liam hadn't grabbed her arm. "What on earth was that?"

He bent down and picked up a stake sharpened at one end. "Looks like there's going to be a bit of fencing going on round here."

Julie got her breath back after the strength of his grip on her arm. "Go on then, show me your javelin throw."

He felt the weight of the pole in his hand. "You must be kidding. Break my shoulder if I even tried. I've got a better idea, I'll go and put it with all those others over there."

"Oh, go on," Julie begged. "I've never seen a javelin thrower in action. I'll cook the tea tomorrow night."

Liam looked at the pole he still held in his hands and was horribly tempted. "Make it a curry?"

"Vindaloo special."

"OK, but don't get in the way."

Julie remembered the ignominy this young man had suffered in international competition. "Need a marker for your feet?"

"If you like."

Julie carefully laid the strap of her bag across the path. "There you are. Where's the safest place to be?"

"Just about right where you are."

Liam paced back from the bag strap and told himself this was just a bit of fun. He was throwing a fence pole for the hell of it and if he caught his foot in that lethal strap he'd probably break his leg. The pole was ridiculously heavy but he wasn't planning on throwing it very far. It was as he started his run he knew things were not as they once were. At one time he would have felt fit and ready for this. Now too many bits of him were wobbling and he could have sworn his thighs were slapping together. This was an elephant impersonating a lemming and something had to be done about it. Even if he never threw a javelin again, he couldn't live with all this surplus flesh shaking all over him. His mind was so distracted he quite forgot about the marker on the path and when it felt right he just flung that pole as hard as he could. He hopped along on his left foot as the wobbles subsided.

Julie watched Liam attentively and thought he was quite an impressive sight. "Brilliant!" she cried and would have clapped her hands but her arms were full of flowers.

Liam looked down at his feet. That treacherous bag handle was half an inch in front of his left foot. "I did it," he announced so matter-offactly that Julie thought for one hideous moment that he was referring to Debbie. "Will you look at that. Miles behind the marker."

Julie obediently looked down too and thought they had very funny miles in County Londonderry.

"Come on, let's pace out the throw."

Julie tagged along behind and admired his rear view as he paced across to the pole.

"Fifty three yards," he declared. "Not bad for a fat alto throwing a fence pole."

"So what does a soon-to-be-thinner alto throwing a proper javelin hope to achieve?"

Liam picked up the pole and shrugged. "I have been known to pass the hundred metre mark. Unfortunately not in competition in front of any judges and it would have to be one of my better days."

"And thinner days?"

"One more weight joke and…"

Julie looked up at the barbarian leaning on the pole and was glad to see he was laughing at her. "Yes?"

Liam put the pole back with its fellows. "Come on. And don't forget it's curry tomorrow night."

*   *   *

It was noted among all the festival staff and most of the residents of the village part of Brockleford that young Liam McGuinness was back in training. It was also noticed among the office staff that Liam McGuinness was on a diet. He was very nice about it but not even one of Sigs' legendary chocolate cakes could tempt him.

Nick Greenwood was rather dismissive of a man who felt he had to go running for miles and stop eating cake just to make himself more attractive to the women in the office but there was no doubt about it, Liam was definitely attracting them. Even Sigs had taken to asking his advice about her proposed fitness regime. Nick Greenwood sought out Stella McGinty in her office.

"What are you doing about the temps?" he began abruptly.

"Should I be doing anything?"

"I mean in the autumn. You aren't seriously proposing to keep McGuinness on are you? I mean Julie's all right, quite a decent kid, but he's a bit of a troublemaker."

Stella sighed silently. She had known this would come, but she had hoped it wouldn't come until nearer the autumn, but she had started it all off by engaging a new cat to set among the pigeons. "Do you have a complaint about Liam's work?"

"Well, no," Nick had to admit and hated being put on the defensive. "But I think it's a bit slipshod. He's done in about four weeks what it takes Sigs two months to do."

"Sigs has other duties as well. Besides which maybe Liam just works fast." Stella carried on playing out the rope, waiting to see how long it would take Nick Greenwood to hang himself.

Her adversary was not that stupid. It never crossed his arrogant brain that a competitor had been chosen deliberately but he knew when Stella McGinty was preparing for battle.

"Forget I mentioned it," he said charmingly and went to talk to Phyllis.

*   *   *

It was again not a good day for Phyllis. It had all started with a phone call from her son to say that his girlfriend had dumped him after five years of non-marital bliss. To add insult to injury she had taken the cat with her and Phyllis knew how much her son doted on Harley the cat. She had no option except to invite him for the weekend, which she knew would upset Fred as their son was a vegetarian and Fred, most emphatically, was not. It wasn't even as though she could appeal to her daughter for help as the first grandchild was about to be produced. Thankfully within wedlock.

"Phyllis!" hailed a voice from the doorway.

"Hullo, Nick, what can I do you for?"

He didn't notice the frown on her face behind the glasses. "Just wondered if you could give me a clue how much is left in the equipment budget? I've been thinking for a long time we ought to get some decent equipment in this place. Thought I'd put in a word with Stella."

"Budget meetings in January," she intoned and didn't take her eyes off her computer screen.

Nick acknowledged this was going to be harder than he had thought. "It could mean something a bit more up to date for you as well. You must be sick of that old spreadsheets system by now."

"I've got used to it. Do you want something, Nick?"

He really didn't know why she was so scratchy these days. "Have you any idea when Stella's going to fire McGuinness?"

"Didn't know she was. Go away. I'm busy."

"Well, after he got Debbie knocked up and everything."

"Did he?" she replied vaguely. "I thought Debbie had given up on that idea since she made it up with her boyfriend."

Nick could have screamed. He slammed the door on his way out as he knew that would upset Phyllis and he strode blindly along the corridor back to the main office. Just one decent break in his life, that was all he wanted. One chance to get out of this place and make a name for himself. He couldn't understand why Ted Ellerby had taken such a shine to Liam. That tongue-tied peasant hadn't even said one polite thing about the cello sonata that had been written for him. It was too upsetting to speculate what Liam McGuinness had done to get that sonata but Nick couldn't believe it was all innocent. What with Ted and Debbie both notched on the proverbial bedpost it seemed this Irishman just didn't care. But, then again, he didn't seem to be showing any interest in Julie. Nick was still plotting about Julie when Sigs passed him in the corridor.

"Ted's back," she told him. "Wants to see you at the Manor this afternoon."

*   *   *

Nick sat stiffly on the sofa in the drawing room at the Manor and watched Ted Ellerby prowling round.

"It's like this," Ted said eventually. "You know it's all set up that when I snuff it this place becomes a museum and research library?"

"Yes," Nick answered slowly, wondering what was coming next.

"Well, fact is, I want to change things a bit."

Nick nearly groaned aloud. He could see it all now. The whole kit and caboodle willed to some dreadful redheaded Irishman. "In what way?"

"First of all I'm not going to wait as I'm sick of getting letters from students and so forth so I want to get the library going now. I only need the harness room to work in so I'm going to have some of the outbuildings converted to make a proper place of it and get all the stuff over from Lotty and Dotty too. Now, you are a musicologist, I have already asked you to write my biography when a line can be drawn under the last chapter and you have agreed. I've been trying to get things sorted out and dated for you, you know what I'm like for never throwing things away, and I just wondered if you could spare a couple of weekends to get the manuscripts in order before all the things from Lotty arrive."

Nick thought things were definitely improving. "Of course. When had you thought?"

"Whenever you like, but not too far away. Check your diary and let me know."

"Could spare you this weekend if it helps," Nick offered then hoped that didn't sound too desperate.

Ted barely seemed to be listening. "Good. I'll carry on writing dates on things as best I can and then you can get weaving with some sort of thematic catalogue before it all gets out of hand."

It was a different Nick Greenwood who sauntered back across the green. Biographer and compiler of thematic catalogue to Sir Edward Ellerby. He was going to make it after all. He passed Labrador Cottage just as Liam was locking his car.

"Another trip to the publisher?" Nick called cheerfully.

Liam jumped. That was the first civil thing Nick had said to him for nearly a week. "Another one. Should be getting on for the last."

"Did you know Ted's back from Santa Fe?"

"No."

"Yes. Just been to tea at the Manor. I'm going to get to write the catalogue of his works. And the biography."

"Congratulations."

"You going back to the offices?"

"Not yet. Just want to dash in here first."

"Right-oh. See you in a bit."

Liam watched Nick Greenwood swagger across the cricket pitch and wondered what on earth Ted Ellerby had slipped into the tea. He had never seen Nick so polite and so charming before. A shudder passed through him and he shot into Labrador Cottage for a comforting cup of peppermint tea.

*   *   *

"Must say Nick was in a good mood this afternoon," Julie announced at the supper table. "Which is funny really as he was in a foul mood all morning."

"Can beat you on that one. I know the reason. Going to write the thematic catalogue and biography of Ted."

"There's something going on," Julie decided. "I mean what was all that he was saying about Ted turning his home into a library?"

"We'll have to ask him next time we see him." Liam concluded and looked sadly at the meagre plate of food Julie had given him. Sometimes he hated being on a diet.

Julie was still trying to persuade Liam it was his turn to wash up when she was interrupted by the banging of the door knocker. She answered the knock on the door and smiled politely at Ted.

"Hullo, hear you've been buttering up Nick Greenwood."

"Yes, pompous little ass. He lapped it up. Liam in?"

"Just putting on the pink Marigolds."

"Lovely." Ted preceded Julie into the kitchen. "Ah, glad you're here. How's the sonata?"

"An unforgiving swine. How was Santa Fe?"

"Very pleasant. Tell me, how long do you propose to wear that silly gold thing in your ear?"

"Until I remember not to lose my temper."

"No, that's not what I mean. I remember Stella had her ears pierced not so long ago and she had to wait a certain time before she could start to wear proper ear rings."

"Six weeks. And half a bottle of surgical spirit. I'm not doing it again."

"Good because I only bought you the one. Went to a Navajo reservation in New Mexico. Fascinating people. Hold out your hand."

Liam, delighted but embarrassed, did as he was told. He looked at the silver ear ring he had been given. "Thank you. That's very generous of you."

"Oh I know. And here's a necklace to match. Julie, stop bothering that kettle and come here a minute. I was going to get you some ear rings too but then I thought I don't think you wear them so I bought you a bracelet."

Julie accepted the dainty silver and turquoise bracelet with a smile. "Thank you. You're spoiling us again."

"No more than you will earn one day."

Liam was afraid something like this would happen. So far in Ted Ellerby's debt he wouldn't be able to refuse. He turned the ear ring in his hand and watched the turquoise bead slide along the loop. Jewellery for tourists made by one of the most repressed peoples on Earth. "Does everything have a price?" he mused sadly half aloud and then blushed to realise the other two had heard.

"Oh yes," Ted assured him. "Tea tomorrow at the Manor. Both of you."

*   *   *

It was quite a gathering at the Manor for tea the next day. Julie and Liam were the last to arrive as the latter had thought it might be polite to try out the silver ear ring and had then had to spend five minutes stopping his ear bleeding.

The housekeeper showed them into the drawing room where Dotty and Lotty were admiring the views of the garden from the French windows and Sigs and Stella were sitting on the sofa looking as though they had just stepped into fairyland.

"It's like something from Agatha Christie," Julie muttered to Liam. "Any second now the great detective will burst upon us and all will become abundantly clear."

"I hope so, because I haven't got a clue."

Ted didn't keep his guests waiting long and he was chuckling to himself as he led the bewildered sextet across the courtyard of the manor house to what had once been the stable block.

"Come along in," he encouraged and dived into the first building.

Seven pairs of eyes eventually adjusted to the gloom of the row of stalls that still smelled of horses although nothing equine had lived in them for nearly half a century.

"Welcome to the Ted Ellerby museum and archive," the composer announced formally. "I knew you'd never understand. I have hired an architect and signed contracts with a firm of builders just this afternoon now that planning consent is granted. These buildings are to be converted into a proper library and research archive. Something to keep you all going when I've kicked the bucket. My solicitor's working on the finer points, but all that concerns you at the moment are the employment prospects. Come along."

They followed along behind. Through the stalls, under the ladder to the hayloft then right into the harness room. In this last room, some semblance of civilisation had been introduced. There was a table, a chair, a pile of manuscript paper and dozens of boxes all over the place. There was a second door which opened onto the courtyard and a window opposite with a cobweb-encrusted view of the fields.

"This is where I do my writing," Ted said simply. "This is where I like to work. I like the fact it smells of centuries of horse harness. I like to imagine all the conversations that must have gone on in here between the grooms and this is where I want all of my manuscripts to be kept. I've brought most of them in already."

"Oh my God," Stella muttered. "He really has lost it. Ted," she began sternly. "I've told you before that you mustn't keep your manuscripts in the outbuildings. If you don't go and put them somewhere dry and mouse-free I really am going to take them all along to the bank to go in the vault."

Ted, with the experience of friendship, ignored her. He looked at the young man gazing out of the window. The mane of hair hid the silver ear ring but Ted knew it was there, he had caught a glimpse when the wind had flung those curls all over the place. He knew Liam would never be to him what George had been, but it was nice to dream.

"Anyway," he said sharply. "Lotty and Dotty, I want the contents of your attic over here when the building work is finished and, Liam, I want to offer you the job of curator. Starting in the autumn when your contract with Stella runs out."

There was a stunned silence. "What?" Liam asked faintly.

"Just that. I said I would call in my debt and now I'm calling it. The price of the favours I have given you is that you will take charge of my memory when my body is gone."

"But I don't know anything about being a curator."

"Then you shall have to learn. Right. Enough bombshells for one day, I think. Let's go and see if there's any of that elderflower cordial left. Come along."

Stella caught up with Liam. "You've heard Nick is writing the biography? Looks like you and he will be having to work quite close together over this one. Do I congratulate?"

Liam had a feeling there was some sort of plot afoot in Brockleford and he wasn't sure if he liked it. "You can tell me just what Ted's up to."

"If I knew that, I'd be chairman of Mensa. Humour him. He'll have forgotten all about it by next week."

Liam shot her a hard look but there were no secrets in her face. Maybe he was just paranoid. He blamed it on his upbringing. But there was definitely something going on.

Stella brought up the rear of the cavalcade and began to hope that things would work out all right now Ted had made up his mind to keep hold of Liam by legal means. All they needed now was something large, spectacular and commercially viable from the scheming composer.

CHAPTER FIVE

In which tea and cakes are served at a garden party

Stella McGinty never wanted to hear the words "commemorative volume" ever again. It was already two months behind schedule and it seemed there was no way that book was going to be ready for its planned launch date. She looked up from her desk to where the mocking calendar assured her July had indeed begun and the festival was little over six weeks away. It was a relief that the fuss in the office seemed to have died down since Debbie had apologised to Liam for naming him as the father of her baby. Stella McGinty felt more and more often that she would never understand the young.

She flicked through the pages again. It wasn't so much that not all the editorial corrections had been made, it was just the attitude of those damned publishers. Did it matter if the curly bits round the chapter titles were different for chapter six? So some of the footnote numbers were a different size from the others - so what? Stella was fed up with the whole stupid idea. It had been Nick's brainchild in the first place then he had delegated with the consummate skill that was peculiarly his own and it had finished up with the office temps, who really shouldn't have had to do much more than file bits of paper and make tea, rushing all over the place and almost having to rewrite chapters themselves. Stella looked at the last few sheets on the heap. Those two had certainly made a cracking good job of the index anyway.

The office door opened and Nick stuck his head in. "Gather there's a bit of a crisis on?" he asked smoothly.,

"Come in and close the door." Stella invited and steeled her heart against the Greenwoodian charm. "This book. I've got the list of the finer points sorted out now but there is still the small matter of the photographs you wanted. Dotty and Lotty have sent over what they think is the best option, have you looked at them yet?"

Nick ran a hand through his hair. "Good God! Do you think I've got time to deal with those two old fools? Get one of the juniors to do it."

Stella just managed to bite her tongue in time. "Nick, this whole project was your idea. I have followed up your suggestions for authors, Dotty and Lotty have worked hard to find you those pictures. Do you seriously think it is a good idea to pass over the job of choosing them to a couple of juniors? Besides which there is the matter of the photograph you wanted of the manuscript. How are you getting along in that department?"

Nick had genuinely forgotten but he wasn't going to admit as much. "Oh, can't find a half decent photographer for love nor money."

Stella refrained from commenting about the need to book a photographer a little in advance for most occasions. "Well, what do you suggest?"

"Get McGuinness to take the manuscript to a copy shop in Chester or somewhere. There must be one. They can do a colour photocopy of the thing and then the printers can work from that."

"Hardly. A colour slide is what is needed apparently."

"I haven't got time to deal with that now," Nick proclaimed again. He got abruptly to his feet. "Is there anything else you can't cope with?"

At certain times, Stella mused, authority had to be exerted and she was, after all, the director. "I can cope perfectly well, Nick, but tidying up after you is not one of my jobs. Now, you put a decent colour slide on my desk by Monday afternoon or the whole thing is off. All right?"

Nick didn't reply. He slammed the door on the way out and fairly shrieked across the office, "McGuinness! Get the manuscript for *Maytime Wedding* off your boyfriend, and get me a colour slide of the opening page by Friday morning. Go on. Move it." He got some satisfaction seeing how Liam's face flushed scarlet, but there was no denial, not so much as a scowl or a clenching of the fist. Nick was triumphant. It had taken a good few weeks but at last that Irishman knew who was the boss.

* * *

Ted Ellerby recognised the signs as soon as he opened his front door in response to the ferocious jangling of the bell.

"OK, what's Greenwood said to you now?"

"Oh, everything," was the not very helpful reply. "He now wants a colour slide of *Maytime Wedding* first page by Friday. Today is Wednesday. How the hell am I going to get a photographer to do their fecking stuff by Friday?"

Ted had seldom seen such rage but he wasn't fazed. "Liam, you are getting yourself into a state again. I suppose Greenwood referred to me as your boyfriend again?"

"Yes."

"Don't take it to heart so. You and I both know it isn't true so let those gossips say what they like. You are an attractive young man and I lived with one of my own sex for forty years. People are putting two and two together and making ninety five. Come in a minute, or we'll have the chickens up the stairs again and they do make such a mess on the carpets."

Liam followed his host along the corridor to the kitchen. "I'm sorry. It just makes me angry."

"I know. Goes with your hair colour. Don't let Nick Greenwood get to you. Coffee?"

"No. Thank you."

"Still dieting?"

"Yes."

"Well at least sit down at the table until you've got a civil tongue in your head. No, better idea, go and walk round the garden for five minutes. And don't come back until you feel better."

After ten minutes Ted made coffee for himself, remembered Liam liked tea, and went out into the garden with the drinks. He found Liam sitting on the broken seat by the fish pond, elbows on knees, head down and morose eyes glaring at the inoffensive fish.

"Here," Ted hailed him. "Put this in your pocket and then get this tea down your throat. I don't care what sort of a diet you're on."

Liam realised it wasn't any kind of herbal tea but he was thankful that at least it wasn't the dreaded coffee again. He looked inside the envelope he had been given. "What's this?"

"Colour transparency of the opening page of *Maytime Wedding*. I had the whole thing photographed about ten years ago when I had a daft idea of producing a facsimile. Now get up and let an old man rest his aching bones."

Liam dutifully sat cross-legged by the side of the pond and took the mug of coffee from Ted. "But you knew Nick would need a photograph so why didn't you give this to him weeks ago?"

"Because I wanted to make the little bastard sweat. Didn't occur to me he'd delegate. Again."

"How does he get away with it?" Liam enquired of the fish.

"He has a certain charm. You've seen his attraction for the women?"

"Except for Julie."

"Ah, now Julie is a little on the slender side for Nick's taste so tell her not to get any fatter."

"Slender? The woman's anorexic."

"Do you really mean that?"

Liam was surprised by the sharp concern in the other man's voice. "No, not really. But I'm sure she doesn't eat enough. I keep feeding her marmalade sandwiches at the least appropriate times but it doesn't seem to be doing any good." Liam sighed and looked away across the garden. "It's no good. I want to move our relationship on to the next phase. I've tried not to because I think if I put one foot out of line she'll smack me round the head, so I walk round her on eggshells."

Ted's mind went back over half a century to when a fresh-faced young man had joined the bomber crew as the rear gunner and the two had lost months of their relationship as they had both been afraid to say anything. At least Liam's object of desire was socially more acceptable, even these days. "Maybe you should say something. Drop a few hints. She may not smack you round the head."

"True," he conceded. "She might play along, even let me go as far as buying a ring for her finger and then dump me when something better comes along."

"Do you trust her so little?" Ted enquired sadly.

"I trust all people so little. I learned a lot about traitors and friends while I was growing up and it wasn't always as easy as the ones who had the rosaries in their pockets and those who didn't. No, we made an agreement. Friends for the summer with no messy complications. I'll wait and see what the autumn does."

Ted looked at the young man dreaming across the garden. His dark blue eyes had lost their angry sparkle and he was smiling as a fish came and nibbled the finger he had stuck in the pond.

"I must go. Thanks for the coffee and the photo. And the time. My mother always used to send me out into the mountains whenever I got mad."

"Sounds a very sensible woman. I should like to meet her one day."

Liam turned away as the two got to their feet. "She doesn't go anywhere much. Not since she was shot in the back and paralysed."

Ted wasn't sure what to say. Condolences seemed ridiculously inadequate and not even expected.

"And do you know the worst part?" Liam asked and wouldn't look at the man by the pond. "The bullet was meant for me. Thank you for my tea. I'll bring the photo back soon as I can."

*   *   *

They all stood respectfully round as though a dear friend was laid out in state on Stella McGinty's desk. No one dared touch as fingers were still sticky with chocolate cake but it was an awe-inspiring moment in a life.

"Is that it?" Debbie asked when she felt the reverent silence had gone on quite long enough. "That's the book we've all been so worried about? But the pages aren't even stuck together."

"It's an unbound copy," Stella explained kindly. "The publishers have sent us one in advance and I thought you might all like to have a look at it. Nobody to take it home, please, it might never reappear. And please keep it clean."

Julie licked her fingers clean. "What colour is the binding going to be?" she asked as she picked up the pages.

Nick glared jealously and snatched them away from her. "Red. And the dust jacket's going to have the photograph of the first page of the opera manuscript superimposed over a Brockleford landscape. I'll take this back to my desk and study it carefully."

"Be the first time you have," Sigs muttered under her breath as Nick so grandly left the room.

Julie felt thwarted. She had been hoping to have a look at the pages since she and Liam had worked so hard to get the entire book ready.

"Nick!" Stella roared. "Get back in here please! We need to discuss the launch"

The proud father of the literary baby came trotting back but minus the pages. "Sorry, getting carried away."

"Right, for the benefit of those of you who haven't suffered a Festival before, I shall explain a few things. Ted's house will be open again for the public to look round and he's agreed with the builders that the conversion work will be put off until after the Festival so there aren't workmen crawling all over the place. Tours of the house are always guided, Nick and Sigs split them between them and Ted keeps well out of the way. This year, I would like Julie and Liam to join as guides so I'll arrange with Ted for Sigs to take the two of you round sometime so you know how the tour goes."

Nick's voice was heard to mutter something about bedrooms but the others all ignored him.

"Garden party, chaps. Annual bash for the dear old farts of the Friends of the Brockleford Festival. Best bibs and tuckers all round. Friday week so the office will be closed that afternoon except Debbie has offered to look after the phones. I've booked the usual spread from the usual caterers so there shouldn't be any hitches and Ted has promised us his usual strawberries. Report to the Manor at two o'clock then, party kicks off at two thirty. Right, I think that's all for now. Back to work. Julie and Liam, can you hang on a minute, please." Stella waited until her audience had been reduced to two and then she continued mercilessly. "Now, you two presumably haven't had any dealings with the Friends before. They are mostly Ted's age, some a little younger, they are all without doubt his groupies and will not take to any criticism of him or his music. I'm sure I can trust you two to be discreet but I think I'd best warn you some of them can be, shall we say, a little difficult. They will probably criticise anything and everything either to your face or, more likely, behind your back. I must ask you to keep your mouths shut in the face of any such criticism and just remember they put a lot of money into the festival coffers and most of them are personal friends of the chairman. Oh, and, Liam, could you tie that hair of yours back for the occasion? I don't really want ginger bits in the strawberry jam."

*   *   *

The Mediterranean garden was a positive haven that evening. The plants had all been watered with the aid of a bucket and measuring jug and it was really very pleasant to sit among the scents of soggy herbs and talk about nothing. It had been a fraught day and it was getting dark before Julie realised that the rather pleasant tickling on her arm wasn't the clematis being friendly, it was a mosquito having its tea.

She slapped her arm and squashed the offending insect. "Rotten creatures. I'll have a bite the size of a golf ball soon."

"You must taste nice," Liam mused innocently then caught the glare she shot at him. "Sorry, I wasn't intending to take a bite."

"Good." Julie leapt to her feet saying things about TCP and raced up to her room. She wished Liam wouldn't look at her like that. It melted all her resolves never to get involved with anyone ever again. It was only for a few more weeks then she would be gone. Liam was going to be stuck in Brockleford as the curator for Ted's museum so that left the world for her. She really couldn't decide where to go. She leaned on the windowsill as she rubbed ointment into the bite on her arm and looked down at the garden. Liam was still sitting there, smiling wistfully to himself as he so often did. Julie had painted her own picture of the enchanted world of mountains and leprechauns where Liam went when he dreamed. Ointment administered, Julie went to the kitchen to make the lemon tea. It was going to be hard to keep Liam as a friend. Try as she might, she had got fond of him and she wanted to move their relationship onto the next level. But she was afraid he might yell at her or go off in a huff. So she walked round him on eggshells.

*   *   *

Stella McGinty called a council of war only a few days later.

"Right, just to confirm all the rumours and memos that have been going all over the place. Book launch on August the fifteenth at St Bart's and it's a three-line whip for that one. I want everyone to attend and you will be helping by handing round the food, pouring drinks and generally being nice to all the important and press who will be attending. The Chairman has accepted his invitation and is bringing some of his wealthier friends with him. Put on a good show for this one and maybe, just maybe, the festival will get a few donations out of it. No jeans to be worn, ladies and gentlemen, and I want to see Nick and Liam strangling themselves with ties. Shoes are to be polished, any hair more than six inches long is to be tied out of the way and I will not tolerate even the lowest of jinks on this occasion. Are you all quite clear on that?"

"I haven't got a tie," a sulky Irish voice muttered in the background.

"Fifty pence each in the charity shop on the High Street," Stella responded smartly. "And if you don't get one by yourself then I am choosing it for you and my colour sense is notorious. Idem if you have nothing but jeans in your wardrobe."

She saw the look of mutiny on Liam's face and nearly laughed. This was going to be easier than she had hoped. Threaten a barbarian with a collar and tie and he was putty in your hands. "Of course, whoever manages to persuade Ted to come along as well will be excused the worst aspects of the dress code. But not the jeans." She looked straight at Liam and caught his smile. "Fancy a bit of a challenge?"

"Got to be better than wearing a tie. When do you want me to go?"

"Not just yet. We'll get the garden party over and done with first. No point in having you on the books if we're not going to make use of you, is there? We've all been trying for over a year and I don't think Ted's that much of a sucker for redheads."

*   *   *

Julie had always imagined garden parties were synonymous with straw hats and china teacups. Certainly the hats were there in abundance but the cups were a sad disappointment. It wasn't that they weren't china, it was just that they always seemed to be used and she was getting a little tired of carting tray loads of the offending vessels to the kitchen.

The Manor looked quite resplendent for the garden party and Ted Ellerby was on his best behaviour. Julie had only once seen him misbehave when he pinched Liam's behind just as that young gentleman was successfully negotiating a plate of cucumber sandwiches around the milling throng. The cucumber had narrowly avoided becoming instant mulch on the herbaceous border and Julie could see Liam had said something quite profane to the offender. Ted just grinned unrepentantly and Liam had retired to the kitchen to look after the dishwasher.

Julie carried yet more mucky cups to the kitchen to find Liam flopped at the table with his legs stretched out. She sat in another chair at the table. "Hot out there," she mused. "You coming out again?"

"When Ted comes in."

Julie watched as Liam opened the steaming dishwasher and unloaded clean crockery and stacked dirty with considerable dexterity but she didn't say anything.

"Problem is, I can't decide whether he's being kind of paternal or whether I'm being incredibly stupid and missing the point. I'd like to think it's harmless, I like the old geezer in a way. But I'm getting a bit nervous about taking up a curator job here in the autumn. Keep it to yourself but I've applied for a job in Geneva."

"Geneva? Wow! What sort of job?"

"Admin for an international orchestra. I don't think I stand a chance really, my German and French aren't that good and they did ask for at least one to be fluent."

If Liam went, Julie thought treacherously, she could stay. "Well, good luck. I'll miss sharing the cottage with you." He looked round at her over his shoulder and for a breath-taking moment Julie thought she had gone too far. She relaxed as his smile was more of a grin.

"And I'll miss you too. Won't be the same without black lace petticoats among the washing. Anyway, I've not even been called for an interview yet." He stopped abruptly as Sigs arrived in the kitchen.

"Can we have some more clean cups out here, please," she asked rather sharply, put out that she hadn't quite heard what was being said.

Julie realised she would have to leave the comparative cool of the house. "There's a tray load here."

"Go on then, get them across to the table. Liam, angel, Stella wants you to go and help serve the food. All the old ladies are asking where the charming gentleman with the ponytail has gone to." Sigs flopped at the table too. "And I shall rest my poor sore feet for a few minutes in here. Can I do some washing up, or anything?"

"Instructions on top of the machine; I've just been putting them through on the quick wash, seems to work OK," Liam told her and reluctantly followed Julie out into the baking garden.

The heat hit him like a solid wall and he wished he'd brought a hat. Fair-skinned redheads could only tan their skins to a certain extent and Liam knew that all he could hope for from now on was more freckles. He saw Ted approaching from one direction so he set off in another and joined Stella at the cake table.

"Sigs has taken over the washing up. Need anything taken round?"

"Strawberry gateau, if you wouldn't mind. Do warn people it's got nuts in it, don't want anyone keeling over."

It seemed that the members of the Friends of the Brockleford Festival had no objections to nuts,

"And who are you?" one elderly lady demanded in cut-glass tones of the young man so patiently warning of the perils of nuts.

"Liam McGuinness, just here for the summer."

"Oh, so you're the one Ted was talking about. Quite a promising alto he reckons. Of course you'll never compete with George. Did you ever hear George? No, I shouldn't think so, you can't have been much more than a baby when he died."

"I was thirteen," Liam protested. "And it so happens I went to a recital of his when I was twelve. One reason I took up alto singing."

The octogenarian face creased into a myriad smiles. "Well, I never did. Which recital was that?"

"Belfast, July 1983."

"Oh, that one. Yes, I remember it quite well. He sang that enchanting cycle of Ted's. *The Kindness of Ravens*. You must know it. That was the premiere as I remember. Of course, poor George didn't have long to go after that. So tragic. Are the strawberries in that gateau quite fresh?"

"I believe so."

"Oh good. I'll just take another piece. Anyway, do run along with the cake before it melts."

Liam set off among the party guests and met up with Julie near the fish pond.

"How's the strawberry gateau going down?" she asked

He looked at the wilting sandwiches on her tray. "About as well as the fish paste from the look of it. I don't think I've ever been so hot in my life."

"Now that is because you are a delicate bloom from the misty loughs of Ireland," she told him and smiled.

Liam began to wonder if there was some enchantment afoot among the flowers. He had never seen her look so pretty before, nor ever noticed just how nice a smile she had.

"I'll take you there one day," he heard himself say and didn't know why. At least two police forces had told him he would be a fool ever to cross the Irish Sea again.

Julie thought poor Liam did look rather flushed and his eyes were all out of focus somehow. "Are you all right?"

"I'm fine, why?"

"You look as though you're about to faint."

"I'm just hot," he excused himself. "But I think I'll pick up some of the dirty cups and escape back to the kitchen for a wee while."

Julie loved it when he forgot he was supposed to be civilised and started talking Irish. "Me too. I might come from the tropics of Devon but this heat really is a bit much."

Ted was also rather worried about Liam McGuinness but guessed it wouldn't do him any favours in Liam's book if he went across and spoke to him considering what he had said after the episode with the cucumber sandwiches. But it was stiflingly hot in that garden and Liam had been out in the sun with no hat on for quite a while. With noble thoughts of offering headgear if nothing else, Ted bravely walked across to where Liam and Julie were chatting together as they stacked up cups on a trestle table.

"Liam, are you all right?" Ted asked.

Julie grinned. "Been out in the sun too long. He's going to have terrible freckles by tomorrow. Come on, dreamboat, let's get these cups to the kitchen."

Liam wasn't feeling at all well. He had never been able to take the heat and his only hope was that he could make it to the sanctuary of the kitchen while peering through the sea of dancing green dots in front of his eyes. It was fortunate, he later thought, that he had the sense to take his weight off the trestle before he tried to pick up the tray loaded with cups. He was about to sweep the others' concern aside in a macho show of something but he wasn't quite sure what. Those green dots suddenly all fused together and there were red stripes wiggling among them.

*   *   *

"I'll give you one thing," Julie's voice remarked from a long way off. "You've certainly got style."

Liam clutched his aching head, encountered a cold hand and a bag of something unidentifiable and realised he was flat on his back on Ted's sofa. "Oh, God. Tell me the worst."

Julie reclaimed her hand from the bag of frozen peas and let Liam hold them to his own head. "You fainted. Beautifully. In front of the entire gathering of the Friends of the Festival you went a funny shade of purplish white and then went thud into Ted's outstretched arms. I'm only glad it wasn't mine as I'd probably have dropped you."

"You're kidding me," he pleaded.

"Sorry. You've probably just been out in the sun too long. Phyllis has rung up her hubby on his mobile as he's out on his rounds somewhere and he'll drop in if he's got time. How do you feel now?"

Liam knew he couldn't begin to describe the dread, the horror and the sheer blind panic that were starting to take over from the headache and the nausea. "So how did I get here?"

"Nick and Sigs carried you."

"This time you've got to be kidding?"

"Not at all. Let's face it, Nick is the only bloke here under fifty and Sigs isn't what you might call a seven stone weakling."

"Julie, if I have to face any of them again I am going to die."

"No you aren't, silly. You've probably got a bit of sunstroke and you passed out in the heat. Couple of days' rest in the cool and you'll be fine."

There came a knock at the door and Sigs poked her head in. "How are you feeling, sweetie? I must say you certainly know how to go in style. Quite the most dramatic thing I've seen for a long time. How's the head?"

"Aches a bit."

"Thought it probably would. Fred Bond's here. Want him to take a look at you?"

Liam started to sit up and was going to refuse but those green dots were starting to come back. He thudded back down again with a groan which the two women interpreted as an affirmative.

*   *   *

Liam was ordered to his bed and told not to get out of it until Sunday afternoon at the earliest. To his disbelief, but immense solace, Nick Greenwood personally took him back to Labrador Cottage in his car. Through the blinding headache and the crowd of green dots he had been dreading a weekend at the Manor with Ted as nursemaid.

Julie couldn't help wondering if Liam was rather accident prone. In the space of about two months he had pulled a muscle and gone down with sunstroke. Maybe he was just careless, she thought charitably. He was no trouble as a patient. Spent most of the weekend either fast asleep or drinking water and didn't seem to want any company. Julie was a bit sorry as she liked gossiping with Liam but she took the opportunity to go back to her neglected cross stitch. She was heartily sick of stitching peacocks' tails by Sunday evening and was glad to be interrupted by the banging of the door knocker. She knew who it was as there were two dogs barking on the doorstep. With a dread sense of déjà vu she rushed upstairs and put the toilet lid down before she opened the front door.

"Hullo, dear," Dotty hailed her. "I've made some fig rolls for Liam. And for you, of course. How is he?"

"Asleep probably. Come on in a minute."

Liam was far from asleep and he thought it might be prudent to go down the stairs before those two well-meaning ladies and their dogs came up to visit him in bed. It was too hot for pyjamas and he hurriedly pulled on track suit bottoms and a vest then gingerly negotiated the stairs for the first time in nearly forty eight hours.

"There you are!" Dotty cried in greeting and gave him a kiss on the cheek. "My, you don't look at all well. Are you sure you haven't got a temperature?"

"What I've got is sunburn," he admitted sheepishly.

The two sisters exchanged a triumphant glance. "We've bought you a present," Lotty said proudly. She handed across a straw hat with a green ribbon round it.

Liam knew the gift was well meant but he had always looked dreadful in hats. "Thank you."

"Don't just thank us, make sure you wear it." Lotty told him. "Has Julie been looking after you all right? We would have come across ourselves but you know what Lady and Billy are like."

Liam managed to wrest his trousers free from Billy's teeth. "Julie has been amazing. Quite a good little nurse."

Julie blushed and wished she hadn't. "You've done nothing but sleep since you got here. Anyone for coffee? Except Liam who prefers tea."

They all sat round the kitchen table with the back door open onto the paved courtyard and two hot dogs lying in the shade of the garden wall with their noses very close to a bowl of water. Tea and coffee were left to cool in mugs and even the fig rolls seemed to be melting in their tin.

Dotty fanned herself with a newspaper. "It really is quite ridiculously hot these days and the weather man says it's going to get worse. I don't know how I'll ever keep my vegetables alive if it goes on much longer."

"Would you mind if I gave some of these fig rolls to Nick?" Liam asked after a long silence. "It's just that he did give me a lift home on Friday and I suppose I ought to go some way with the hand of friendship."

"He'll bite it," Lotty warned. "It's up to you. I suppose it couldn't hurt. Does he like fig rolls?"

"I should imagine he'd eat anything that was free," Dotty remarked cynically.

*   *   *

Nick Greenwood was euphoric in his triumph. He had not only made sure Liam McGuinness was forcibly taken away from the Manor but the stupid Irish fool had even gone so far as to thank him and give him some quite delicious biscuits. Things were just starting to work out perfectly and if his eyes hadn't deceived him when he went looking, there was a letter from Geneva on Stella's desk and it was asking for a reference.

Stella summoned Liam to her room first thing Monday morning. "Sit," she told him rather too formally. "Tell me, are you happy working here?"

"It has its moments," was as far as he was prepared to go without knowing what all this was about.

"Leaving aside the strained muscle, the sunstroke and two Ellerby works written for you, what would you say you've gained from your time here?"

"Are you going to fire me?" he asked before committing himself further while realising it really didn't matter if she did as he had the job offer from Ted anyway.

"I might," Stella replied and tried not to smile as she worked out just what he was thinking. "It depends how you answer my questions."

"Well, I've learned how to sort out an archive. Ticket allocations, student helpers, writing letters of all sorts, got to grips with the word processor and the photocopier. You've said that I'm going to be trained as a guide for Ted's house and will have to do some ushering at concerts."

"And what do you think you've put back into the Festival?"

"A sorted-out photo archive?"

"Nothing else? Nothing more personal?"

"What do you expect me to say? I've not been here long enough."

Stella allowed herself a small smile to remember the tongue-tied young man who had sat in that very chair and blushed. Liam McGuinness had certainly blossomed. She picked up a piece of paper and waved it vaguely in his direction but kept it out of reach. "I've been asked to write a reference for you. Geneva now is it? Be a bit different from Brockleford and I'll miss the convenience of your car. I presume you haven't told Ted?"

"Not a word."

"Right. Well, it seems they're interviewing in London next week so I'll fax across the reference. I'm not trying to put you off in any way but you must realise that if Debbie decides she's not coming back after she's had her baby then I'm more-or-less obliged to offer Julie first refusal on her job. For one thing you have had Ted offering you the curator job and for another Julie has shown no sign of itchy feet."

Liam nodded consent and stood up to leave the room. His attention was distracted by the glimpse of a red tractor trundling across the landscape visible from Stella's office window.

"I don't want to stay in Brockleford. It's a funny place. Maybe you'll think I'm mad, but it's the kind of place you come to just to get away from something and if you're not careful you'll be stuck here for ever."

Stella knew exactly what he meant. "As Ted so eloquently puts it: 'Is Brockleford the last refuge of all the hope-less people in the world?' You hang on to your hopes, young Liam. I wish you luck in whatever it is."

The conversation was halted before it got too intense. A series of shrieks from Sigs in the outer office sent Stella rushing to investigate. There was a huddle of women round Debbie again but Nick was still sitting at his desk. His face had gone deathly white and he looked as though he had seen a ghost. Stella didn't know what to do first but help was at hand.

"Liam, go and find out what's wrong with Nick, I'll see to Debbie."

Liam went reluctantly across to where Nick Greenwood was almost shaking. "What's the problem?"

"Oh, God. It's a disaster."

"Come along to the kitchen and I'll make you some coffee."

"Thanks, old chap."

Nick felt a bit safer when his audience was completely male and the kitchen door was closed. "It's Debbie."

"What about her?" Liam enquired as he spooned instant coffee into a mug. If there was one thing he had learned it was how to make coffee.

"She's engaged to be married."

Liam was puzzled. He didn't think Nick had been coveting Debbie particularly and couldn't see that this news was any reason to be so upset. He made the coffee and almost had to wrap the other man's fingers round the handle of mug for him. He guessed that if he didn't say anything then clarification would follow.

"I went out to the pub on Saturday night. Just the local so I could walk home and, well, OK, it was stupid of me I suppose, but I drank a bit too much."

Still baffled, Liam made himself some camomile and spearmint tea and swirled the bag round in the mug as the narrative continued.

"I met Debbie on my way home. She'd been crying and was all upset so I invited her in for coffee and, you know how these things go, and she is one of the best. But you know that anyway. Fact is, I can't remember a thing about it. I couldn't tell you now whether I went to bed with her or not and how the hell can I find out who she's engaged to?"

The proverbial penny dropped and Liam gulped tea to hide his amusement. He scalded his tongue and nearly swallowed the tea bag but at least it quenched the desire to giggle. "You think it might be you?"

"Are you completely stupid? I've been there once and don't want to do it again." Nick realised his audience was now completely baffled. "I've been married before. The Decree Absolute came through on Friday and Saturday was by way of a celebration."

It was hard to shake off the inbred Catholic revulsion to the concept of divorce but Liam had long ago renounced his faith. "Sorry, I didn't realise. Want me to go and find out for you? I'll get Julie to do it, be a bit more subtle."

"Would you? Thanks."

Six paces away from the kitchen, Liam met Julie heading in the opposite direction.

"Sigs has gone to buy some celebratory buns. I've been sent to make the coffee. What's going on with Nick?"

"He thinks he's engaged to Debbie."

Julie put her hand over her mouth to hide her smile. "What?"

"Just so. Apparently he got paralytic on Saturday night and thinks he proposed to her on the way home from the pub."

"Brilliant! Can we make him think that a bit longer?"

Liam had forgotten about the vindictive side to Julie Hutchinson. "You mean he isn't?"

"No, it's that boyfriend of hers."

"The one who beats her up? Is she doing the right thing?"

"She seems to think so. Says he's been quite a reformed character since she became pregnant."

"Now I'll bet she never said that."

"Why not?"

"There are too many syllables in 'reformed character'."

"Well, all right. I think the expression was 'really nice' but does it matter? We could wind Nick up something rotten and I still haven't forgiven him for propositioning me twice."

Liam remembered how the other man had taken him into his confidence and felt a bit of a traitor. "I don't think we should."

"Oh, you stuffy-knickers! Why not?"

"Betrothals aren't laughing matters, as well you should know."

Julie couldn't believe he was being such a prude. "Well, who rattled your cage? Just because your tart dumped you there's no need to lose your sense of humour."

"Who says I ever had a sense of humour?" he snapped and stalked off back to the kitchen.

Julie watched him go. Another spectacular McGuinness huff. She estimated thirty minutes and a jam doughnut to get over it.

"Found out anything?" Nick asked anxiously.

"You're OK, it's her boyfriend."

"What? Roger? But he beats her up."

Liam shrugged. "That's what I said too. But apparently he's changed since he learned about the baby."

"Roger Day will never change. You ever met him?"

Liam shook his head.

"He'd make you look small. Very pleasant most of the time but got a temper on a two-inch fuse. Plays for the cricket eleven in the summer. You must have seen him from your house. Fast bowler."

Liam didn't know a fast bowler from a slow one but he had seen a very large cricketer. "That's Roger Day? The blond guy? With the outward dimensions and apparent charm of a telephone box?"

"That's him."

"Jesus."

"Quite." Nick was recovering from the shock. He put down his empty coffee mug. "Right, well, back to work. I suppose you'd better get on and organise the whip-round. I can't imagine it'll be a long engagement." Nick went out and the mug stayed behind.

Julie came in and Liam guessed she had been loitering outside. "Got over your paddy yet? I'm sorry, I shouldn't be rotten to you."

One look at those huge green eyes and all resolves were gone. "I'll forgive you. On condition you eat my allotted doughnut."

"I can't eat two doughnuts."

"Then take one home for your tea. I've missed two days of training as it is and you know how easily I get fat." He saw the gleam in her eye and knew he had done it again. He batted the end of her nose with a teaspoon. "Your sense of humour will be the death of me."

The door flew open and Julie was thrust rather embarrassingly close to Liam.

"Oh!" Sigs exclaimed. "Sorry, do excuse me. Can you bring the plates for the doughnuts when you come?"

"We were just…" Julie began. "…Talking," she finished lamely to the closed door. She looked up and realised it was now her companion who was amused. "Now that you find funny. I don't understand you at all."

"That is because you laugh at other people and I laugh at myself. Do you want me to stay in here with you for an indecent length of time, or get out now?"

It was horribly tempting but Julie wasn't ready to set herself up yet. "Hop it," she said, but her voice wasn't as sharp as she would have liked.

Liam grinned amusedly. "See you later," he said rather too loudly as he left the kitchen.

Phyllis' face appeared round the door. "Oh, it is you. I wondered who it was."

Fortunately salvation was at hand. "Been asked to make early coffee to celebrate Debbie's engagement."

"Really? I must go and congratulate her."

Left alone in the sanctuary of the kitchen Julie let her breath out. It had been a bit too nice, being squashed against several stone of javelin thrower. If only she could be certain he had quite liked being jammed against a few stone less of her.

CHAPTER SIX

In which the weather turns unbearably hot but nobody goes swimming

July got ever hotter. It even got to the point where Liam felt obliged to buy a baseball cap to keep the sun off his head when he went out running in the mornings and evenings and his straw hat with its green ribbon became a common sight round the environs of Brockleford. He wished he had stopped caring long ago what he looked like in hats.

There was another round of doughnuts when the first bound copy of the commemorative volume arrived at the office. Stella sent Liam off to the Manor with it to show it to Ted and reminded him that the price of failure was the wearing of a tie.

Liam had no intentions of having to endure the almost-forgotten agony of formal dress. He wasn't too confident of his powers of persuasion and thought some moral support could be useful.

"Can I take Julie?"

Stella returned the smile. "Bodyguard? It's the hat that does it. Go on then. Go and butter up Ted."

"He'd fry if I put butter anywhere near him."

Stella watched the jaunty young man walk back through the office and she shook her head to remember the rather gauche bumpkin who had come for an interview. In a week's time he had to go to London for another interview and, if her hunch was correct, in the autumn he'd be off to Geneva. Only problem was, nobody had told Ted yet. Better to wait until after the job was secured, she told herself and went to make sure her office window really was open because there certainly wasn't any air coming in.

*   *   *

Liam and Julie found Ted Ellerby hard at work in his harness room. He looked up at his visitors with that slightly out-of-this-world look peculiar to creative minds in mid flow but then he smiled wearily.

"Do come along in and sit down. To what do I owe the pleasure on such a boiling hot day?"

Liam passed across a plastic carrier bag. "Sample of the book. Stella thought you might like to have a look at it."

"A good-hearted woman. Let's go and see if Mrs Dobson has left anything for us in the fridge, shall we?"

The fridge in the kitchen revealed the treat of some home-made lime cordial and a pot of ice. The kitchen faced north, the windows were open and it was pleasantly cool inside. All three, each hoping the others wouldn't notice, slipped off their shoes and plonked bare feet on the stone quarry tiles of the floor.

Ted looked intently through the book while the other two cooled off with tumblers of cordial. "Very smart volume," the composer pronounced. "It's so flattering to see such things written about one while still alive. How are the plans for the launch coming along?"

"Fine," Julie assured him as she could sympathise with Liam's aversion to ties especially in that weather and was going to do the best she could to help. She borrowed Liam's hat so she could fan herself. "We've got to go over there tomorrow to look over the hall but Stella doesn't think there'll be any problems. Sure we can't tempt you along?"

"I find such functions so tiring at my age," was the honest admission. "Santa Fe nearly killed me."

Liam looked at the other man over the rim of his glass. "If you don't fancy the walk I could always take you there and bring you back in my car."

One more look like that, Ted thought, and he'd agree to anything. "That's very good of you but it's not the walk, it's all the standing around and speechifying that's the problem. I'll think about it. The other thing is, I've just started an opera."

The other two were suitably impressed. "Your third?" Julie checked.

"Correct. I know it's not an original idea but I'm basing it on *A Midsummer Night's Dream*, only it's all up to date and the fairies are actually drug dealers."

"Sounds a bit heavy," Liam remarked as he filled up his glass from the jug on the table.

Ted pushed his own glass across for a refill. "It appeals to me, that's all. The nobles have turned into business executives, the rustics are a bunch of street kids and I'm putting it all in Belfast during the Troubles."

"Why?" came the sharp query from the man who had left the sanctuary of a small hamlet to live with his grandmother in Belfast for the sake of his education.

"Because the whole point of the story is that there is a message of hope at the end. Now, Liam, I need your expertise on these matters to get a few facts straight."

"I threw in Catholicism and I left Ireland."

"Would you then deny your childhood?"

"If I could. Why bring in things you know nothing about?"

"I know about war. I helped to bomb Dresden into oblivion when I was about your age."

"Then set your opera in the war you know about. Turn your fairies into the crew of a Lancaster and make the nobles a bunch of Nazis."

Ted considered that very carefully. "It could almost work. We'll have all manner of VE day fiftieth anniversary celebrations next year and I'm planning on finishing it for next year's festival so I could work it in with that. Good idea of yours. Will you sing the lead role for me?"

Liam gulped his cordial too hard and coughed a few times. "Are you serious? I have had a few lessons from Anna. There's no way I could consider taking on an operatic role. Besides which, don't you think a counter-tenor would be rather out of place in such a setting?"

"That's the whole point of the Puck character. He could be anything. The other characters are going to be real enough but I want him to be nothing. A dream. A spirit. A ghost of your own imagination, but not a real person, fairy or what have you. That's why an alto is ideal. Some sort of hermaphroditic costume and a vocal range that could be sung by a man or a woman. The whole point about the character is that gender doesn't matter. It's something in your own mind."

"Sounds weird," Liam decided. "I'm flattered you asked, but I can't see me being ready to sing in an opera by next year."

Ted had to acknowledge that it was a daft idea. This was a former choirboy who had 'had a few lessons from Anna'. He was quite right really. "Well, will you at least sing it on disc?"

Liam knew this was not the time to mention Geneva. "Tell you what, you get it written then I'll take it along to Anna and if she falls about laughing then we'll give up the whole idea."

"You can come and see it now."

Feet were reluctantly pushed back into half-cooled shoes, then hats were put back onto heads and the blistering heat of the yard was braved. The harness room was stifling in spite of having the window and the door open and Liam hoped he wouldn't faint again. Once had been enough but twice was too awful to contemplate. Ted let Julie sit on his chair to save her skirt from the ignominy of the floor but Liam thought his jeans could cope with dusty tiles. The two visitors looked at the booklets of manuscript.

Liam stared hard at one passage sung by the character of Puck. "You have a wicked sense of humour, Sir Edward. This cannot be sung by mortal voice."

Ted knew exactly which bit he meant. "George could have done it with his eyes shut."

"Maybe, but George was the acclaimed master. I wouldn't even like to try, I'd rupture something."

"I'm not rewriting it. You either get yourself up to standard or you don't sing it."

Liam rather resented the other man's bullying tone. Nobody had bullied him like that since his father had gone away and he wasn't going to put up with it now. "OK, I won't sing it. Doesn't bother me." He casually tossed the pages back onto the table. "Come on, Julie, or Stella will think we've got lost."

Julie thought Liam was being unspeakably rude but fought shy of saying so in front of Ted. She got up from the chair and smiled at their host. "Thanks for the cordial and everything."

Ted barely heard her. There was a mutinous sparkle in the indigo eyes of Liam McGuinness and Ted knew he had been right in his assumption that there was a core of steel to this easy-going redhead. "All right, you win. I'll sketch out an alternative just in case. But I still say that by the time this opera is staged you'll be singing it and wondering what all the fuss was about. Care to run through it now with the piano?"

"I'll show it to Anna first if I may?"

Ted gave back the pages. "You may indeed. When are you seeing her again?"

"Wednesday evening."

"Good, good. Oh, and tell Stella I'll come to the launch."

"You will?" Julie asked before she could stop herself.

"Yes, I might as well. But I want you, McGuinness, on standby. Just in case I faint. You owe me one for the garden party."

*   *   *

Ever since Nick had found out about the prospect of Geneva, he had become quite friendly towards Liam and had no qualms in whisking the manuscript pages from his grasp.

"What's all this then?"

"Ted's writing an opera."

"Good God! At his age? What's the title?"

"He never said. Stella in?"

"Office." Nick sat down with the music and didn't even watch Liam walk away.

Stella looked up when someone knocked on her door and Liam came in. "Ah. Mission accomplished?"

"Successfully. He'll come to the launch on condition there's a chair to hand. So, no tie, right?"

Stella McGinty knew when she was beaten. "OK, no tie. Well done, must have been a masterful piece of diplomacy."

"Julie helped."

"Quite a double act." Stella handed across a piece of paper. "Just rescued this from the fax in time before anyone else saw it. They've changed your interview day next week. Told Ted yet?"

Liam looked at the paper and suddenly didn't want to go. "I'll see if I get offered the job first. By the way, Ted's writing an opera."

Stella sent up a silent prayer of thanks. "Let's hope he sticks around long enough to finish it."

"He was talking about next year's Festival."

Stella could see it all now. A new Ellerby opera and hundreds of people fighting for tickets. Salvation, it seemed, was at hand. And if Liam went to Geneva, Julie could get on with the publicity. "Did you see the manuscript?"

"Been allowed to borrow what there is of it. Nick's got it at the moment. Ted had a rather ambitious idea that I'd be singing it by next year. He's completely mad."

"Oh, I don't know. You try your best and keep Ted sweet. The Festival needs something like that and you can always come back from Geneva."

"True," Liam admitted. He went back to his desk vowing that once he had broken the spell of this enchanted place there was no way he would ever return. Unless, he realised, a certain pair of green eyes started to make promises.

*   *   *

St Bartholomew's church hall was like an oven.

Sigs peeled off her linen jacket and flapped the neck of her dress. "Oh my goodness, I hope the mercury's gone down a bit by next month or we'll all be keeling over in here. Right, here's your sketch, Julie. We've got to fit in two buffet tables, a promotional display board or two and another table for the book to be displayed on. I think Stella's idea was that Ted could sit at the table with Nick and the two can sign copies if anyone's interested. Which they probably will be. Liam, sweetie, have you got the tape measure? Your trousers are the scruffiest, be an angel and measure up the floor for me, just to make sure. Then if it's all OK I'll get on and hire the display stands."

The two women wandered around while Liam bad-temperedly measured and envied them their cool sophistication. He felt like a wrung out dishcloth and was sweating in his thinnest jeans and a sleeveless T shirt yet there were those two in their floral dresses looking as cool as so many cucumbers. He had a sudden image of himself wearing a floral dress, snorted with laughter, inhaled dust and started coughing and wheezing.

Julie fetched him a glass of water from the kitchen. "Here. I don't know what you're giggling about anyway."

He didn't really want to tell her and hoped a sheepish grin would suffice. "Sorry. Just an idiotic idea that came into my head."

"Are you all right, sweetie?" Sigs enquired. "We don't want you fainting again and you do seem to be rather a delicate flower."

Julie looked at the well-developed torso and arms of the javelin thrower and wondered where Sigs got her ideas from. "No he isn't. He's just going for the sympathy vote."

A taunting breeze was stirring as they left the hall.

"Road or river path?" Sigs asked the other two.

"A walk along the river sounds nice," Julie admitted.

"Oh good, I was hoping you'd say that."

The river stank in the heat and the path was cracked but the three all tried to believe it had to be better than walking along the road.

Sigs looked at the turgid water and sighed. "The river always looks so tempting, doesn't it? Does either of you swim?"

"I learned at school," Julie offered vaguely. "Can't say I liked it very much. Liam?"

"Bit like you. Certainly wouldn't catch me going into that river."

"Should hope not," Sigs retorted. "If the current didn't get you then you'd be smashed to bits on the weir a bit further along."

"What weir?" Julie asked.

"You mean you haven't seen it? Oh, we must digress a little on the way. Perfectly charming spot for a picnic when it doesn't smell so bad but ghastly if you fell in." She tripped over something in the grass. "Oh, damn it. Who left a bloody fence pole in the way?"

Liam and Julie exchanged a look and a smile. "I'll put it with the others," Liam offered.

"Thank you, sweetie. Those blessed poles have been there for years and I'd swear all the local yobbos come and throw them around."

At the end of the field, a sign to Brockleford Village directed pedestrians over a stile to the left and through a small wood. Sigs climbed over the stile on the right and doggedly followed the River Walk route.

"It's not far," she assured the two who tagged along behind as they trekked through a field of dozing cattle.

The field seemed to go on for ever, then over another stile and Sigs stopped walking. "There it is."

The two strangers to Brockleford looked at the weir and were glad they hadn't been lured into the river. Even in the hot weather when the river was deceptively sluggish on the surface it was roaring over that weir with a frightening force.

"There've been two people drowned since I came here. The council used to put up notices warning people not to swim in the river but some local hooligans would always come and take them away. There's been talk of fencing off the weir for years now but nothing ever gets done round here."

Liam looked across that treacherous stretch of water to where the field on the other side shimmered in the heat. It was all so far removed from the cool, misty loughs of Ireland and a sudden stab of homesickness made him bite his lip. It had been a long time since he had felt the wind howl down the Sperrin mountains to where the sheep huddled together to try and keep warm.

Julie's gaze was fascinated by that torrent of water. It was mesmerising in its ferocity and the noise was incredible. She had noticed that roar the last time they had walked along the river but had mistakenly assumed it was traffic on the nearby road.

Sigs smiled to look at them. They reminded her of how she must have looked when she first saw that weir. It had been an evening in a late March, frost glittering in the moonlight and if it hadn't been for that injured badger on the path she would have ended her misery there and then with one short step into the water. But that had been a long time ago and both she and the badger were over their injuries. At least the badger was. Sigs sighed quietly and wondered what sort of a mess it would have made of her carpets by the time she got home that evening. It wasn't as though she hadn't tried. Every night she put it out and every morning it came back for its breakfast.

"We'd better go," she told the others quite sharply. "Just try not to fall in the river unless you happen to have a lifeguard with you. And even then I wouldn't give much for your chances."

Julie turned away from the river and shuddered in spite of the heat. She spun round too quickly, put her foot in one of the cracks on the ground and thudded into Liam. He, smiling under the brim of his hat, set her upright again.

"Drunk again, Miss Hutchinson? Whatever will the neighbours think?"

Julie to her annoyance felt herself blush and she seriously wondered if there was some kind of enchantment in this place.

"Sod the neighbours, it'll be Stella who skins us if we don't get back pretty sharpish," Sigs cautioned them and set off at a cracking pace across the field of sleepy cows.

* * *

Liam sat down in the chair opposite Stella's desk and announced flatly, "They've offered me the job."

Stella felt oddly cheated, but slightly relieved if she had been honest. "Can't say I'm surprised. You going to accept?"

"Do you think I should?"

If he had asked her to marry him, Stella could not have been more astounded. "You're asking my opinion? I'm terribly flattered but I don't know that I can help very much."

"I hoped you'd be impartial. Julie wants me to go so if Debbie leaves she can have her job. Nick wants me to go because he can't stand the sight of me and I've just got this bad feeling that when I tell Ted he's going to burst into tears on my shoulder."

"Whoa! I didn't realise there were all these implications. Forget all those others. What do you want to do?"

Liam's smile was wry. "Go to Geneva. The job sounds perfect, the people all seemed very nice and not one batty old woman among them, the salary is the stuff dreams are made of."

"But?" Stella interrupted kindly.

"But I like it here. I like the batty old women and this whole crazy set up even if Nick does bug me more than I should let him."

"And how long before the charm wears off? How long before you're sick to the back teeth of fending off Ted's advances, putting up with Nick's bitching and wishing there was more going on in this one-eyed town? I'd give a bright young thing like you a year and then I think you'll hate yourself for not going to Geneva."

Deep inside, Liam knew she was right. But he would still miss them all. "I suppose I'd better go and talk to Ted."

"Break it to him gently. He never really got over George."

*   *   *

Liam declined Julie's offer of moral support and went to the Manor on his own after work that evening. He walked there to try to settle his nerves but it didn't help. Ted was out in the garden, dozing by the fish pond and suddenly looking his seventy four years. He stirred as footsteps crunched on the dry grass and he shaded his eyes from the sun so he could see who it was walking so slowly up to him.

"Liam! You caught me in a sleepy moment. Lovely to see you. Fancy a drink? I've nearly got that blasted opera finished. Never written one so fast in all my life before." He didn't like the way Liam just sat quietly at his feet and contemplated the fish for a while. "Bad news? Something gone wrong at home?"

Liam stirred the water and several fish came across to nibble at his fingers. "No. To me it's good news, I suppose, but not for you."

Ted knew at once what he meant. "You're leaving?"

"In the autumn. I've been offered a job in Geneva."

Ted looked slightly down at the young man who had finally raised his eyes. The early evening sun made his already red hair the most incredible colour and Ted gave in to weeks of temptation and touched those tangled curls.

"Geneva, huh? Well, that's not so bad. Couple of hours from Heathrow and I can visit you.

Conversely three hours from Heathrow and you can visit me."

The sunlight forced Liam to squint as he looked at Ted. "Fact is, things are going to be getting pretty busy from now until I go so, in a way, I've come to say goodbye to you now. I'll make sure you get all your various bits of music back. And thank you for adopting me. And I'm sorry I won't get to be curator of your library."

Ted took his hand from Liam's hair and gently stroked the other man's rough cheek for a second. "Any use me putting your salary up?"

"No. Sorry." Liam hoped that errant hand wasn't going to stray much further and he began to wish he had brought Julie after all. "I'd better go. I left Julie cooking the tea."

"Cooking? In this weather?"

"Well, OK, washing the salad vegetables."

"She looks after you well. You'll miss her, won't you?"

"I'll miss everybody from you to Billy. But I think it's the best thing if I go."

Ted stood up beside his visitor and knew there were no powers of persuasion he could use on this stubborn Irishman. Liam McGuinness was going to go and there was nothing he could do to stop him short of committing an arrestable offence. "Will you swallow your revulsion and let me give you a hug?"

Liam forced himself not to run away. It wasn't that much to grant after all. "Go on then," he said, and prayed.

* * *

"How did he take it?" Julie asked as she tried to shake the lettuce over the courtyard, let go of the cloth and green leaves went everywhere. "Oh, bother1 I'd just got that washed."

"I'll rescue it for you."

"Well, don't bend down too much. Don't want you fainting again."

Liam looked up from his lettuce garnering. "I see. Now I'm too thin for fat jokes we're on to the fainting jokes are we?"

"Certainly are. What monumental decision have you made?"

"I'm taking the Geneva job. Just had a long talk with Ted and he agrees it's the right thing for me to do."

Julie was learning to be bold. "Just a talk?"

Liam was learning to outface her. "Well, OK, a bit of a snog but I declined the offer of sex."

Julie flung a cherry tomato at him. "That is gross!"

"Well, you started it," he pointed out and picked juice and pips from his hair. "You've got a lethal aim with vegetables. Ever thought of going in for the shot putt?"

"And you're too fat to duck out of the way!" Julie took the lettuce from him and knew that if she didn't ask she would be wondering for ever. "You didn't really get that cosy with Ted did you?"

Liam saw a chance. "What does it matter to you?"

Julie saw what was coming and backed away. "I was just curious. Sorry. None of my business,"

Just for a split second Liam hated her. It seemed the cool Julie was never going to yield. She obviously didn't care two hoots for him and he was a fool to think she ever would. "Need anything else picked up from the floor?"

Julie guiltily wiped a dribble of tomato juice off the end of his nose. "No, thank you. And I'm sorry I threw a tomato at you." She didn't know how to get through his reserve without making a complete fool of herself. "Do you want to wash your hair?"

It crossed his mind to tell her she could wash it for him as a punishment but he wasn't sure he could cope with the cranial massage from her. Just a few more weeks, he told himself and it would all be over. He could go to Geneva and forget all about Julie. If only it could be that easy. He nearly offered some gentle words of devotion there and then but she had turned away and was washing the lettuce all over again. A tomato pip cruised slowly down his cheek.

"I'll go and stick my head under the tap. Won't be a minute."

Julie heard the kitchen door close and she hurled the innocent lettuce leaves into the bowl. Just a few more weeks and it would be too late. She wished she had the courage to tell the truth but she was so afraid of being rebuffed. With a sigh of resignation she got on with the coleslaw.

Liam came trotting down the stairs and back into the kitchen shaking water from his fringe just as she lost the battle. Liam had never imagined Julie could cry. She did it as she did everything else: quietly, unobtrusively and rather formally. He hesitated for a split second between rushing forward proffering a slightly grubby handkerchief or trying the cheerful tactic.

"What's all this? I didn't really snog Ted in the garden."

Julie half screamed, half growled and bolted out of the back door. Too late she realised she had run the wrong way. There was nowhere to go. Brick walls and paving slabs surrounded her and the rotary dryer nearly took her head off as the hot wind sent it into motion.

*   *   *

Phyllis Bond was fulfilling her self-appointed obligations as wife to the doctor and had brought round some baby clothes for Freda Sewell. Not that she needed any really as this was her sixth but it afforded the opportunity to look round the house and see how things were generally. The sixth was fractious in the heat and Freda was trying to get her youngest child to bed and be polite to Mrs Bond at the same time. Eventually she had to give up the polite idea and hope the nosy old bat wouldn't mind looking out of the bedroom window for a while.

Phyllis didn't mind at all. Labrador Cottage was next door and there were some enlightening items of underwear drying on the line in the back courtyard. Her attention was diverted when Julie shot out into the yard as though the house was on fire. The poor girl roamed the tiny area for a while like a caged tiger and Phyllis was quite sure she was crying. So where was her fellow lodger? These men were never around in a crisis.

The fretful infant in the background was forgotten as the object of Phyllis' scorn came out into the yard. She didn't like to think what was going on as the front of his hair was all wet. To her annoyance neither of them said a word but she guessed they had had some form of a row. Julie was cowering against the far wall and she jumped when Liam put his hand on her shoulder.

"Go on, say something," Phyllis muttered.

It was all getting quite fascinating. She was gazing up at him and he was gazing down at her and any second now Phyllis would have the best bit of gossip that anyone had brought into the place for months. Mind you, they all suspected that those two couldn't share a house and keep it platonic. Wasn't in human nature that kind of thing.

"Go on, do something," she told the players quite sharply. "Don't just stand there like a pair of fools." They were talking now. Mumbling rather as she couldn't hear a word of it. They looked so perfect together and now he had her face in his hands and was gazing right into her eyes. Wonderful. Now, all he had to do was lower his head a few inches.

*   *   *

Two people in a paved courtyard got the frights of their lives when a sash window rattled at an alarmingly close proximity.

"I know it's not the done thing," Mrs Sewell's voice announced, "but I do like to keep the window open at night."

Phyllis could have screamed.

Julie and Liam looked up at the noise and both saw Phyllis Bond duck for cover behind the curtain. They exchanged a look of horror as they realised what their little tableau must have looked like to someone at the upstairs window next door.

"She'll never swallow the onions and black fly story," Liam cautioned. "Honest to God, I thought I'd upset you. Never occurred to me it had anything to do with onions."

Julie's right eye was still incredibly sore. "Are you sure there aren't any bits of fly left? It still stings."

He had another look. "There's no fly left at all. Not so much as a wing."

"We'd better go and eat."

"True. Want me to finish off the onions for you?"

"They're done." Julie glanced up towards Mrs Sewell's back window. "Reckon she's still watching?"

"She'll watch until we go back indoors and then she'll probably put a glass to the wall."

There was a pause.

"It's just to wind up Phyllis, right?" Julie checked

"Just so."

"No messy entanglements? Friends such as we used to have?"

"Right."

Phyllis smiled to herself. She always knew she had been right about those two.

* * *

Debbie sidled up to Julie in the office the next morning. "I'm so glad you and Liam are getting things together at last," she muttered confidentially. "You really should think about getting married. I love being engaged. Which reminds me, I've written out a wedding list. Will you pass it round for me? Looks a bit funny if I do it myself."

"Yes, of course." Julie took the sheet of paper from Debbie and smiled to herself. It had worked perfectly. She was now guaranteed safety from Nick, any vicious rumours still hanging on about Liam and Ted had been superseded and altogether the scene in the courtyard had been worth it. She looked at the list. "What do you want me to do? Pass it round so we can get you something each or would you rather there was a collection for something a bit more expensive?"

"I don't mind," Debbie admitted. "Is he really good in bed?"

Julie gulped a bit. "Pardon?"

"Liam. Phyllis said you were all over each other and any minute she expected you to be at it like a pair of rabbits against the back garden wall."

Julie shut her mouth with a snap. "I'll just go and photocopy the list," she declared and bolted for the sanctuary of the toilets.

*   *   *

Liam had been out on various errands that day and Julie didn't see him until she got back to Labrador Cottage in the evening with her blushes etched into her cheeks. She was rather relieved to see the Saab parked outside the gate as it meant she could get this over and done with before she lost her nerve.

"Have you heard what Phyllis has been saying?" she squealed at the young man unloading bags of shopping into the fridge.

"Humour me. I've been stuck in a jam on the motorway for an hour."

"She said we were, well, almost, you know, out in the yard last night."

Liam was rather tired and fractious and it wasn't helped by the fact he knew Ted was coming to hear the rehearsal of the cello sonata that evening. "Julie, we organised a very public stage kiss. I defy even Phyllis Bond to make something out of that."

"But she has."

"Stop getting hysterical. Next you'll be saying she's turned it into full blown carnal knowledge."

Julie knew her face had transcended scarlet but she had to make him share in the embarrassment. "Like two rabbits standing up against the wall."

"Can you do it standing up at all?" he wondered aloud. He derailed that train of thought before it got too interesting. "Maybe I'd better buy a book on the subject."

"You are incorrigible," Julie told him. "I'll pay half towards it and we'll leave it lying around next time Phyllis invites herself over."

*   *   *

It was just as they had feared. Nudges and smiles all round as soon as they walked into the church. They had seriously considered going along separately but had decided that would be worse. It didn't help that Ted was there early, sitting on a high stool in front of the orchestra.

"At last," the composer cried in greeting. "Our lovebirds. Come along, let's hear how the sonata is coming on then I may even stay and listen to the Berwald."

Ted Ellerby had to admit to himself that the cello sonata was progressing remarkably well. There were one or two passages that the soloist persistently got wrong but that was forgivable. He was rather pleased in a way that Julie and Liam had finally got round to everyone else's way of thinking. At least it probably meant Geneva was out of the question. Which meant Anna could keep up the good work, which meant that the premiere of his new opera should feature a rather promising young alto in the lead role. Ted sighed quietly. Who was he trying to fool? Liam was nowhere near ready to take on such a part. Maybe he should stick with the cello. Ted winced as Liam hit a totally wrong note at the end of a run. Maybe he should stick with throwing javelins around.

The composer had the grace to applaud the efforts of the musicians. "Not bad at all," he told them. "Well done all of you. I'll just go through a few things with Liam if the rest of you would like to take your break."

Nick hated the way Ted so assumed control whenever he was around but he didn't think it would be a good idea to argue with the composer.

The urn wasn't quite ready yet but the players were all quite happy to stand around and listen to the suffering soloist being made to play the worst bits over and over again until even he was getting them right.

"He's getting much better," Dotty confided to her sister. "And I'm so glad he's got together with Julie at last. Do you think they'll be getting married?"

"So far as I know he's still going to Geneva in the autumn," Lotty replied crisply and wished her sister could keep her feet on the ground a bit better.

"Oh. Well, perhaps she'll go too. I'll miss them."

"Why don't we wait and see what happens?" Lotty advised before her sister got too emotional and started making wedding cakes.

*   *   *

The two gentleman paused at the door of Brockleford church. They had called first at Labrador Cottage then, on getting no reply, at the house next door and the lady with all the children had assured them that Mr McGuinness was in the church on the other side of the green. It had seemed a bit unlikely somehow after what they had been told about the Irishman but their chief had told them not to hang about over this one.

One of them looked over his shoulder to make sure everything was as it should be. "Ready?" he asked his companion.

"OK. Think there'll be trouble?"

"Probably. Bit of an unknown quantity in Brockleford this one. Pity the chief wouldn't wait for the advisor from Ireland."

There was a slight commotion behind them then a redheaded young woman lunged for the door.

One of the men held her back. "Hold on a minute, Miss. You can't go in there just yet."

"But I've got to. You don't understand."

"You can go in when we come out again. Now just go and wait over there for a minute. We won't be long. It could turn nasty and we don't want you getting hurt."

The young woman, like most of the residents of the village, looked at the cars parked on the green and her gaze travelled on to the surrounding policemen. "OK, I'll wait," she agreed.

"Good girl. Just get right out of the way. We shouldn't be long." The man swore profanely as another car arrived with its lights still flashing. "Get that idiot to turn the lights off," he commanded one of the men behind him. "We don't want this one getting away from us. Got to show the Met we're one up on them."

*   *   *

"Curious lighting effect," Dotty remarked aloud when Liam joined her, Lotty and Julie for tea break. "Do you think it's an electrical storm?"

Several pairs of eyes had been diverted by the strange blue lights that flashed through the windows of the church. It lasted too long to be lightning even though the weather had become very oppressive. Ears strained to catch the sound of welcome thunder but all was silent.

Fists clenched round plastic cups when the church door opened and a very large, authoritative gentleman strode in.

"Good evening, ladies and gentlemen," his voice boomed across the church. "Is Liam McGuinness here?"

Three women glanced at the man who made up their quartet; he certainly didn't seem to know the gentleman but he sighed once as though this enquiry wasn't entirely unexpected.

"Over there," Nick told the arrival without giving Liam a chance to say anything. "The one with the red ponytail."

The gentleman strode across to Liam, stopped in front of him and thought it must be his lucky night. Not a sign of a show of resistance. He showed his police identity card and introduced himself. "You are Liam Declan McGuinness? Recently of Flat 4, 29 Belvedere Road, Catford, now of Labrador Cottage, Brockleford?"

"Yes."

"We'd like you to come to the station to answer a few questions."

"About?" Liam asked and suddenly he wasn't the rather placid musician any more.

"Tell you when we get there."

Liam put down his tea and said to Julie, "Take my cello home, please. This could take some time."

* * *

Dotty put her hand through Julie's arm as the door closed behind Liam, and Lotty followed behind just to find out what was happening. "I'm sure it's all a dreadful mistake," she consoled. "You'll see, he'll be back here in just a few minutes."

Ted Ellerby shuffled across to join them. "Is this a joke?" he asked faintly. "Something someone's cooked up for a bit of fun?"

"Not so far as I know," Julie admitted and her voice shook. It was all over Brockleford that she was Liam's girlfriend and now he had been taken off by the police. What on earth was going to happen to her? What on earth was going to happen to Liam?

The eerie blue lights started up again and the tell-tale sirens told the innocents what the reality had been behind the supposed summer storm. Nobody spoke and nobody moved. It was all just too dreadful to contemplate. The orchestra was divided into those who were aghast to think there had been a criminal living in Brockleford village and those who were indignant at such a miscarriage of justice. Everybody jumped as the door banged again.

Ted stared a bit harder. His eyes were going. Certainly this arrival had a lovely long red ponytail but this one was definitely of the female of the species and it wasn't young Liam coming back again to laugh at the joke.

Nick took one look at the well-proportioned figure, the blue eyes and the shining hair of the young woman and strode across. "Are you looking for someone?" he purred.

"Sir Edward Ellerby," she declared in a brash American tone. "His housekeeper told me he'd be here."

"I'll take you across," Nick offered. "May I know your name?"

She didn't answer. Just looked at the doddering old man standing with an almost as old woman and a skinny bitch with brown hair.

"Are you Sir Edward Ellerby?" she challenged him.

"Yes," he admitted and thought she was a bit young for a groupie.

"I'm Adelaide Anderson. Your grand-daughter."

CHAPTER SEVEN

In which the festival is almost halted by a scandal

"I don't know what to do first," Sir Edward Ellerby admitted to the gentleman sitting beside his bed. "On the one hand I've got young Liam carted off to God knows where and on the other hand there is Adelaide calmly eating me out of house and home."

"Let's start with Adelaide, shall we? She's probably the easier of the two to deal with. You are quite certain she's your granddaughter?"

"Unquestionably."

The visitor to the bedside paused, then decided he could probably risk being a bit forward. After all, he had been dandled on the celebrated Ellerbian knee as a baby. "My father never even let on that you'd been married."

Ted looked away towards the window. "It didn't last very long."

"Did my father even know about it?"

"Oh, yes. He was one of the witnesses. So were the rest of my crew. It was a wartime thing, very hasty. She was an ambulance driver; I, as you know, was a bomber pilot. Neither of us expected to live very long."

"And there was a child?"

"Must have been. I never saw her. The wife left me for some smart GI in 1944. Probably something to do with me palling up with George."

"I'll go and talk to Adelaide."

"I wish you'd talk to the police. It's been hours since they carted young Liam away and I'm not sure he can stick up for himself as well as Adelaide can."

"Do you know where they've taken him?"

"Don't have a clue. Brockleford nick's only a part-time thing."

"I'll start there and see how I get on. You're quite sure you want Adelaide to wait a bit longer?"

Ted's mind was beginning to feel a lot easier now his solicitor was here. "Perfectly."

*   *   *

Julie sat at the kitchen table in Labrador Cottage and listened to the crashes and thuds going on upstairs. She dared not look at Lotty and Dotty whose house it was that was being so systematically turned over. Much to Lady's delight there was a very handsome German Shepherd sniffing all over the place but no matter what she did with her eyes and her tail, the other dog was at work and wasn't going to give her so much as a second look until he was quite finished.

"Anything?" the policeman at the table asked his fellow who had just come down the stairs.

The arrival shook his head. "Clean as the proverbial whistle." He could see quite well what was going through the canine head of his companion. "OK to let the dog go now?"

The policeman nodded. One word from his handler and the dog had no hesitation in inviting Lady out into the yard. She, in a shameless show of licentiousness, almost threw him out there.

"Hope you don't mind," the dog handler said to Dotty. "He won't do her any harm."

"Nice to see her enjoying herself," Dotty remarked. "Few years ago, sonny, that would have been you and me."

The policeman at the table looked at her sharply for a moment, saw beneath the wrinkles and the faded eyes and realised that Miss Dorothy de Grys must have been quite a beauty in her day. "A few years ago, Miss de Grys, I would have been fighting him for you."

Dotty beamed and pushed the biscuit tin forwards. "Another fig roll, Inspector Reilly?"

"Don't mind if I do. Thank you. Right, at this stage I'll keep things as informal as I can so perhaps we can all have a little chat about Mr McGuinness."

"He hasn't done it," Dotty supplied. "Whatever it was. Is. What is it anyway?"

"Now that I can't tell you just yet." The Inspector decided he might get some sense out of the daft old girl. She seemed bright enough, just not quite on this planet. "What do you know about Liam's family?"

"They've got two water spaniels. Lovely dogs but very smelly. I think he said he lives on a farm somewhere. Can you remember, Lotty?"

Lotty sighed. Really Dotty was getting so vague these days. "A hamlet near the Sperrin Mountains. Wherever they are. Ted told me that Liam had told him his mother's paralysed but I don't know whether it was an accident or illness."

"Ted who?"

"Ellerby. Sir Edward. The gentleman who was with us when your colleagues took Liam away."

"Bit of a confidant is he, this Sir Edward?"

The two sisters looked at each other but didn't say a word.

"I see. Maybe I'd better go and have a word with him."

"He's not very well," Dotty cautioned. "This dreadful woman turned up just after Liam went away and said she's his granddaughter. Poor old Ted nearly had a heart attack on the spot. Nick took him home."

"And who's Nick?" Inspector Reilly was quite right. Mad old women were often a good source of information.

"Our conductor." Dotty lowered her tone and leaned conspiratorially close to the policeman. "Whatever you do, don't ask Nick anything about Liam. He doesn't like him because Ted does and he'd tell you Liam did the bank robbery just to get him put in prison."

The charms of Dotty de Grys were fading. The Inspector turned his attention to the young woman who hadn't said a word even when it was obvious a load of strangers were in her bedroom and virtually ripping open the mattress of her bed. Her eyes were sharp, her face almost scowling and her body defensively upright on the kitchen chair. Julie Hutchinson would probably lie to save her boyfriend but she had to be worth a try.

"I'm sorry about messing up the house," he started nicely. "How long have you and Liam lived together?"

The green eyes glared. "We share the house. We do not 'live together', all right? We moved in here in May. Before that I'd seen him once when we came here to interview for our jobs."

"And what has he told you about his family?"

"Nothing. His mother writes him letters but he never shows them to me. Nobody else writes to him. Not personal letters anyway."

The Inspector had got the measure of Julie Hutchinson. A decent, honest young woman completely out of her depth, but she wasn't going to tell him any lies. She might miss out a few bits here and there but she couldn't make anything up to save her own life, let alone that of someone else.

"Where does he put these letters from his mother?"

"I have absolutely no idea. Somewhere in his room I should imagine."

The dog handler bawled up the stairs to the searchers to make sure they found some letters.

"You don't go in his room at all?"

Shock and horror registered on her face. "No I do not. Well, I scoot in there and grab the pile of washing when it's my turn to do it but that's all."

"And does he ever go into your room?"

"Just for the washing. If I let him. Which has only happened about twice."

"And how often is he here alone?"

"Every Thursday evening when I go to my aerobics class. Apart from that I don't know. I'm not his keeper."

"And there's no telephone here?"

"No, there's a public box on the other side of the green."

"And neither of you has a mobile?"

"No." Julie wanted them all to go away. She wanted to be left in peace so she could go to bed and cry. She wanted to sit in the Mediterranean garden and watch the cricketers doing their practice. She wanted Liam back where she could look after him.

Lotty hated to see Julie look so upset. "Would you kindly tell us what this is all about? I think you owe us at least that much. It's quite obvious Julie knows nothing about any of this. I mean you arrested him under the Prevention of Terrorism Act. Just because the poor thing comes from County Londonderry is that any reason to lock him up? I know Brockleford is rather over-populated with bigoted xenophobes but I didn't think that extended as far as the police force. And from your accent you're a native of Liam's home country anyway."

"Let me assure you, he has not been locked up. He's just been called in to answer some questions."

"No he hasn't, you arrested him. I followed you out of the church and heard you. Are you going to charge him with anything?"

"Probably not."

"So why has he been arrested?"

The Inspector wasn't to know that Lotty could withstand interrogations by a whole classroom of five-year-olds. One policeman didn't stand a chance.

"We just wanted to make sure he hasn't been a naughty boy," he parried and hoped that would do. Lotty de Grys, he thus found out, showed no mercy.

"Give me some examples. Are we talking about making bombs? Shooting people with a pea shooter? Kidnapping the vicar because he double-booked the church hall? You're not being very helpful are you, Inspector Reilly?"

Tim Reilly was satisfied these people were innocents. Belligerent and hostile, but innocent. He guessed he could trust them with the truth. "As you observed, Miss de Grys, I come from Strabane and I've known Liam a long time. He comes from a large family which is of great interest to nearly every police force in the British Isles. His father and two of his brothers are locked up in the Maze and McGuinness senior is doing life with a recommendation that he serves at least thirty five years. Believe me, for scum like that, thirty five years isn't long enough. Liam has had two other brothers and one sister shot dead by the Protestants. A second sister vanished without trace some time ago and foul play is very strongly suspected although there is no evidence and she has never been found. His mother was injured in a shooting incident in which Liam was the intended target but she got in the way."

The other three at the table looked at him as though he had gone green, and furry whiskers had suddenly sprouted out of his head.

"No," Dotty corrected him gently. "Liam went to Cambridge. He got a sports scholarship with his javelin."

"And before he threw javelins he threw things at soldiers."

Lotty thought this had gone on quite long enough. "So if he's as bad as you say he is, what on earth is he doing in Brockleford living a perfectly normal life? I mean, quite frankly, you couldn't hope to meet a nicer young man."

"He got out. Left the family home, went first of all to live with an aunt in Coleraine and then when things caught up with him there he moved on to his mother's mother in Belfast. He was last in trouble with the police at the age of sixteen and that was his father's fault. We haven't heard a whisper about him since. But you must understand, with a family like that, all the police forces in Britain are keeping an eye on that one."

"Let's get down to details," Lotty encouraged. "Exactly what his he supposed to have done? Specifically? Here in Brockleford?"

"He applied for a job abroad and the people ran the usual checks which triggered off a tiny cog in the large machine of Scotland Yard,"

"It's an orchestra in Geneva, for pity's sake!" Lotty exclaimed. "And they offered him the job. And that still doesn't answer my question."

Tim Reilly really couldn't believe this old dear was so cool in the face of such a crisis. "Have you ever been in the police, Miss de Grys?"

"No, but I used to teach in primary schools. Wonderful training. So, the answer to my question is?"

"Nothing specifically. I got the Met to pick him up a few times when he was in Catford but he was still living clean then. We'll probably just put him through the mangle once more and if nothing pops out he'll be cleared to go to Switzerland."

"But that's dreadful!" Dotty cried, nearly in tears to think that poor Liam was being horribly tortured to see if anything 'popped out'. Whatever that meant. She hoped the policeman didn't mean it literally.

"He's used to it by now."

Julie wanted to weep at the idea of Liam being abused in some way. She had always closed her eyes and her ears when nasty things happened in police cells in dramas on the television. Now she wished she had had the nerve to look as she might at least have had some idea.

A rather self-important looking policeman bustled into the kitchen. "Found the letters, Guv. Think we could be on to something."

The Inspector sighed. "Pity. This was one McGuinness I was hoping would make it. Let's be out of here."

The policemen all left Labrador Cottage without the sirens and lights going on their cars and all around the green the net curtains were allowed to drop back to rest on their windowsills.

"Come on, dear," Dotty said to Julie. "We'll help you get this place straight."

They had got the downstairs tidy when the door knocker rapped again.

"I'll go," Lotty declared.

A sheepish handler was on the doorstep. "Sorry to bother you. Can I have my dog back, please?"

*   *   *

Liam wrapped the coarse blanket round himself as he huddled on the bed, and tipped his head forward so his hair would hide his face. The cell at the police station stank as though every previous occupant had performed every bodily function in it and his stomach was churning even though it was empty. He had played this game before, even if not with this particular police force, and knew the worst thing he could do was lose his temper. So he had to go along with it and pretend he really didn't care. Didn't care one bit if they took his clothes away to see if there were any traces of explosives on them and left him with only a blanket for an embarrassingly long time. Didn't care when he was bodily searched inside and out just in case he had hidden anything somewhere and samples were obtained by various methods for DNA analysis, just in case he had done anything that could tidy up police records. He had begun to think he was through playing this game. They hadn't picked him up for over six months and the last time had been half an hour in Catford nick.

This was the worst he'd ever known. First they had tried the unsubtle approach then, presumably having got the measure of this supposed terrorist, they had gone for the humiliation bit. Liam sighed. It didn't matter really. He had met it all before and no doubt he would meet it all again.

The cell door crashed open but he wasn't going to raise his head to see who it was. He didn't want to know. He cowered away as something soft was hurled across the cell at him.

"Put these on," he was told. "You've got a visitor."

* * *

The solicitor had never met a terrorist either and looked with some alarm at the tall young man with the split lip and the magnificent red hair down nearly to his waist.

"You must be Liam. Ted asked me to come along. I'm Richard Davison, Ted's solicitor. My father was his solicitor before me."

Liam accepted the proffered hand. "Good of you to come. But you needn't worry, I've been here before. They've got nothing on me."

Richard Davison so wanted to laugh at the rather unfortunate turn of phrase considering the young man had had all his garments confiscated and was clad in a paper boiler suit. He wished he could look half as good in a police issue boiler suit but he had never had the height to look that good in anything.

"This time I'm afraid they might have. Something to do with your mother's letters."

There was a pause while Liam remembered he must never lose his temper in a police station. "They've taken my mother's letters?"

"'Fraid so. Went over your house with a fine tooth comb."

"How's Julie?"

"She's all right. Got Lotty and Dotty with her."

"Good. And Ted?"

"Ted, I'm afraid, is a little under the weather. Of course, you missed Adelaide."

Glad of the relief, Liam sat at the table opposite the solicitor. "Who's Adelaide?"

*   *   *

Julie was habitually dozing over her cornflakes the next morning after about the worst night she could remember when the door knocker tapped politely. For a moment she wished she hadn't insisted Lotty and Dotty left her alone yesterday evening. She knew it wasn't them as there was no scuffling and barking. Somehow she wasn't surprised to find Phyllis Bond on the doorstep.

"Oh dear. You do look dreadful. Did you sleep at all last night? Of course you must have been worried sick. What time did Liam get back?"

"He didn't," Julie managed. "I don't know what time he'll be back. Inspector Reilly said it could be a while."

"Oh, well, yes, of course it can be when they're charged with terrorist offences. I must say I'd never have thought it of Liam. Always seemed such a nice boy although I must say I've never been too sure about men who have such long hair. And, of course, decent men just don't wear ear rings."

"He hasn't been charged. The police are perfectly entitled to hold him this long without charge. Now, please would you excuse me as I need to have my bath or I'll be late for work."

Phyllis wandered into the kitchen. "Of course it must be so hard for you. What with him had up for bombing half of London and you almost his wife. Will you have to go to court and testify? Someone told me they had found drugs and all sorts here yesterday. Went over the whole place with half a dozen dogs and dug up the garden and everything." Her experienced eyes swept the kitchen. There it was, just as she had expected. A pretty little diamond ring on the dresser and just the right size for a dainty thing like Julie.

Phyllis parked herself at the table. "So how are you coping? I heard you had Lotty and Dotty with you last night. Ever such a sweet couple but no good in a crisis."

Julie thought of Lotty's cool composure but didn't bother to argue. It was quite obvious Phyllis wasn't going to go. She picked up her cornflakes. "I must have my bath. Do make yourself some coffee if you're staying."

"Why, thank you," Phyllis beamed. "I'll just make myself a quick cup then we can walk along together when you're ready." She halted Julie and handed her a small object. "Here you are. I expect you'll want to wear this at last to prove your devotion."

Julie, without thinking, took the ring. "It's not mine, it's Liam's. I'll put it in his room."

Julie paused in the doorway of the back bedroom. Lotty and Dotty had put the things back more or less where they thought was the original place as Julie hadn't wanted to go in there. She didn't want to go in there now. That was the most violated room in the cottage and she didn't want to see what those people had done to it. With a supreme effort of will, she pushed open the door and went in. Dotty and Lotty had certainly tidied up. She guessed Liam would have one of his celebrated huffs when he saw how everything was folded neatly, hanging straight or just simply stood in a line. The occasional glimpse Julie had seen had reminded her more of a bomb site than anything else.

Thinking of bomb sites made her pause. What if Liam really had done something dreadful? She knew so little about him. All she knew she had learned from Inspector Reilly, but her instincts had made her fond of her fellow lodger. She tossed the ring in her hand, smiled quietly, and put it on the bedside table. The place felt funny without Liam. She had missed hearing him fidget in the night, snuffling along to the bathroom in the morning, thundering down the stairs for his breakfast. The time had come to trust him and tell him the truth. On the other hand, how much did he trust her? Not a thing had he told her about himself and he could turn out to be a terrorist yet.

"Are you all right?" called a voice from downstairs. "I can't find the sugar."

"Blue jar on the dresser. I'm fine, thanks." Julie, and cornflakes, shot into the bathroom.

*   *   *

Liam was awoken from his light, hallucinatory sleep by the scent of tea. He half sat up on the hard bed and his tired eyes focussed on the plastic cup being held out to him. He recognised that hand. Tim Reilly had turned up at last. Now things would get back to normal with any luck.

"Here you are. Just how you like it. Black tea, no sugar. Well the hair hasn't changed but what the hell has happened to your face?"

Liam groggily sat up on the bed and took the tea. "Bit of an accident. I was wondering when you'd turn up."

"Been on the case since yesterday. Have they run all the tests?"

"Embarrassingly."

"Thought so. Where are your clothes?"

Liam shrugged. "Didn't like to ask. They're not as well organised as your lot or the Met." He flinched as his face was tilted up by the chin and the light hit his eyes.

"Hm. Not as subtle either. You going to complain?"

"Complain? Since when did I have any rights?"

"They've got no call to go bashing your face against walls, I don't care what you've been hauled in for."

"It was an accident. Besides which they haven't charged me yet. But you'll never guess, I've got a solicitor."

The other man sat beside him on the bed. "Since when?"

"Since Ted Ellerby adopted me."

"You've got a good bunch of friends here, Liam. I was hoping you and I wouldn't be meeting like this again."

"You and I have been meeting like this since Paddy and Flynn got me in trouble for throwing things. I have no faith this will be the last time, have you?"

"Now then, I hope you're not going to let this lot get you down? How long have we known each other?"

"Since I was five and you were a rookie constable."

"Right. I've locked up a third of your family and seen another third buried."

"How is Ma?"

"Missing you. But at least I can go back and tell her you've got in with a good crowd here. And you've got a decent and honest girlfriend at last."

Liam snorted into his tea. "If by that you mean Julie Hutchinson, I'll tell you now it'll take an oxyacetylene torch to get through that one's exterior."

"Don't you go kidding yourself. That girl's got a soft spot for you if ever I saw one."

"Said so, did she?"

"Well, no. But I can tell these things."

"Hm."

"Drink your tea and we'll get the formal interview over and done with. Then I should imagine you'll be home in time for lunch."

Liam looked up and watched Inspector Tim Reilly leave the holding cell. Theirs was a curious friendship. The policeman and the son of the murderer. Theirs was a friendship that had nearly cost him his kneecaps on several occasions. But if there was one thing Liam McGuinness never did, it was grass. And Tim Reilly had learned at least that much.

* * *

Stella McGinty looked up from her desk in response to the polite knock on her door. "Julie!

Wasn't expecting to see you today. Any news of Liam?"

"No. And that's what I want to talk to you about."

Stella waved the younger woman to the chair in front of her desk. "Fire away."

"I don't know if Inspector Reilly spoke to you yesterday but he's known Liam for a long time and says it's unlikely he'll be charged with anything. And I just know Nick's going to try and persuade you to sack him so I've come to ask you not to."

Stella had to admire the other's courage and didn't like to tell her Nick had already asked her the same thing that morning. "All I've heard is the gossip. Tell me the truth."

"Liam comes from, well, not a very nice family. But he's not like the rest of them. This Inspector Reilly has been keeping an eye on him for years and says he hasn't even got a driving offence. It's just that every so often he gets arrested like he was yesterday just because of who his family is. It really isn't fair and I don't think he should lose his job because of it."

"Well, all I can do, in all fairness, is wait and see what happens. If they charge him with something then I'll have to think very seriously about what I'm going to do."

"But even if he's charged it doesn't mean he's done anything. You can't sack him if he's charged. How will you feel if it goes to court and then he's let off?"

"Go home, Julie. You're in no fit state to come in to work and, as you say, certain parties are going to be revelling in this. Tell you what, go and visit Ted. I've heard he's not too good and I'm sure you can cheer him up."

"But I've got a lot of work to do."

"Go home," Stella repeated kindly. "And rest assured I won't sack Liam without good cause. I don't suppose you know if this will affect Geneva?"

"I've no idea," the miserable Julie admitted. "Just one thing. Please don't tell him I came and saw you and made a fool of myself like this."

"Oh, I'll tell him all right. I'll tell him you stuck up for him no matter what."

Julie started to panic. "No, don't. Because then he'll think that. It's just that, if he thinks I like him then... Never mind. Just don't tell him. Please?"

"All right then. I'm sorry, I thought you and he had something going."

"Well we haven't. Not really." Julie could feel her face getting redder and redder. "I'll be back tomorrow. Thank you."

Stella smiled indulgently as the distraught Julie positively fled back out through the outer office and the door banged behind her. Liam McGuinness was going to know the torment that poor creature had gone through if she had to write to him in prison.

*   *   *

"Breakfast, Grandpa!" a remorselessly cheerful voice cried. "Someone came to see you but I sent her away again. Told her you weren't up to visitors."

"Who was it?"

"Oh, some skinny bitch. Think she said her name was Julie."

Ted Ellerby looked at the young woman standing beside his bed and wished she would go away. Adelaide Anderson had done nothing to endear herself to him. She was loud, bossy, and, worst of all, his granddaughter. He had a good idea why she had suddenly turned up, didn't want to encourage any sort of friendship, he just wished she would go back across the Atlantic and stay there.

"Well, you can just go and fetch her back again."

"No way. She was nearly in tears as it was. Don't want hysterical women weeping all over you. We've got to get your strength back again so you can come and see Mom and Grandma."

"Down the drive, turn right and keep walking. When you get to the village green you will see a row of cottages on your right. The pink one is called Labrador Cottage and Julie Hutchinson lives there. Go and get her and bring her back. Now."

Adelaide hadn't expected a seventy four year old raging gay to be so forceful. She had thought he would be some dreamy old guy who would be glad to have some young company. She had been prepared for him to be a bit put out to find he had had a child and would probably want to keep the child of this child a secret from all his gay friends but she wasn't going to give up. Silly old sod. Didn't he know it was time he died? All she had to do was make sure his attorney knew there was a living family who were entitled to inherit the lot then, so far as she was concerned, the best thing he could do would be to drop dead quietly and discreetly.

"Labrador Cottage?"

"That's the one. Go on."

It wouldn't do to cross him this early in their relationship. Adelaide banged down the breakfast tray where he couldn't reach it and slammed out of the room.

Ted got slowly and stiffly from the bed. It was about time he got up or his old bones would get stuck. Besides which there was the opera to finish. Funny thing, this Adelaide. Reminded him of her grandmother. She had been a regular bossy boots too.

*   *   *

Julie was interrupted in mid cry by the thundering of the door knocker. "Go away!" she shouted as loudly as she could.

"Grandpa wants to see you!" came the answering bawl.

"Oh, no," she muttered. She bolted to the bathroom, did the best she could with a lot of cold water, then went bravely to the door.

"You told me he wasn't well."

"He isn't, but he wants to see you. Say, you been crying?"

"Chopping onions."

"Oh, right. Come on then."

Julie hoped her face wasn't quite so red and puffy as she followed Adelaide into Ted's bedroom. She felt rather embarrassed at being in such a private place and was relieved to see that the old gentleman was sitting in a chair by the window and was clad in a dressing gown in spite of the heat.

"How are you?" she asked politely and blinked to try to stop the tears.

"Bearing up better than you from the look of things. Adelaide, be a dear and get Julie some lime cordial, would you? Mrs Dobson will have left some in the fridge. Thank you."

Adelaide stamped out of the room and Ted smiled wearily at his visitor.

"I don't mind if you cry in front of me. Any news?"

Julie shook her head and tried blinking a bit more but a sniff escaped instead.

"Have you heard anything from the police?"

"Not since yesterday."

"Well, I spoke to my solicitor Richard this morning. He saw Liam yesterday and apparently he still hasn't been charged. There's some kind of a hiccup to do with his mother's letters I believe. There are some tissues on the bedside table, do help yourself."

"Thank you."

"The problem is, of course, under the Act he could be held for an extraordinarily long time without charge. Hush, here comes Adelaide."

Adelaide thrust a glass at Julie. "Here you are. Have you eaten your breakfast, Grandpa?"

"Yes, thank you. And very nice it was too. Now, would you mind doing another little errand for me? Dotty has promised me a loaf of bread and as your young body is far better able to cope with the heat than is her old one, would you get it for me? I'd be ever so grateful."

Adelaide nearly demanded to know the extent of the gratitude but thought she should bite her tongue just a bit longer. "OK. Where do I find Dotty?"

"Last Chance Cottage. Down the drive, back across the green again, past the church, left along the high street all the way to the end then down Blackthorn Way. There isn't a name up but you can't miss it."

"Jesus. What kind of a crazy place is this?"

Ted and Julie watched her leave the room and presently the front door banged.

"She seems quite nice," Julie offered lamely thinking of the young woman who had marched silently beside her all the way from Labrador Cottage to the Manor. "And it must be nice for you to have the company."

"She is after my money. Pure and simple. Unfortunately for her it's all tied up in trusts and a foundation so she's not going to get a penny of it."

"Have you told her?" Julie asked, amazed at his calm in the midst of such a trauma.

Ted smiled. "Not yet. Making use of her for a bit first. Which reminds me. Would you mind asking Nick to drop by next time you see him?"

"Of course."

Ted realised she wouldn't ask and probably hadn't even thought of it. "I thought he might like the chance to get to know Adelaide a bit better."

Julie looked up and caught his eye. "That's cruel."

"They deserve each other. Come and sit over here where it's cooler and let's talk of more pleasant things, shall we?"

* * *

"We've got a problem," Tim Reilly told the young man still waiting so patiently in the holding cell.

"A big one or a little one?"

"On a scale of one to ten, I'd say about twelve. The chief constable wants you charged and I, as a humble advisor from the RUC, have no powers to stop him. He's applied to the Home Secretary to have you held for another couple of days and they're really making mountains out of your mother's molehills."

"This is turning into a nightmare. I've lost track. What day is it?"

"Thursday."

"I'll have lost my job by now."

"Probably. I'll go and talk some more to your friends. Just so they know what's going on. Want me to give your love to Julie?"

"You might as well give it to Ted for all the good it would do."

"OK, I'll give it to Ted instead. Cheer up, Liam. I've got you out of worse pickles than this and at least no-one's got a crowbar over your knees yet. I'll go and talk to that solicitor as well, might as well get some use out of him. You've never had a solicitor before. Your luck must be changing."

Liam crashed back down on the bed again when his visitor had gone. He could see the merciless sun was still beating down and he looked at the pattern it made on the wall opposite the tiny, high-up window. If it rained before they let him out, he said to himself, then that was it. Off to the Maze to join the rest of his family.

*   *   *

Tim Reilly didn't recognise the young woman who opened the door of the Manor. "Good morning. I wonder if I may speak to Sir Edward Ellerby?" he asked politely.

"That way," she told him in a New York accent and jerked her thumb over her shoulder.

Ted Ellerby rose from the sofa in the drawing room when the visitor walked in. Although he hadn't met this compatriot of Liam's before, he recognised the arrival from Julie's description. "Ah, Inspector Reilly. I've been hoping you would turn up. Any news?"

"I'm sorry. It seems likely he's going to be charged this time."

"Then what happens?"

"Magistrate's court, probably remanded in custody and then we wait for a trial. Which could take months."

"Do they have any evidence?"

"They're getting it."

"Ah, the old adage. Throw enough mud and some of it will stick."

"I'm afraid so."

"Poor Liam. What happens about Geneva?"

"I expect the Chief Constable will inform them."

"Which means?"

"They'll tell him the job's not his any more."

"And then?"

"If we're unlucky he'll give up the fight and just go down like the rest of his family."

Ted thought of the architect's plans lying neatly rolled on the desk in the study. He remembered the feel of the young man in his arms in a sunny garden. "Oh no. I won't let that happen to him. You have my word."

*   *   *

Julie trailed back to work on Thursday. For some reason she was immensely cheered to see Dotty sitting at Liam's desk tussling with the word processor.

"Damn thing!" Dotty shrieked and hit the innocent machine on the monitor. "Why won't you do as I asked you? Oh, flaming Norah! Give me a typewriter any day of the week. Hullo, Julie dear. Any news?"

"No, sorry."

Stella came rushing in late that morning. "Nick, Sigs, my office. Now."

Two people scuttled out from behind their desks and Stella's door slammed.

Those left in the office looked at each other.

"I'll go and get some doughnuts," Debbie declared. "Can someone lend me some money?"

Dotty caught the piece of paper the printer spat out. "Have a look in my purse, dear. Oh, no! I can't send this letter out. Look at it. It's all in italics."

"You must have changed the font," Debbie explained kindly as she headed towards the door.

"What font? I never touched the flaming font! Julie, help!"

Debbie just got back from the bakery before three sober-faced people came out of Stella's office.

"Go home. All of you," Stella rapped. "This year's festival is cancelled. Off. Kaput. Go on, the lot of you. Take the day off and come back tomorrow when I've decided what to do."

Debbie looked forlornly at the bag of doughnuts she was holding.

"Come on," Julie said to her. "Come back with me for some coffee. You too, Dotty."

The other two beamed. "Why thank you, dear," Dotty replied. "I must say I wasn't looking forward to a day with this horrible creature getting its fonts in a twist."

"Anything any of us can do?" Debbie asked Sigs.

She cleared the frown from her brow. "Not unless you can talk some sense into Adelaide Anderson."

"That reminds me," Julie remembered. "Nick, Ted wants you to go and meet Adelaide. He thinks you might get on well with her."

Everyone looked at Nick.

"Go for it," Stella advised. "The Brockleford Festival is relying on you. Now, what have you got in that bag, Debbie? Unless my nose deceives me it's cinnamon doughnuts."

"I'll go and put the kettle on," Sigs announced. "Good luck, Nick."

Dotty looked sadly at the word processor lurking on the desk like a technological delinquent.

She wished Liam would come back and rescue her from this purgatory.

*   *   *

Nick Greenwood well remembered the woman with the red hair. "Ah, Adelaide. We meet again. Nick Greenwood, I saw you on Tuesday evening."

Adelaide looked at the dark hair and grey eyes of the man on the doorstep. Not bad. Pity he'd gotten a bit fat. She looked him up and down, paid particular attention to the folds in his trousers and smiled. "Hi. Come to see Grandpa?"

"Yes, please."

"So long as you don't try to talk him into going ahead with the festival. I told that Stella McGinty it's all off. He's in no state to do anything about it. For Christ's sake, he's seventy four and I've got an airplane seat booked for him next week."

Nick acknowledged this was going to be a battle. He fixed his most charming smile, carefully studied her from her red hair to her gold sandals and raised one eyebrow in his best imitation of a sophisticate. "Wouldn't dream of it. What are you doing this evening?"

Adelaide caught the raw promise in his eyes. "Why wait for this evening?"

*   *   *

No matter which way he turned his head, Ted couldn't get those notes in focus. He wiped his eyes on his hand again and had another look. It was no good. No matter how hard he tried this *Midsummer Night's Dream* just wasn't working. He screwed up the sheet of paper he had been working on and dropped it onto the floor to join the dozens of its fellows that rolled around in the hot breeze stirring the dust on the harness room floor.

He planted his elbows on the table, rested his chin in his hands and looked out across the courtyard. Even the chickens were too hot to move.

He thought again of Liam, sitting cooped up in a cell; angry, disillusioned and probably slowly roasting to death. Inspector Reilly had made it all sound very normal, but it wasn't. He had been full of praise for Liam who had broken away from his family and turned his back on their activities but, it seemed, for the rest of his life he was going to be punished.

A vision darted into his mind. A solitary figure on a bed in a cell. Tormented by a chain of ghosts that came from his past. No present and no future. The creative mind of the composer got to work. The *Midsummer Night's Dream* was hurled onto the floor and the grey head bent industriously over the blank sheet of manuscript paper on the desk.

*   *   *

What the hell is this?" Adelaide asked and picked up one of the sheets of paper that were blowing around the courtyard.

"That is your grandfather's latest opera. Rescue it!"

Adelaide and Nick raced round the yard and scooped up all the bits of paper including the screwed up ones that were bowling out of the harness room like deranged footballs.

"Got the lot?" Nick asked and took the bundle from Adelaide.

"Reckon so. You sure you want to talk to him now?"

"Even more so."

"Then can we go back to bed?"

Nick groaned silently. He had never met a woman like her. He had got up that morning feeling quite cheerful in spite of the heat and she had reduced him to a shattered wreck in little more than half an hour. "If you like. How well do you get on with your grandfather?"

"Oh, OK I guess. And don't you forget what I said. No festival talk."

Nick didn't make any promises. He went across to the harness room where Ted was hard at work. "Morning, Ted. Why is your opera all over the courtyard?"

"Get out!" Ted bawled. "Get out, go away and don't come back until I tell you. Can't you see I'm working? I can't possibly cope with you now. Go on, hop it."

Adelaide hooked a triumphant hand through Nick's arm and her eyes gleamed. "Come on then, lover boy. Would you mind if I tied you up this time?"

Nick Greenwood really couldn't believe the things he had to do for the festival.

* * *

Liam tossed irritably on the hard bed. He was beginning to forget what his room at Labrador Cottage looked like. It was dark again but he couldn't remember whether that meant it was nearly Friday or nearly Saturday. They'd given him fish for his evening meal and it was lying heavy in his stomach. His head ached, his eyes were sore as they never turned out the lights in the cells and he wanted nothing more than to have a shower and to wash his hair. They had given him back his clothes and his ear ring when he explained politely that he didn't want the hole to close but his necklace they had put in one of their sealed little bags along with all the other bits he had been told to hand across. His shoes wouldn't stay on his feet without their laces so he had taken to padding around barefoot, but there wasn't really anywhere to pad to. Just a tiny little cell. Or, if he was lucky they let him stray as far as an interview room where they went through his mother's letters with him so often he had almost memorised them and he was quite sure they had. The way they could twist her innocent words and her snatches of gossip was frightening.

He gave up all hope of sleep and sat up on the bed. His hair and shirt were soaked with sweat and sticking to him horribly and he stank something dreadful. There was a blinding blue flash, the lights went out and the thunder went off like a bomb outside his window. He listened while his pulse rate returned to normal. Yes, he could definitely hear it. The raindrops were lashing down outside, battering uselessly against the parched earth and rattling like rubber bullets on his window.

He twisted his hair up on top of his head to try and cool his neck a little and wondered what the Maze looked like.

CHAPTER EIGHT

In which a book is finally launched and a fence pole is thrown

"Oh, what's it done now?!" Dotty shrieked as yet another mangled envelope was spewed onto the floor. "Oh why did Debbie have to be away this morning?"

Julie picked up the envelope from the floor and pressed the reset key on the printer. "Have another go," she encouraged.

"Thank you, dear. Oh, why did they have to send Liam to prison? It's just not fair."

Julie went back to her desk and didn't answer. It was Friday, it was raining as though it would never stop and there was still no word of Liam. Stella had got ever grimmer throughout Thursday and now she had called Nick and Sigs into her office again. Debbie had gone for an ante-natal check up and Dotty had been called in to get the invitations for the book launch sent out. The Festival might be in jeopardy but there was no way Stella was calling off the launch. Normally Julie liked having Dotty in the office but today all the older woman could do was grumble and shriek much to the annoyance of the other workers.

Dotty looked across the office at Julie. The poor thing always looked so tired recently. Of course she was worried sick about Liam, but then they all were. It didn't help that Adelaide was keeping Ted virtually under house arrest and nobody had seen him since he had gone such a peculiar colour at the orchestra rehearsal and had been taken home by Nick. That wasn't true, Dotty reminded herself. Nick and Julie had both seen him but it seemed Adelaide was doing a very good job of discouraging all callers. Oh, why wouldn't Liam come back? He understood printers. Men were good at that sort of thing. The printer beeped pitifully and its display panel assured the distraught Dotty that it really did need a new print cartridge.

"Now what does that mean?" she asked it.

A freckled left wrist adorned with a frayed leather bracelet reached past her. A hand flipped up the top of the printer and took out a small black and green box. "It means it wants its breakfast. Bit like me, really."

Dotty looked up, flung her arms round the arrival's neck and didn't care if his hair was sopping wet and all over her face. She inhaled the scents of shampoo and aftershave as she delightedly kissed his cheek. "Welcome back. Was prison really bad?"

Liam saw Julie was looking at him and smiling but she wasn't going to leave her desk in an emotional outburst such as Dotty had displayed. He returned the kiss on the cheek. "It wasn't prison. Just the police station."

"And?" Julie asked, holding her breath. She went scarlet as Liam crossed the room to give her a kiss on the cheek too.

"Released without charge."

"Oh, I am glad." It was no good. She had to do it. And Dotty wouldn't tell anyone. She gave Liam a small hug. "Missed you. I've had to do my own washing up these past three nights. What have you done to your face?"

"Bit of an accident. It's nothing."

"Does it hurt?"

"Not any more."

Dotty had to smile. They looked so sweet standing there in each other's arms and without a thought for anyone else in the world. She heard ominous footsteps thudding along the corridor. "Liam, dear, I hate to interrupt, but you've taken away my print cartridge."

Liam let go of Julie and looked at the box in his hand just as Phyllis walked in. "You're right. Sorry."

"You're back!" Phyllis cried. "What happened?"

"Released without charge. I've come to see if I've still got a job here."

"I mean what happened to your face?"

"It was an accident."

"It's a nasty bruise. What have you put on it? I've got some cream in the first aid box if you think it would help."

"I put some witch hazel on it. It'll be fine."

Phyllis gave him a hug too. "Been awfully quiet without you. Welcome back."

Liam would have bitten his lip to stop himself grinning like a loon but his top lip was split and he was afraid it would start to bleed. "Thank you. Must say I wasn't expecting quite such a warm welcome."

"Well, don't expect it from everyone," Phyllis cautioned. "I'd better check with Stella and see if you're entitled to be paid for two days at the police station. What did they do to you?"

He shrugged. "Nothing much. Just wanted a few details about some things."

"I'll go and tell Stella you're back. She's incarcerated with Nick and Sigs again. It's just too dreadful to have the festival cancelled at this late stage."

"Cancelled?"

"Julie, fill him in. I'll go and talk to Stella."

*   *   *

Stella McGinty looked at the young man sitting in the chair on the other side of her desk and thought she had done this before. His red hair was rain soaked, his expression was inclined to the miserable and that dreadful bruise on his face really didn't do him any favours at all.

"No charges at all?" she checked.

"None."

"Can this be verified with the police?"

"With the Chief Constable himself."

"Well, some people would call me a fool but your job's safe for the time being. Any news from Geneva?"

"No."

"Well, that's maybe a good thing. Right, you sit here a minute." Stella opened her door and summoned Julie into her room then firmly shut the door in Phyllis' face. "Now, possibly more than last time, I need you two to do your double act. I don't know what Adelaide Anderson has said to her grandfather but he's agreeing with her all down the line that the festival should be cancelled. Or so she says. I haven't been allowed to speak to him personally. Nick hasn't done much better although God knows he's tried. So, Liam, I don't care what you do. Just get the festival going again before the end of today or I've got to start cancelling concerts."

She dismissed the pair of them and watched as they left the offices, walking a bit closer together than they used to do, she noticed. And from the smile on Phyllis' face she had reached the same conclusion. The two women caught each other's eye and both knew the other was thinking of hats for weddings.

*   *   *

Liam looked at the familiar sights of Brockleford as he walked beside Julie. She hadn't said very much to him but she wasn't exactly walking two feet away from him as she had done before. Maybe there was a bit of hope here after all. He just wished he wasn't so tired he felt drunk and slightly out of the real world.

"Got any ideas?" he asked.

Julie forced her mind to concentrate on the task in hand and stop remembering the feel of that hug he had given her. "Only one," she admitted and went scarlet.

"Care to share it?"

She paused. It had seemed a good idea when it first occurred to her but now it appeared rather ludicrous. "Are you any good at flirting?"

"With Adelaide?"

"With Ted."

*   *   *

Adelaide Anderson took one look at the man on the doorstep and asked bluntly. "Who the hell beat you up?"

"Is that any of your business? I've come to see Ted."

"He can't see anyone at the moment."

Liam hoped Julie's plan would work. Personally he had his doubts. "Is he blind or dead?"

"Just who the hell are you?"

"Liam McGuinness."

"But you're supposed to be in prison. Oh my God, you're an escaped convict."

"I am nothing of the sort. Now, are you going to let me in or do I sit on your doorstep and wait? And I'll tell you here and now that I can wait for a very long time."

"You picket my doorstep and I'll call the cops and then you really will go to prison."

"You call the police and I'll tell them you're holding an old man hostage to suit your own material gains. Let me in, you money-grubbing little bitch or I'll stand here and shout. I presume Ted can still hear?"

Julie had never thought to see Liam be so terrifying. If he had looked at her and spoken to her the way he was with Adelaide, she would have run a mile. Clearly this was a side of his personality he liked to keep hidden. In the meantime all she could do was hope Liam was playing a part and doing it beautifully so far but this was the easy bit. She followed behind him as a thunderstruck Adelaide let them in. To Julie's unspoken admiration, Liam didn't falter. In a sudden switch of mood he went from scary to flippant as he went straight to the drawing room, bent over the man at the piano and kissed the top of his head.

"Now, what's all this about the festival being cancelled?"

Ted Ellerby nearly fell off the piano stool. He looked up into the indigo eyes of the man leaning over him and had to smile. He had a feeling he knew what was going on here and he would never get another chance like this. He returned the kiss on the lips, being very careful not to hurt that dreadful injury on Liam's face. "Spoke to Richard this morning. Bet you're glad. Anyway now the weather's broken I think we can safely go back to coffee."

Liam hadn't been expecting the kiss but he heard Adelaide stirring in the background so maybe it would be worth it. "Couldn't spare me a biscuit, could you?"

"I think there may even be some fig rolls left. Adelaide, coffee."

"Yes, Grandpa," she snarled and left the room. So that was Liam McGuinness was it? The gossip was obviously true but she reckoned she could cope with that.

"You," Ted told Liam, "are incorrigible. I suppose Julie put you up to it?"

"Yes. Sorry."

"Please don't apologise. I was rather enjoying it. No charges according to Richard. Here, sit beside me and let's do this in style."

Liam reluctantly did as he was told. "No charges at all. Thanks for sending in the cavalry by the way." A septuagenarian arm found a snug niche round his waist and didn't show any sign of moving even though Adelaide was out of the room.

"My pleasure. Now, while all this is very nice what exactly are you hoping to achieve?"

"If Julie's got it right, you'll find out very soon."

Footsteps were heard approaching the drawing room. Ted rested his head on Liam's shoulder and hoped 'very soon' wouldn't come too quickly.

Adelaide came back into the room prepared for battle. "Coffee," she announced and banged the tray down on the table. "Over here."

Liam gently extracted himself from Ted and got to his feet. "I hear you've called off the festival."

"Too darned right I have. Grandpa's going back to the States with me next week."

"Is that a reason to call off the festival?"

"Wouldn't be a festival without him."

For a sad, fleeting second the thought crossed Liam's mind that one year it would have to be. But not for quite a few years yet, he hoped. "What's the real reason? Don't want to lose any of the money he's got? I just hope you don't try to talk him out of my inheritance. Never mind, I'll take him along to our bed in a minute and find out then."

The colour drained from Adelaide's face. "You'll do what?"

"Shag him senseless, sweetheart. It's what I do best. Isn't it Ted?"

All Ted could manage was a half-articulate grunt but Adelaide thought he was agreeing.

"My God!" she screamed. "And you called me a money-grubbing little bitch."

"Which you are. It's just that I grubbed it first." Liam triumphantly returned to the piano stool with two cups of coffee. He had to hand it to Julie, she'd certainly got the measure of Adelaide Anderson. The American woman was getting quite hysterical by this time. He put the cups on the piano and gave Ted a possessive cuddle. "Now clear off. The festival is not being cancelled and you're not taking Ted off to America."

"You going to stop me?"

"Yes."

Ted and Julie looked at the two redheads sizing each other up across the drawing room.

Guessing he would never be able to do it again. Ted slid a rather intimate hand up the inside of Liam's thigh. "I think I can cope with the festival," he assured his granddaughter. "Now that I've got Liam back."

Adelaide bolted from the room and look of triumph was exchanged.

"I think the festival's back on," Ted remarked.

"Can I have my leg back now?"

Ted gave the thigh a final pat. "If you must. Anyone ever tell you you've got legs like a horse?"

"Goes with the mane," Julie put in. "Liam you were wonderful."

He blushed and shifted away from Ted. "Any biscuits going?"

*   *   *

Liam leaned back as he sat beside Julie on the bench in the Mediterranean garden. The seat had been so wet they had had to put bin liners over it before they could sit on it but they wouldn't have sat anywhere else. He looked at the cricketers splashing around rather miserably on the drenched pitch and didn't envy them having to play their match that night. Little spurts of water shot up as they pounded along and all their trouser hems were muddy.

"Don't know why they don't cancel the game," he remarked to Julie.

"Dedication," she offered and the bin liners crackled as she shuffled a bit closer to him to get away from the clematis that was dripping on her.

"I suppose you want to know why I didn't tell you about my family?" he asked and hoped the banging of his heart wasn't audible now she was sitting so close to him.

"Not really," Julie admitted truthfully. "I don't think I'd tell such things to someone I didn't expect to share a house with for very long."

"Are you ashamed of me?

"No. I admire you for turning your back on it all. I pity you because you must be for ever living with the dread that one of your relatives is going to be released and come and get you." Julie just stopped short of saying what else she felt for him. Another drip forced her ever closer and she could feel the heat of his body now.

There was an awkward pause. Liam knew he could move up the bench a bit further but he didn't really want to. "When did the car come back?"

"It never went away. I hope you don't mind but I gave them the key. I got the feeling it was either that or have the fire brigade chop it up into little bits. Then they just turned a dog loose in it. I'm afraid Lady quite fell in love with him. The policemen wanted to know how you could afford such a car. They didn't believe me when I said you'd won it."

Liam couldn't look at her as he confessed what half the police force were probably still wetting themselves laughing about. "Oh, I won it. But not for any athletics competition. It was after that fiasco in Stockholm where I'd been eliminated for falling over the line. Me and some of the other blokes in the team hit the clubs and I got, well, more than slightly paralytic. There was this contest being held in one of them. A free translation of the Swedish is 'Mr Beautiful Bum' and the others made me go in for it."

Julie nearly shrieked with laughter. "You didn't!"

"Honest to God. Stripped right down to a borrowed G string and half a bottle of baby oil. I was drunk out of my mind at the time."

Just for a moment she allowed herself to try and imagine what he must have looked like but as she had never seen a man wearing less than swimming trunks and then only in the appropriate venue, she failed miserably. "One day," she started, realised she had murmured aloud and stopped, red-faced.

"What?" he asked amusedly and looked into her scarlet features.

"Nothing."

"Get me drunk again and I might."

Julie caught his eye and saw he was laughing at her. "Forget I spoke, all right?" She couldn't look away now. "Sorry, I was just trying to imagine..." It was a lost battle. She closed her eyes and leaned those last few inches towards him.

*   *   *

Adelaide Anderson stretched herself lazily across her lover in their bed and soundly kissed his mouth. "We'd best get up and go check on Grandpa."

"He'll be fine. I don't know what you're worried about. But you're right. We'd better get up. I've got to get that programme book finished today now the festival's on again."

Adelaide giggled and chewed at his ear. "You and your stuffy festival."

"It's not. Just you wait until you see me conduct the premiere of Ted's cello sonata."

"I can." Adelaide sat up in the bed and gathered her hair behind her neck. "What are we going to do about McGuinness?"

Nick idly rubbed her back. He had thought he had seen the last of Adelaide after the festival was reinstated but then she had called him out of the blue and invited him across. Wary that she might try to get everything called off again he had felt obliged to comply but he had a suspicion that she hadn't rung him because she loved him. "Do we have to do anything about him?"

"He's been in trouble with the cops, right?"

"I don't know the details but they seem to have something on him."

"Well find out what it is and we'll see about planting some evidence. Then all we have to do is get him taken away and sent to jail for a good long spell and Grandpa won't have his boyfriend any more, will he? So he can come back to the States and be with his family."

Nick had teased Liam often enough about his relationship with Ted but Adelaide's bitterness was genuine. "This is starting to sound pretty serious."

She looked him straight in the eye. "Believe me, I am serious. That guy stands to cheat me and my family out of what is ours and I'm not going to let him. So you go talk to your friends and find out just what you can."

*   *   *

Julie woke late on Saturday morning and yawned quietly. She listened hard but there were no sounds of movement from Liam's room so she guessed he had gone out for his morning run. A smile crossed her face as she remembered the previous evening. After the scene on the bench, more rain had driven them indoors where he had told her all about his family while she had stitched peacocks' tails. So she had told him about hers, but it hadn't been half so exciting.

She rolled out of her bed and went to look at the weather. The sun was out again, puddles were glittering in the light and, all in all, things looked pretty idyllic. She took a leisurely bath and sat down to her Saturday cornflakes feeling superbly at peace with the world. The spoon banged her nose and breakfast went everywhere when there came a loud thud from the back bedroom.

Liam caught Julie in the act of mopping breakfast off her blouse when he walked into the kitchen. "What have you been doing? Playing with your food again?" he asked her tenderly and they exchanged a greeting kiss.

"I thought you were out. Thank goodness I didn't start singing in the bath."

"I've never head you sing in my life," Liam commented as he reluctantly let her go again. "You've got no idea what a luxury that bed was last night," he told her as he got on with making his habitual morning mug of blackcurrant tea. "So what's on the agenda for today?"

"Oh, you know. Shopping, washing, usual Saturday things."

He caught her to him by the waist and they kissed a bit more. "God, I can see life with you is going to be exciting."

"Until you go to Geneva," she pointed out rather bitterly.

"Until I go to Geneva," he agreed. "To be honest, I don't know what I'm going to do. Why couldn't you have thrown yourself at me before I applied for the job?"

"Why couldn't I..." she started indignantly then realised he was laughing at her. Her smile became wry. "Friends for the summer?" she quoted ironically.

"Something like that. And will you get your thieving hands off my bananas."

*   *   *

Ted Ellerby called at Labrador Cottage just as the washing machine emptied its drum all over the kitchen floor.

Julie opened the door to him. "Oh, hullo. Come along in a minute. Sorry, we've just had a bit of an accident."

Ted followed her along to the kitchen where Liam was mopping water into a bucket. "See what you mean. Want me to go away again? It's just that young Nick has taken my keeper out for the day so I've made good my escape. I thought the three of us could go out for the day as well, but I see you're in mid crisis."

"Won't take long," Julie replied rashly. "And a day out sounds lovely. We can always do our shopping tomorrow."

Liam wrung out the cloth again. "And when do we telephone the plumber?"

"Isn't he lovely when he's all banal?" Julie enquired of Ted. "Let's leave it. Let's do something mad and foolish just once in our lives."

Liam had had quite enough of things mad and foolish in his life. "Let's get the water off the floor at least," he recommended just as the door knocker rattled again.

"I'll get it," Ted offered. "I'd help with the mopping but I don't think I can bend that far any more."

Tim Reilly and Ted Ellerby looked at each other for a few seconds.

"Thought you'd be gone by now," Ted remarked, not unkindly.

"Flight doesn't leave until tomorrow. Got Liam sorted out extra quick this time. Are they in?"

"Washing machine's just flooded the kitchen floor. We were going to go out for the day. Want to come along too?"

"That's very good of you. Maybe we'll get Liam to take us somewhere in his car. Seems a pity not to use it after he went through so much to win it."

"Humour an old man. He hasn't told me this one."

Liam raised his head from the bucket. "What on earth is that noise?"

"If I didn't know any better I would say it's the sound of our Sir Edward having a good giggle. Wonder who it is that's so amusing him?"

The kitchen door opened and Ted came in still wiping the tears of laughter from his eyes. "All done in here? Come on then, young Liam, fetch your car keys. Or may I call you Mr Beautiful Bum?"

Liam looked up wildly and guessed. The police inspector was hit square in the face with a very wet floor cloth. "And you once accused me of being a grass!"

Tim Reilly remembered the days when this young man's weapons had been more lethal than a sodden cloth. "Assaulting a police officer is it now, McGuinness?" he enquired mildly.

"Only those who deserve it. You coming on the picnic too?"

"I am that." Tim allowed himself a little smile. It would be good to see the face of Colleen McGuinness when he told her, quite truthfully, how her son was getting on.

*   *   *

Debbie slunk up to Julie first thing Monday morning. "You can't deny it now."

"Deny what?"

"You and Liam. Roger says he saw the pair of you snogging your heads off in your front garden on Friday night."

Julie didn't go even slightly pink. "So?"

"So nothing. I'm happy for you. Here's an invitation for the pair of you even though the wedding is ages away. I didn't think you'd mind sharing one now. And we can't afford to get that many printed."

Julie quite liked Debbie in her own uncomplicated way. "Thank you. And I'm happy for you too. How's the baby coming along?"

Her magnanimity was her downfall. Debbie was still telling her all about it twenty minutes later when Stella arrived.

"Anyone seen Nick this morning?"

Heads were shaken all round.

"Oh well, I'm sure he'll turn up soon. Can someone send him to my office when he gets here? And, Liam, try to sort out the mess Dotty's made of that mailing list; those invitations need to be in the post by this afternoon. Oh, and do me an edited list of just the names would you and fax it off to the Chairman. Copies for me and Sigs."

Julie wasn't surprised when Liam had been at work with the word processor for five minutes, mouse frantically whizzing all over the place, then he plaintively raised his voice.

"Can someone please tell me what Dotty's done to this machine?"

"She merged the two lists," Debbie explained. "When she shouldn't have done. She wanted to print out one lot of envelopes instead of two and thought it would be easier."

"She hasn't merged anything. She's lost half of it by the look of things."

"She renamed it something, but I can't remember what." Debbie leaned over Liam from behind to see the screen better, held his hair out of the way with one hand and sent the mouse scuttling along the list of file names.

Julie nearly went and wrenched the two of them apart. She knew envy when it stirred in her soul but rationality told her the emotion was misplaced. She didn't have any ties on Liam. Friday night they had got a bit carried away with the kissing and cuddling and Saturday had been a day of sunshine and laughter with Ted and Tim. Sunday had been shopping, getting the plumber booked, cleaning up the cottage and then going to the separate beds without so much as a kiss on the nose. Now here they were. Just as they had always been. Friends for the summer. She had no idea if Liam was deliberately playing it cool so he could leave her without a qualm in the autumn, if she had kissed him so hard she had hurt his bruises more than he admitted and he wasn't risking it again, or whether he just found her a total failure and rather unattractive after all.

Her attention was distracted when Nick arrived. He hobbled rather than walked and sat very gingerly at his desk looking for all the world as though he had had a first, disastrous, ride on a horse.

Debbie abandoned Liam and went across to Nick. "Are you all right?"

"Just about. Stella in?"

"Yes. She wants to see you. Are you sure you're all right?"

Getting up was obviously as painful as sitting down had been. Nick staggered over to Liam and muttered something in his ear before progressing very slowly to Stella's office.

"What's up with him?" Sigs asked curiously. "Liam, where are you going?"

"Nowhere," he replied as he left the room.

The others all looked at each other and Sigs pointed a biro at Julie. "We're relying on you to find out what's at the bottom of all this."

*   *   *

"I don't believe you!" Julie shrieked across the supper table that night.

"Honest to God, Julie. I was sitting on one of the toilets, with Nick half naked in front of me and rubbing Savlon onto his behind."

"You've got to be making it up. Oh, poor Nick."

"Poor Nick? Since when?"

Julie gave up the struggle and wept with laughter over her plate. "And what was wrong with his, um, him?"

"Whiplashes."

"No," Julie pleaded as her ribs started to ache. "You're making all this up. Why are we laughing? It can't have been easy for him. I mean how did he get whiplashes there anyway?"

"I didn't like to ask but he was calling Adelaide some strong things, I can tell you."

"I'm definitely going to buy that book."

"Will you let me look at the pictures?"

"I thought you'd gone off me."

"I thought you were just being nice to me because the police had let me go and if I tried it again you'd belt me for sure."

Julie gently pulled his head forward by the hair and softly kissed his mouth. "Now, where did I leave that whip?"

*   *   *

Nick Greenwood had cause to bless Liam McGuinness's discretion although he fancied that prude Julie had sometimes had a smirk on her face so he guessed the Irishman hadn't been as discreet as all that. But so far as anyone else ever found out, a wasp with malice aforethought had found its way into the pile of clothes Nick had left on the chair in his bedroom overnight and had come to rest in a pair of trousers.

By the time July had blistered its way into August, everyone had more or less forgotten that Nick's garments had been invaded by a wasp. Ted Ellerby had given up his *Midsummer Night's Dream* idea and was engrossed in the bitter lament which he had entitled *After the Dream* where his hermaphroditic Puck had been called to account and left in some sort of purgatory. Nobody had been allowed to see any of the manuscript but they all agreed it was wonderful to see him writing again. Stella McGinty crossed everything that could be crossed and hoped the music world would welcome a new Ellerby opera.

The early days in Brockleford seemed like a dream to the two who lived in Labrador Cottage. They barely had time to concentrate on their relationship, and certainly didn't have time to visit Ted. Lotty and Dotty had no time to come across to see them, and the weeds were slowly winning in the Mediterranean garden. Liam got a letter from Geneva confirming his appointment and a starting date of 30th September. He took Julie out for a meal in Brockleford's Chinese restaurant to celebrate and she believed then that their relationship wasn't going to last beyond the summer.

*   *   *

"What are you wearing to this do, then?" Julie asked Liam through his bedroom door.

"Scarlet. What about you?"

"Orange. Come on, be serious." She jumped as he came out and bumped into her in her dressing gown. "Oh. Not a suit then?"

"I don't possess a suit and Stella has let me off the tie. Go and get some clothes on or we'll be late. Anyway, you'd look ridiculous in orange."

Julie refrained from making remarks about redheads who wore scarlet. She hurriedly changed into her floral dress, kicked on her white shoes and decided she didn't need a cardigan. Somehow Liam always looked good no matter what he wore. There he was in dark grey trousers and his white sleeveless

T shirt and no doubt going to look far better dressed than half the men in suits at the launch.

"Aren't you taking a coat?" he asked her as she galloped down the stairs to join him. "It'll be late by the time it finishes."

"You are turning into my mother." Julie took her cotton jacket off the peg in the hall. "Happy now?" She watched as he shrugged on his own jacket and took something out of the pocket.

"Would you wear this, too? And, yes, I do mean with all the implications."

Julie looked at the silver and diamond ring in his hand. "Are you proposing marriage?" she asked incredulously.

He flushed. "Yes. Julie, if you'll marry me I'll take up Ted's curatorial job and Geneva can stuff itself."

Julie panicked. "No. I'm sorry. I love you dearly but I don't want to marry you. Well, I do, but…" she felt the hot waves of embarrassment sending her red from the chest up. "Because if you got to hate it here then it would be my fault and I'd feel guilty for tying you down. No. You go to Geneva and if we both feel we can't live without each other then I'll come out and join you. It's the best chance you've got for getting away once and for all and I won't let you throw it away. Oh dear. I'm sorry. I'm not handling this well, am I?"

Liam, disappointed and feeling rather foolish, put the ring back in his pocket. "No, you're not, and neither am I. Come on, or we'll be late."

"We could take the car."

"Not worth it. Anyway, after what you've just said I fully intend to come home drunk."

The two marched sullenly along the river walk in silence. Julie really couldn't see what he was getting so huffy about. She had done just about the least selfish thing she had ever done and here he was sulking. It wouldn't have been quite so bad if he had at least offered her a new ring instead of the one his previous fiancée had posted back to him.

Liam felt a complete idiot. He had been hoping to get the chance to explain that this second hand ring was only a temporary measure and he fully intended to get her one of her own choosing at the first available opportunity but she hadn't even given him the chance. Last chance to get away indeed. As if she thought he didn't recognise a rejection when he heard one. Any pathetic excuse would do for a thick Irish potato. He rather spitefully let her trip over the fence pole on the path and didn't offer to throw it out of the way.

*   *   *

Stella McGinty couldn't believe how well the launch was going. The church hall was exquisitely decorated and laid out, the festival staff were all perfectly charming, and Stella could feel herself relaxing as each perfect minute ticked by. She thought Liam and Julie were being unusually frosty towards each other but she really didn't have time to worry about the office temps. They were certainly already too professional to let any personal squabbles show to an outsider. Debbie was being a bit woolly again and had gone into maternity dresses long before she could have needed to just to get the sympathy vote, but that was just Debbie. Stella began to hope that the dramas were all over. Somehow, she couldn't quite believe it.

Food gone, the guests began to leave, most of them having parted with money in exchange for a signed copy of the book. Stella couldn't honestly have said she was sorry to see them go. But with a share of the profits going into the festival coffers, she wasn't going to complain too much.

Suddenly, it seemed, the guests were all gone and only the staff were left looking at a messy hall.

"Can we clean up tomorrow?" Nick asked plaintively. "I'm whacked." Nobody mentioned, but several thought, that he had spent the entire function sitting at a table signing books while they had been circulating with refreshments and generally getting very tired legs and arms.

"I should think so," Stella agreed. "I did mention the possibility to the vicar and we're none of us dressed for clearing up. Let's all get on home."

"Via the Manor," Ted insisted. "You must all come for a drink to celebrate. Thank you, everyone. It isn't often one gets to be so celebrated in one's lifetime."

The two with dogs to collect from their sanctuary in the kitchen of the church hall were among the last to leave and Lotty realised one other person was hanging back, glaring rather balefully at the retreating Julie Hutchinson. She put the lead on Lady who had been having a nice snooze beside the cooker and asked, "Care to walk with us, Liam? We'll take the river path as the road is a bit dangerous for the dogs."

"Suits me," he replied gracelessly.

They hadn't even got as far as the first stile before the two sisters had found out their friend had had his proposal of marriage turned down. They each put one comforting arm through his and nearly sent him mad with their conflicting advice while Billy and Lady joyously pursued anything in sight until they forgot what it was.

Julie looked across the river and wished she hadn't got caught up with the rest of them. Liam looked quite magnificent with the setting sun turning his hair the most wonderful shade of auburn she had ever seen. Away from the hygiene restrictions of serving food at a party, he had taken off the black ribbon which repressed the curls that had been washed only that morning and his hair was all over the place again. It spoiled the image somewhat to see he had a rather short, slightly elderly, lady on each arm but it looked to be more fun that having to walk along the dusty road with the others. Stella and Sigs were busily tearing the launch to pieces, Nick and Adelaide were wandering along with their arms round each other and that left Julie with Debbie and Ted. One had absolutely no conversation whatsoever and the other was walking rather slowly.

"Want me to shout at Liam to go and get his car?" Julie enquired kindly.

"No, don't worry. I'm walking at this speed because I am content, not because I am tired. It's been a lovely afternoon and I'm glad I agreed to come." Ted desperately wanted to find out what had happened between Julie and Liam but with Debbie ambling along at his other side he didn't dare ask.

"Wish we'd gone on the river path now," Julie lamented. She realised they had lost Debbie and looked back. "Oh, the idiot child. Debbie! Get back from the edge."

"There are some lovely dragonflies here. Come and look. Is it true they only live for one day?"

Julie and Ted exchanged a smile of resignation and went to join Debbie who was watching the mayflies darting about. Julie got quite mesmerised in the end but the chatter of the other four was getting distant and she pulled on her jacket as the sun's warmth was being replaced by the evening cool.

"Come on, Debbie. You can come and watch the mayflies another day."

Debbie turned reluctantly from the enchanting insects and turned her ankle in one of the cracks on the ground. "Whoops!" she declared and grabbed Julie's arm to steady herself.

Julie wasn't expecting Debbie to be so heavy and she staggered one pace the wrong way as Debbie's weight sent her off balance. Her foot hit a loose piece of bank and she just heard the start of Debbie's scream. The end of the scream was lost in the sound of the water rushing over her head and roaring in her ears. From a long was back in her memory she remembered her swimming lessons and tried to get back to the bank. There was nothing for her to grab hold of. The few bits of vegetation just tore out of the dry earth but she carried on paddling desperately as the current got hold of her and she started to be swept towards the weir.

* * *

Three people and two dogs stopped walking when they heard the screaming start.

"Oh my God," Lotty intoned. "Sounds like Debbie's fallen in the river."

Billy and Lady thought this was wonderful. Their owners dashing back along the path, over another stile and into a field of cows. Something worried them. Nobody was playing. They lay side by side in the grass and whimpered.

"Oh, hell's bells," Dotty wailed. "It's Julie. Can she swim?"

"Not that well," Liam told her and tried to quell the rising panic. He could see the others had gathered on the bank on the other side but there was nothing for Julie to catch hold of and she was too far out for them to reach her. Sigs and Stella were a little downstream, lying on their fronts, waiting with arms outstretched to try to catch her. Nick and Ted were desperately hunting for some sort of branch or rope or anything they could throw out to her. Debbie was screaming and Adelaide was running for help towards the village as fast as she could in three-inch heels.

"Fence poles!" Liam cried.

Dotty and Lotty thought he had gone completely mad. First of all he took off his jacket and for a ghastly moment they thought he was going to take a foolishly heroic dive into the river to try and save his sweetheart. Then he shot off back along the path and didn't even stop at the stile.

"My goodness. He hurdles too," Dotty remarked. "Oh, dear. I do feel so helpless. What can we do?"

"Keep up with them in case she washes over this side. Where do you suppose Liam has gone?"

"I thought he said 'fence poles'."

"Funny thing. So did I."

"Should we take his coat?"

"Might be prudent." Lotty picked up the discarded jacket upside down and didn't notice the small, shiny object that fell out of a pocket and neatly lassoed a buttercup.

Both sisters swore afterwards that the ground fairly shook when Liam came thundering up behind them. He had a fence pole in his right hand and didn't stop for any pleasantries.

"Nick!" he bawled across the river. "I'm going to throw you this pole. Try to get her to grab it."

Nick waved back that he had understood and watched attentively as the other man barely slowed his pace.

Liam ran on ahead until he could hear the weir roaring its murderous intent then he jogged back from the bank, desperately trying to get enough oxygen into his aching lungs to make him do this last run. The pole was heavy, the river a good sixty yards wide and he had only made fifty three the last time he had tried this stunt. If he foot-faulted on this run he would be the one to go over the weir but there was nothing else for it.

Sigs and Stella had almost caught Julie but they didn't have the strength to hold her. They were nearly in tears as the struggling Julie started to tire but had the sense not to waste her energy by screaming.

"Keep your heads down," Ted told them. "Liam's about to throw a pole across and it could go anywhere."

The two looked across to the opposite bank to see Liam careering towards the river with the fence pole raised to his shoulder.

"I hope his brakes are good," Sigs muttered.

Stella thought she had never seen anything more spectacular. Liam's red hair was flying in the wind and it was the image she had had in her mind when she had first seen him. The barbarian throwing the spear at the hordes with a faintly obscene sounding cry as he launched the pole at the very edge of the river.

The pole hurtled over the water, Dotty and Lotty got the same idea and rushed to grab Liam before he toppled forwards. The three of them fell in a heap backwards and an anxious Billy and Lady came galloping across to make sure they were all alright.

Nick Greenwood watched that piece of wood come flying towards him as though it was happening in slow motion. It was frighteningly surreal to see a fence pole whizzing through the air like that. The pole landed with a thud near his feet and he grabbed one end, got as near to the river as he dared and held it out. He had a vague idea that several elephants were all hanging on to his trouser belt but the pole was an encouragingly long way into the river.

"Grab the pole, Julie!" he shouted at the bobbing head.

Julie didn't hear the words but she saw a miracle extending across the river and she caught it. There was a lurch and a bump and then she was being hauled from the water in a very undignified manner. There were no conscious thoughts in her mind. Just an acknowledgement that she was on dry land and people were piling clothes all over her.

Stella and Sigs let go of Nick as soon as they realised Julie was safe and they got her bundled into their jackets. Debbie and Ted didn't have any jackets to offer but they hung around sympathetically just in case.

Nick had forgotten all about Adelaide running to get help as he took Julie in his arms. "Come on, you're alright," he consoled her and led her away from the bank. "I've got you now. You're quite safe."

Stella looked across the river to where Liam had got to his feet more quickly than Lotty and Dotty could do. He was standing and watching as Julie was escorted by Nick and it was a scene that etched into Stella's mind. Liam's hands were on his hips, his hair was streaming behind him as the wind had picked up and a large black dog stood beside him with her nose against his thigh. It was a wild, savage image, and Liam wasn't smiling. Just before she turned to follow the others back to the road, Stella noticed the barbarian was kindly helping two old ladies to their feet.

CHAPTER NINE

In which a cello sonata is ultimately performed on a trombone

Liam had only ever been in Julie's bedroom twice. Two nervous dashes from the door to the neat pile of washing on the floor and then he had kept his eyes firmly fixed on the objective in case she had left something frighteningly feminine lying around. Now here he was, two o'clock on a cool August morning, sitting on her bed while she cried in his arms and chattered all sorts of nonsense in her hysteria. Poor Julie, not only had she had the experience of falling in the river and believing herself a few minutes away from a nasty demise, she had also had to suffer the examinations of Fred Bond, the sympathies of Phyllis (who was clearly annoyed she had driven to the book launch and so missed all the drama), Sigs and Stella but also the howls of anguish of a distraught Debbie who had blamed herself for the whole thing. He admired Julie, he really did. She had gone for a bath, come back downstairs to assure the gathering in the cottage that there was nothing wrong with her and had then gone to bed. Fred Bond had invaded her bedroom when he got there and Phyllis had tried to go with him but her husband wouldn't let her although he had accepted Stella's offer to be a kind of chaperone. Liam hadn't liked to intrude, he had certainly never wanted company when he had stared a nasty demise in the face, but he had looked in on the slumbering Julie at regular intervals during the evening. It had started at half past one. At least, it had first woken him at half past one. The muffled crying from the front bedroom. So here he was. Two o'clock in the morning and wishing he was in his own bed and fast asleep.

"Try to get some sleep," he pleaded with her. "It's over now. You've had a fright and a bit of a swim and what you need now is some sleep."

"I can't."

"Course you can. Go on, do as you're told. Or I'll get Fred Bond round again."

"Don't you dare," she managed, and closed her eyes.

Liam knew perfectly well she wasn't asleep. He nearly fell on top of her as his own body tried to shut down for the night. There was nothing else for it. Thankful it was a double bed in the front room, he lay down on top of the duvet beside her and left his hand a prisoner in her grasp.

*   *   *

Julie woke in the morning and for a while couldn't remember a thing except she had had a bad dream. Her next conscious thought was that the pillow was a bit lumpy so she gave it a sleepy thump.

"Ow!" it said.

Julie sat bolt upright and realised she had gone to sleep with her head on Liam's shoulder and there he was, wearing nothing but a pair of shorts and stretched out six foot four on her bed. Her momentary panic subsided when she worked out she was under the bedclothes and he was on top of them so he hadn't taken advantage of her, but it was a bit of a shock.

"What are you doing here?" she hissed desperately.

He sat up beside her and pushed the hair from his eyes. "Sorry," he whispered back. "Didn't mean to go to sleep. I'll go and make you some coffee."

"Why are we whispering?" she murmured softly.

"I don't know. You started it. How are you feeling?"

"As though I fell down a mountain. You?"

He decided not to mention a residual ache in his right shoulder. "Me? Nothing wrong with me but thank you for asking. I'll go and get that coffee."

"Thank you." Julie watched him go and had to smile. She couldn't help but wonder who had been the more embarrassed to find they had been sharing the bed. It had been so sweet of him. But then he was sweet. Not like Nick. There were enough memories lingering for her to recall that it had been Nick who had fished her out of the river. Liam had gone off in a sulk along the river path and had last been seen chatting with Lotty and Dotty with two dogs running all over the place. Julie guessed he must be hating himself now. His sweetheart had gone tumbling into the river and he hadn't been able to do a damn thing to rescue her. But was she still his sweetheart? She smiled benevolently at the young man who brought her a mug of coffee and who knocked at the door before he came in.

"Thanks. What's the time?"

He looked at her clock. "Just gone seven. If you're sure you're all right I'll go out for my run."

"You go, I'll be fine."

"Sure?"

"Yes. Now, hop it. Go on."

Liam knew when he had been dismissed and went unenthusiastically to get ready for his run. She could at least have thanked him for throwing the pole across. But all she could do was go on about how Nick had saved her. He paused in the middle of tying one of his laces. How the hell could she have known? She would have had water in her eyes and her ears, probably couldn't hear anything and in too much of a panic to know what was going on along the bank. So she didn't know. Just thought he had been so upset at her refusal to marry him that he had left her to drown. Problem was it wasn't the kind of thing that came up in conversation. He couldn't exactly go and lean nonchalantly in the doorway of her bedroom and drawl in his most debonair tones, 'Oh, by the way, Nick couldn't have fished you out if I hadn't given him the pole to do it with'. He put his door key round his neck on its piece of string and trotted down the stairs. He had been throwing things around for most of his life. His father and brothers had abused the talent and abused him if he dared try to refuse. He had thrown countless means of destruction but never before had he used his prowess to save a life. It gave him a funny feeling inside and he felt a smile cross his face as he left the cottage. Oddly enough he had forgiven Julie for her refusal of his proposal. He understood why she had done it. He hadn't thought he ever would.

* * *

"I can't do it."

Liam bumped into Julie from behind as he hadn't been expecting her to stop so abruptly. "Yes you can. Go on."

Julie baulked at the stile. "I can't. What if I fall in again?"

"I'll walk nearer the river, you can stay the other side and then I'll fall in before you do."

"Why didn't we bring your car? There'll be all sorts of things to take back when we've finished clearing up."

"What? Two table cloths? Besides which, you can't spend the rest of your life refusing to walk beside rivers."

"Can we go back and take the road instead?"

"No. Now get on with you before I pick you up and carry you."

"You couldn't."

Liam looked at her, looked at the stile and guessed she was probably right. "So you'll just have to walk, won't you."

Julie was determined not to cry in front of him now she was all awake, but she could feel her knees starting to shake.

In an attempt to hide the fondness in his eyes, Liam climbed over the stile and held out his hand to her. "Come on. I won't let you go this time."

Julie, not very sure about all this, took the hand and followed him over the stile. She hung on hard and wasn't going to let go even if he wanted to. The path wasn't very wide, so she either had to stamp along among the nettles at the edge or walk very close to Liam. She chose the latter option but had to let go of his hand so she could put her arm round his waist. Just to keep out of the nettles she told herself. She guessed there must have been nettles on his side too.

*   *   *

"Absolutely sparkling!" Sigs cried delightedly and looked at the two grubby people sitting on the floor in the middle of a clean church hall. "Dear me, you two do look whacked. Was it terribly hard work?"

"No, not really," Julie lied wondering if Sigs even did her own housework.

"Um. Fact is. Can you go home and pop your nightie on or something?"

"Pardon?"

"It's just that the local paper has got to hear about how you were fished out of the river and they want to do a feature on it."

Julie felt herself going pink. "I couldn't. I mean, all I did was fall in. It was Nick who got me out."

"And Liam. Don't forget your blushing sweetheart."

Julie looked at the scarlet-faced young man beside her.

"Oh, my goodness," Sigs realised. "Modest as well. Julie, sweetie, where do you think Nick got the pole from that fished you out? Wonder Boy here threw it across half a mile of river so he could use it."

Julie felt dreadful. Why hadn't the idiot said something? "Liam McGuinness, you are a fool. A dear, sweet fool. You risked ruining your shoulder and your career just for me? And if your offer's still open then I'd like to change my mind."

"I'll wait outside," Sigs told them. "I've borrowed Stella's car so I can run you home. Don't be long." She was dying to know what the 'offer' had been but thought she could probably guess. A strict eye was going to have to be kept on Miss Hutchinson's wedding finger.

Liam looked straight in Julie's eyes. "Sorry, the offer's closed."

"What?" she breathed, hoping he was pulling her leg.

"You were right. I need to get away to Geneva. I can't stay here in Brockleford and I couldn't put it on your conscience that you had made me. Forget I ever asked, OK?"

Julie guessed that was only half the truth but she tried to make light of it. "Are you turning me down now?"

His smile was wry and sad. "Yes, I suppose I am. Will you forgive me?"

"Not immediately," she replied truthfully. "We'd better go."

"Yes. Just leave my name out of your story. There are times when I'd rather not be found."

*   *   *

Stella McGinty was worried. It had been in the local paper and then on the local television news. Twenty two year old Julie Hutchinson hauled from the river by Nick Greenwood, thirty seven, both of them from Brockleford. The council had agreed that it was scandalous that the river still hadn't been fenced off and the local conservation group said it would spoil the natural beauty of the scene. Not one word was written or spoken about how the life-saving pole had got from one side of the river to the other. While Stella was all in favour of modesty, she wasn't that keen on seeing Nick Greenwood elevated to the status of hero when he couldn't have got there without a little outside help. What she couldn't decide was what to do to make things even. She supposed she could start with a call to the Amateur Athletics Association.

*   *   *

"Fan mail," Julie told Liam at the Saturday breakfast table. "Postmarked London and it's not your mother this time."

"Have I no secrets from you?" he asked mildly and took the envelope from her.

She refrained from making cracks about G strings and baby oil but sat down and started reading her own letter. "Oh no!"

" 'Oh no' what? Jesus!"

" 'Jesus!' what?"

"Here shall we just swap?"

Letters were exchanged across the table. Liam read a very short formal note, informing Julie that her mother was coming to see her. It really had been very naughty of her not to write and say she had fallen in a river. Her mother had only found out because a friend of hers that Julie wouldn't remember in Chester had seen it in the local paper and sent the cutting.

Julie had more of a tussle with the handwriting of Liam's letter. He was invited to go back to his old club at Crystal Palace to try out for a team that was going to be needed in a couple of weeks for a competition against the USA.

Two pairs of eyes looked at each other in abject panic.

"What am I going to do?" Julie bleated. "She'll skin me alive for sharing a house with you. She'll tell me I'm nothing less than a scarlet woman."

"You want me to move out?" he offered unwillingly.

"No! Oh, why is it that every time I say anything to you these days you get offended?"

"I'm not…"

"Yes you are. I can tell by the way you screw up your nose."

"I do not…"

"Yes you do. You wrinkle it ever such a little. I'd better get on and do some cleaning and washing and stuff. Oh, help! The festival starts on Monday. I can't possibly have her here then. Help me, please?"

Liam pushed his own dread feelings to the back of his mind. "Right. Now, assuming you don't want her sleeping in your room, and if you're quite sure you don't want me out then I can sleep on the sofa and she can have my bed. I'll even tidy the room up a bit. When's she coming?" He looked at the letter again. "Today?! She doesn't believe in giving notice, does she? I'll hit the supermarket, you deal with the bedclothes. Just bung my stuff anywhere out of the way."

They both shot up from the table at the same time and collided in the doorway. Squashed between Liam and the jamb, Julie knew this was the best chance she was going to get. She grabbed hold of that hair and kissed him firmly right where he had been bruised.

"My hero!"

Liam wasn't sure if he was standing on his head or his heels after that. "Since when?"

"Since for a long time," she told him and started nuzzling.

He loved it when she did that but that morning there were other things to distract him. "Can we save this for later, please? In a matter of minutes we could have your mother banging on the door and I've got to find a diplomatic way of asking Stella if I can have a day off during festival time."

Julie stopped nuzzling. "Oh, shut up," she breathed in his ear and the two got on with some serious kissing.

*   *   *

"Hullo, Mum," Julie said very formally and accepted the maternal peck on the cheek.

"Juliet, darling! How are you? I was so worried. So this is Labrador Cottage is it? My, it's a bit rough. I'm surprised you can cope with it after home. Never mind, I suppose it's almost adequate for one."

"Two," Julie pointed out before she lost her nerve completely. "You'll get to meet my flatmate in a bit. He's just gone to the supermarket."

One tiny monosyllable had given it away. "He?"

"Yes. He. His name's Liam McGuinness, he comes from County Londonderry and we share the house. Nothing worse than that."

"Oh, darling. How sordid. What does Paul think?"

"Paul doesn't know. I broke off our engagement months ago. After he started calling me Cynthia in fact."

"Oh. And I suppose it has nothing to do with the fact you've been living with this, what did you say his name is? Lionel?"

"Liam. No, Mum, it hasn't. Anyway, he's moved out of his room so you can have it while you're here and I've changed the sheets. Let me show you round."

The living room was pronounced "poky", the front bedroom "barely adequate", the bathroom "antiquated" and the back bedroom "a broom cupboard". The kitchen was deemed "not bad for such a hovel" and Julie presently sat her mother at the kitchen table and made her a cup of coffee.

"Sorry it's only instant. I asked Liam to pick up some ground from the deli while he was out."

"Obliging sort of chap, is he?"

"When he wants to be."

"Oh, rather weak-minded. You always did like men without minds of their own. Well, I shall warn you now that I intend to sleep with my bedroom door open so I'll soon know if there's anything going on. Which school did he go to?"

Julie knew it would not be sensible to mention juvenile detention centres, approved schools and the ultimate struggle in a comprehensive in Belfast. "Jesus College, Cambridge. He got a sports scholarship as he's a mean javelin thrower. Doing an Olympic trial some time this month."

"Really," came the purr of approval. "Well you could have said he's quite respectable."

Julie prayed her fellow lodger wouldn't come back with a ring in his nose. That would be just the kind of thing that appealed to his sense of humour that would.

"He also sings alto, plays the cello and drives a Saab. He's not what you're thinking of at all. Probably when he's got as far as he can with the javelin he'll take up his singing training more seriously. Ted, you know, Sir Edward, Ellerby's written two works for him, including an opera."

The front door banged open and Julie tried not to panic. "My mother's here, Liam," she called in warning. She saw the smile on his face and her heart sank. He was going to do something mischievous, she just knew it.

He looked really rather nice and athletic that morning in his jogging trousers and sleeveless T shirt with his hair tied out of the way. The weight of the bag of groceries in his arm gave a nice definition to the muscles and the nails of the hand he offered in greeting were clean.

"Good morning, Mrs Hutchinson," he said politely. "Was it a bad journey up from Devon?"

Eleanor Hutchinson nearly melted on the spot. There was a gentle Irish lilt to his voice, he was certainly extremely handsome and she really couldn't understand how her Juliet could share a house with him and not do anything wicked.

"Pleased to meet you too. I gather you've moved out of your room for me, that's very kind of you."

"No problem." He gave Julie a casual kiss on the cheek as he passed her on his way to the kettle. "Coffee, dearest, or have you had some with your mother? I got the ground you asked for."

Julie didn't dare look at her mother. "Had some, thanks."

"OK. Oh, I picked this up on my way back. I suppose we should have gone together really but it was only the alteration."

Totally puzzled but ready for anything, Julie took the small bag he gave her and unwrapped the bundle inside. Her mother saw it first and swooped like a hawk on a rabbit.

"Oh, Juliet, that is perfectly exquisite. Why didn't you tell me?"

Liam's head popped back from dealing with the kettle. "'Juliet'?"

"Don't even think about it," she warned him. "Mum, can I have that back, please?" Whatever it is, she added silently. She staggered a bit as she was nearly crushed in a maternal hug.

"Of course." The object was passed straight across to Liam. "Now, you just do this properly, young Lionel. None of this casual lark all you young things seem to favour."

Julie looked at Liam's scarlet features and knew his bluff had been called. She silently took from him a ring with a red stone in its setting and put it on her finger. From the look of it he had found it in a charity shop and she couldn't believe her mother had been too transported to notice. "Thank you, darling, it's just perfect now."

Liam caught the glare and knew he would be in trouble when the protection of her mother was gone.

*   *   *

"I wish we'd had a telephone put in the cottage," Dotty remarked to Julie as they tussled with the truculent word processor on Thursday morning. "I mean that way Liam could have rung you last night and you would know whether he was in the Olympics or not."

"It's not that simple," Julie explained patiently. It wasn't Dotty's fault that she always felt bad-tempered these days, but her mother had been there nearly a week, didn't appear to be shifting and was generally integrating herself into Brockleford society. The village part of it, that was. "What he had to do yesterday was see if he's good enough to get in a team for a competition later this month. If he is, and if he keeps it up, then the odds are he'll be off to Atlanta."

"And Geneva?"

"Now there is his problem. He doesn't know what Geneva will say or even if he'll be entitled to throw for Britain or whether he'll have to compete for Switzerland. Whereas Ted, on the other hand, has said he'll sponsor him to go to Australia for the winter to train and will still take him on as curator in the archive."

The hope shone in Dotty's eyes. "Does that mean he'll be staying in Brockleford?"

Julie looked down at her hands. She never wore the ring outside the confines of Labrador Cottage but she and Liam were, secretly, engaged. "I hope so." They had made wonderful plans. A wild, romantic elopement and a secret wedding somewhere in the Celtic mists of Ireland. A long passionate honeymoon in the Emerald Isle full of donkeys and jaunting cars and without a music festival in sight. In the meantime her mother was making plans and they hadn't told a living soul. Julie guessed the elopement would never happen. They'd have a stuffy English wedding in a stuffy English church, her mother would wear a dreadful hat and refuse to speak to her father who would, very properly, give her away. She wondered if Liam's mother would come. Somehow she couldn't imagine her own mother ever having anything to say to a woman who had brought nine children into the world, of whom six were still living even if one of them was missing and two were in prison. Two children were quite enough in the Eleanor Hutchinson book of rules. One was adequate but two were socially preferable. An elder son to inherit and a younger daughter to marry off. Julie, in her more malicious moments, wondered if her mother would have traded her if she had been born a boy. She would have seriously entertained the idea that she had been adopted for the sake of decency but she too obviously had her father's nose.

Julie was summoned peremptorily into Stella's office five minutes after the director arrived at work that morning.

"Sit," came the command. "Liam's on his way home now and he's just rung through from London. He's been asked to take part in a competition slap in the middle of the festival so I gave him a lecture on his duty to his employers and told him we can't pay him for those few days. I've no idea if this will affect Geneva or not. Now, as we all expected, Debbie has tendered her resignation. Do you want her job? I can't in all fairness offer it to Liam as if he's going back into training he won't be much use, will he? So I don't want any heroics from you about letting him have first refusal; he's a total non-starter. Give me your answer by tomorrow because if you don't want the job I'll have to see about advertising it."

The stuffy English church of Julie's nightmares solidified into the flint monster of Brockleford. "I'll think about it. I'll let you know as soon as I can."

"Fine. Off you go. Don't have time to chatter now." Stella watched Julie leave her office. Funny, she'd have thought the girl would have jumped at the chance. Unless, of course, she was planning on going to Geneva.

*   *   *

The choir was giving a concert in the church that night as part of the festival, and Julie's mother, who had ingratiated herself with Nick Greenwood and found him perfectly charming, went to it. Julie had had a few heart-stopping moments, terrified her mother would think Nick was a better prospect than Liam for a son-in-law, but somehow her mother seemed to have accepted Liam's role in her daughter's life. Probably something to do with the fact he had been to Cambridge whereas Nick had only managed to graduate from Bournemouth.

Two relieved people sat on the bench in the garden again and could feel themselves relaxing by the minute.

"When's your mother going?"

"Not soon enough. They've offered me Debbie's job."

"Congratulations. I assume you're taking it?"

Julie looked at the ring on her finger. "Would you mind? I mean where does that leave you with Geneva?"

"It leaves me in Switzerland and you in Brockleford. Julie, it's never going to work out between the two of us. What are we thinking of? You come from a nice family in Devon and I'm as near to white trash as we ever get in this country."

The other thing in which Liam McGuinness excelled, Julie thought, was self pity. Nearly as good as one of his huffs. "Who says?"

"I do. And you can't argue. You've twisted the truth as best you can to make me sound good to your mother, you humour me by wearing that tacky ring when we're alone but you deserve a lot better. How can I ever take you to meet my family? Not only have I been recommended by at least three police forces never to set foot in County Derry again, but have you ever visited anyone in prison in your life?"

"Your mother's not in prison. Nor are your two sisters. They live in a hamlet at the foot of the Sperrin Mountains. And I bet there's a lovely little chapel in that hamlet and a charming Irish priest who would be delighted to marry us."

"There's a gut who's reputed to be a bigoted paedophile who can't keep his hands off choirboys. I wouldn't marry you there if you paid me."

"Got you! So you are still going to marry me?"

He looked at her quizzically. "I'll think about it. You taking Debbie's job?"

"I'll think about it."

Julie went to see Stella the next morning and said she would take the job. Stella was cheered but a little perturbed. She had become quite convinced that Julie would be sticking with Liam in the future.

*   *   *

Ted Ellerby was more than slightly annoyed to be disturbed in his composing by Liam on the Saturday morning. "What do you want?"

"A word if I may."

"Go away, I'm busy," Ted glanced up momentarily and could see Liam was in a bit of a state about something. But Liam was nearly always in states. It was part of his psyche. "Come back tomorrow. Love to Julie."

Liam turned away. There was only one thing for it. He went to find Adelaide.

"Did he talk to you?" she asked.

"No."

"Told you so. He's in the middle of writing and just won't be disturbed. Nick tells me you're going in for Olympic trials this month."

Liam didn't trust Adelaide. Least of all when she was trying to be nice to him. "Next week. Can you lend me a piece of paper and I'll write him a note. It's rather important."

"Sure, come along to the drawing room. That was a good stunt you pulled over the festival but you're not really Grandpa's boyfriend are you? If you were you'd be living here and everything. Heard any more from the police recently?"

"Not a word."

"I kind of liked that Tim Reilly guy."

"I've known him a long time."

"You've been in trouble before? I went through that. Had a phase of dabbling in drugs and once the cops have gotten hold of your name then they just won't leave you out of things. You up for drugs too?"

"Explosives. Paper, please?"

"Right, sure." Adelaide couldn't believe it had been so easy. "But you're not into explosives any more?"

"Not in the slightest. Are you still into drugs?"

"No," she replied warily, wondering where this was going.

"Good. Because if you have any ideas about framing me by planting Semtex in Labrador Cottage you can forget it. Because while you may not be too sure about where the nearest shop is to buy explosives, believe me when I tell you I still know enough low-life to lay my hands on something incriminating very easily and it could just find its way here. Understand?"

She just glared at him, annoyed her little plot had been rumbled.

"And while you're thinking about that," Liam continued, sounding very far removed from the laid back young gentleman she thought she knew, "you may also like to know that Ted's estate is drawn up so tight with trusts a foundation for his archive and library that neither you nor any one person is going to benefit from it. These buildings are already secured as his archive and his money invested to run it. He wrote his Will soon after George died and there's no way he's going to rewrite it."

"It could be contested," Adelaide muttered faintly as she opened the writing desk.

Liam didn't even bother to reply.

Ted Ellerby paused at the French windows. They looked so cute standing together. Two red ponytails at the writing desk and it was so nice to hear they weren't shouting at each other. He went back to the harness room and let them get on with it.

*   *   *

"Liam's gone," Adelaide told her grandfather when he finally surfaced for some lunch. "He's written you a note as he said it was urgent."

"Thank you. I hope you and he didn't use your fists on each other?"

"No. He's a nice guy."

Ted raised one cynical eyebrow but didn't ask since when. He read the note quickly. "Oh my God. Why the hell didn't you give this to me sooner?"

"You told me..."

"Oh never mind. I must get along to the cottage."

Adelaide picked up the note after he had gone. The note she had watched Liam write then left on the kitchen table until Grandpa came in to eat.

Ted,

Sorry about this, but the athletics competition is on the day of the cello sonata premiere. I had to make a choice. You will say I made the wrong one. Will come back tomorrow to talk

L

A silent prayer of thanks went up to heaven. OK so it had been a dumb idea to think she could get Liam McGuinness sent to prison, but she reckoned this would finish him off so far as her grandfather was concerned. Now all she had to do was contact Grandpa's attorney and find out if it was true about what was going to happen to his estate.

*   *   *

"Oh, hullo," Dotty said to Ted when she opened the door of Last Chance Cottage. "Do come on in. Excuse me a minute but I must go and get the bread out of the oven. Would you like a loaf?"

"Thank you."

"Oh, good. Can you drop one off for Liam and Julie for me too?"

"Not today. Is your sister in?"

"Lotty!" she bawled up the stairs. "Ted wants you."

A bemused Lotty came down. "Me? Whatever for? Does someone need a photograph?"

"Charlotte de Grys, ex swing band player, you are one lucky girl."

"I am?"

"You are. Bring your trombone. You've got a cello sonata to learn by next week."

Lotty thought Ted had definitely been overdoing things. "Me? But what about Liam?" She absently caught hold of Billy by the collar before he took a chunk out of Ted's leg.

"Liam, like most men, has turned out to be a crushing disappointment. We shall go right now and get the music from him. Bring your trombone. I'll want you to play it through in case I need to rewrite anything."

Lotty had never seen Ted in such a black mood. She sat nervously in the passenger seat of his car as he drove faster than a seventy-four year old should. Her hands anxiously picked at the battered trombone case and she envied her sister the tranquillity of the cottage and the silent company of the dogs. Not that Ted was saying anything. Just staring ahead through the windscreen with his eyes glaring and his lips compressed. Lotty didn't dare get out of the car at Labrador Cottage but let Ted march up to the door alone.

Ted was glad it was Liam who opened the door. There was no call to shout at Julie and he wasn't sure he could control his rage. It wasn't the innocent Julie who had turned out to be such a traitor.

"Right, McGuinness, give me back the part for the sonata and while I'm about it I'll have back that cello I bought for you too. My God, when I think of all I've done for you and this is how you pay me back? One slight chance you might get on the long list for the Olympics and you turn your back on everything. Make quite a habit of turning your back when it suits you from what I hear."

Liam physically backed away from the man shouting at him on the front step of Labrador Cottage. "I came round to explain…" he started, biting back his own temper in the vain hope Ted would listen to reason.

"When you knew I'd be busy. Music and cello please. Right now. Oh, and I'll tell Anna she's not to coach you any more."

"Now, wait a minute. The arrangements I have with Anna are nothing to do with you. I pay her fairly for those lessons and so long as she's happy to teach me then you just keep your nose out, all right?"

"I think you might find her fees go up when my subsidy is withdrawn. Go and get the music. Now."

Liam, still furious at Ted's attitude, handed across the cello in its case. "The music's inside. Here you can have these as well." He broke the chain when he pulled it from his neck and nearly tore a chunk out of his ear as he got the silver ring out so fast but he slapped the jewellery into Ted's hand. "Now get out of my life you interfering old bastard."

A gnarled hand belted Liam across the face. "Slut."

*   *   *

Julie and her mother watched from the living room as Liam paced into the kitchen and there came a rattle of car keys being picked out of the fruit bowl.

"Oh no," Julie muttered and shot out to the kitchen. "What are you doing?" she asked.

He physically pushed her out of the way. "I am going to get my nose tattooed as you once suggested. Don't wait up for me."

Julie bridled at his tone. "Then I'm coming with you to make sure it's done tastefully."

"Fuck off."

"Don't you speak to me like that. Come on, let's go and find a tattoo parlour. I might even have one myself. Off we go." She bundled Liam out of the front door. "And don't go too far. You know you need petrol."

Eleanor Hutchinson thought her daughter was completely mad. She sighed once then got on with stitching the neglected peacocks' tails.

The two were out for quite a long time but they were giggling when they came back. She put down the cross stitch and went uncertainly into the hall.

"Juliet, I hope you weren't serious about the tattoos. You know I disapprove of anything like that."

Julie, who had been the only girl in her class at college without pierced ears, knew exactly. "It's all right, only Liam had the tattoo. Go on, show her."

"I will not have my daughter marrying a tattooed hooligan."

"Oh, Mum. It's done with vegetable dye. It'll wash out in a couple of months."

Eleanor looked at the patterned blue band round her prospective son-in-law's upper right arm and nearly vomited on the spot. "I forbid you to marry this man," she thundered. "And I forbid you to share a house with him any more. Pack your cases. At once."

Julie backed into Liam's comforting frame and felt his arms, tattooed or not, fold round her. "No."

* * *

Ted Ellerby crossed the green from the church and paused at the gate of Labrador Cottage. He checked his watch but the orchestra rehearsal had finished on time. Barely nine o'clock at night and nobody was sitting on the bench in the garden and no lights were showing. Lotty had rehearsed the sonata beautifully and Ted wondered why he hadn't written anything for trombone before. It had sounded even better than it had on the cello. Or maybe that was because Lotty was the more accomplished musician. Ted sighed and looked at the dark cottage. His conscience had been pricking him for days and he knew he had to apologise to the proud Liam. He had guessed that neither Liam nor

Julie would come to play in the orchestra while the row simmered between the composer and the erstwhile soloist but he thought Julie was being a bit hard on Alan the first oboe who had had to try to play both parts that night. He knew the two hadn't gone away because he'd seen them himself in the High Street at lunch time but hadn't dared approach. And the car was still parked next to the green. Mind you, if what Dotty had told him was true, then something was afoot as Julie had been going in to work with a rather cheap ruby ring on her finger these past few days. It occurred to him then that perhaps the two had gone to bed together but he couldn't quite believe it somehow. Ted didn't dare use the dog's-head knocker in case the two were up to anything but he tapped gently with his fist.

"Who's there? Julie's voice challenged from the darkness.

"Ted. You all right in there?"

A light swung crazily then Julie, torch in hand, opened the door. "Fuses blew when I plugged my hairdryer in. Do you know anything about fuses?"

"Very little. Where's Liam when there's a crisis on?"

"Gone."

Ted's stomach hit the floor. "Gone?"

Julie dived back under the stairs. "Mm. He's staying with his trainer for a couple of days before the competition."

Ted let his breath out. "I owe him an apology."

There came a bit of a fizz and a crackle and the lights came on again. "Hooray! Yes, I'm afraid you do. But I think maybe he owes you one too. Come along in now I can boil the kettle and I'll make you some tea. Proper tea, not Liam's mad herbal stuff."

"I don't deserve such kindness."

"Oh you do. Because if you hadn't quarrelled with Liam he wouldn't have gone off in a temper and if he hadn't gone off in a temper he wouldn't have had his tattoo done, and if he hadn't had his tattoo done my mother would still be here making wedding lists. Liam might owe you an apology but I owe you a vote of thanks. Fig roll?"

"Thank you. Did he really have a tattoo?"

"Not a real one. It's vegetable dye. Washes out eventually."

Ted felt immensely relieved and looked at Julie's hands as she put two mugs of tea on the kitchen table. "So it's true then. You're engaged?"

"Yes."

"Congratulations. Fixed a date?"

"No. It's all a bit complicated and depends on whether Liam goes to Geneva or not or goes back into training. Of course, you threw a spanner in the works because now he hasn't got the curator job to fall back on but I'm sure he'll manage."

Ted cursed himself for a fool. "Of course he's got the curator job. Does this trainer of his have a telephone?"

"Probably. I've got an address if that's any use."

"Thank you. I shall send him a bunch of flowers."

"You wouldn't?"

"Envious?"

"Well, yes. Nobody ever sends me flowers."

"Then I shall send you a bunch too."

Julie smiled at him fondly. "I think Liam's eaten all the fig rolls. I've got a packet of shortbread somewhere."

    *   *   *

The flowers were delivered to Julie's desk the next morning. She took one look at the huge bunch of peach and apricot roses and the green ferny things with them and thought she was going to die from embarrassment. There was a sort of hush in the room and she realised everyone was looking at her.

"They're from Liam," Debbie told her. "Must be."

Julie took the card from its envelope and wanted to laugh. "Sorry. They're from Ted. He said he would but I didn't believe him."

"How lovely!" Dotty cried. "I'll go and ask Phyllis if she knows where there's a vase for them. They are quite beautiful. I'll bring in my secateurs this afternoon and show you how to get cuttings from the roses then you can have some in your bouquet when you get married."

Julie carefully carried her bouquet home at lunch time and smiled as she arranged it in a vase. She read the card again:

You think this is embarrassing? You should see what I sent the other fellah. T.

Dear Ted. Julie looked at her watch and bolted for the stairs. Afternoon concert and she had to be at the church, in her best dress, to show people to their seats by half past two. She missed Liam as she went chasing across the green. Funny to think he was down in London running around a track and hurling his javelin all over the place while she was here in Brockleford and couldn't do anything except miss him.

*　　　　　*　　　　　*

"Look at me," Lotty squeaked. "I'm shaking."

"You'll be fine," her sister consoled. "And when this is all over we're off to the Manor to watch the athletics on the video."

"Oh, why do men always let you down in a crisis?" Lotty lamented. "It should be Liam here getting the butterflies, not me."

Nick crossed the vestry to have a word with the solo trombonist. "Looking very smart tonight, Lotty. All set?"

"No," she protested. "It's no good. I need to go to the toilet."

"No you don't," Dotty chastised. "You only went five minutes ago. Ah, here's Julie. She'll be able to calm you down. Julie, dear, tell Lotty everything's going to be fine."

Supporting her betrothed or not, Julie would have been upset to miss out on the chance of playing in the premiere of an Ellerby work and she was glad the crisis had been resolved. "Of course it will. I hope Liam's getting on all right and hasn't fallen on his face or anything daft. I would have phoned him but I don't have a number."

"I think," Lotty said in a very small voice, "that I would rather fall on my face in the middle of

Crystal Palace than have to go out there and play this piece of music."

"Rubbish!" three voiced chorused.

"Tell me, is Ted out there?"

The others exchanged a look but didn't speak.

"Oh, my word. He is, isn't he. Any sign of Adelaide?"

Nick sniffed. Adelaide Anderson had disappeared as abruptly as she had come and had left him feeling a bit of a fool. Last time he was going to trust a woman with such skinny wrists. He checked his watch, the end of interval bell had rung five minutes ago. "Time to go on. Go for it, Lotty. We're all right behind you."

*   *   *

Lotty was almost out of control as she danced round the drawing room of the Manor that evening. Ted humoured her for a while and danced with her as it had been such a wonderful evening. In spite of Stella's cajoling, which had desisted only when Ted had promised she could blow trumpets over the next year's opera premiere, there had been no big press announcement of the first Ellerby premiere for ten years. There had been none of the razzamatazz that had gone on in the past. Just a small concert among friends in Brockleford church when Lotty de Grys had gone back to her glory days and given the performance of her life.

"OK, we're all ready," Sigs announced.

Six people gathered round the television as Sigs started the tape. It seemed to go on for ever.

Lots of talking, some people did some running and jumping and it was all repeated at least four times from various angles and at various speeds.

"Where's Liam gone?" Dotty demanded as a rather handsome blond American was shown throwing a blue javelin.

"He's not the only one in it," Lotty pointed out. "He's got to have some competition."

"Oh, I suppose so," Dotty admitted and was silent.

On and on it went. More runners and jumpers, quick glimpses of someone hurling a shot putt. Stella was about to suggest that Sigs ran the tape forward when a familiar figure was spotted.

"There he is!" Dotty announced. "Whatever has he done to his hair?"

Six people leaned in towards the screen. "My goodness," Ted said. "Has he cut it all off?"

The object of their attentions was waiting to do his first run. All that remained of the spectacular mane was a curly fringe. The rest seemed to have been shorn to a stubble. There wasn't a stray lock to be seen.

"Now," the commentator told his audience. "First throw for Liam McGuinness of Great Britain. Not been having a good run lately. Eliminated in his last two competitions. Here he goes."

Six pairs of eyes were glued to the screen as Liam hurtled towards that line. As he half turned to throw the javelin, a thick plait of hair could be seen dangling down his back but before anyone could say anything a series of shrill beeps from the television made them jump.

"Foot-faulted again," the commentator told them rather smugly. "Let's just see that again, shall we? Pity really, a young man of enormous talent but just lacks that little bit of control."

"I don't want to see it again," Dotty lamented. "Oh, shut up, you horrible, horrible man."

"It's all right," Julie consoled. "He'll get another go."

"Hated the hair all scragged back," Sigs remarked and nobody argued.

Stella thought the neat young man wearing his country's colours was far removed from the barbarian hurling a fence pole. She rather missed him in a way. A hurdling race was squeezed into the broadcast four times.

"Second throw for McGuinness," they were warned. "Oh, my goodness. What has happened to his hair?"

The barbarian was back. Liam had discarded the bands that had turned his curls into that impressive plait and from the state of it he had torn them out in a hurry. His hair was loosely gathered at the back and curling madly all over the place. He had also found time to put a silver chain round his neck and there was a ring in his ear. As he trotted back to start his run, his Brockleford audience noticed he had taken off the white socks that really hadn't suited him at all.

"Go for it, Liam!" Julie yelled at the screen.

The commentator didn't say a word the whole time Liam was getting ready. He checked the balance of the javelin in his hand and the vegetable dye tattoo on his throwing arm only served to emphasize the barbarity.

"Second run for McGuinness. A young man of such great promise," the commentator droned. Liam went thundering down his run, there were no beeps, just a loud shriek that could have been anything and then that javelin was flying like a fence pole across a river. "Good throw! Yes, I'd say it's going to be a good one." There came a pause. "Ninety two point eight metres! It's a new competition record! Oh, yes! There's an airline ticket for Atlanta somewhere and this young man's name has just been written on it!"

No-one dared look at anyone else. That was it then. Their Liam was going to go to the Olympics. But where on earth did that leave Julie?

CHAPTER TEN

In which the first touches of autumn turn minds to thoughts of farewell

Julie sat alone in the Mediterranean garden that night. It was gone midnight, the only lights were those in the sky and coming from the window behind her, she was nearly asleep as she sat, but she wouldn't have sat anywhere else. It just seemed the right thing to do somehow. Her lemon tea had grown cold in its mug on the bench beside her. She didn't even like lemon tea all that much and without Liam's company it had become unpalatable. She looked across the dark green to where Brockleford church could just be discerned as a dark bulk against the starlit sky. The thought of having to get married in such a place was almost unbearable and she began to think it might be a good idea to agree to Liam's proposal to have a register office wedding instead. It was a pity about his faith but she guessed he wasn't going to accept Protestantism just to please her when his family back home were all staunch Catholics.

Her reveries were broken by the squeaking of the gate. "What are you doing here?" she hissed in case she woke up one of the infant army next door.

"Just couldn't stay away. Got the last train out of London and walked from the station."

Julie got to her feet as Liam arrived at the bench and she hugged him so hard she nearly squashed the flowers he was carrying. "What gorgeous roses," she hinted. "And you carried them here all by yourself, you big jessie."

He worked out her assumption and remembered a post-concert bouquet. "Certainly did. And they're not for you. Ted sent them to me. Along with a necklace and an ear ring, one of which had had to be mended."

"So you're all friends again?" Julie asked and tried not to mind too much about the flowers.

"I have no idea. The flowers and the parcel arrived, my trainer took to barricading his door at night in case my intentions had turned dishonourable, but there wasn't a letter. I didn't know what I was supposed to do. Does it mean the offer's still on for Australia and the curatorial post or not?"

She fondly bunched his hair behind his head and kissed his nose. "Why not speak to Ted? After all, wearing the jewellery on national television gave out a few clues. And the competition record I believe?"

"Ah. You didn't see the broadcast to the end. The last American to go out-threw me by two centimetres."

"So does that mean Atlanta is out?"

"Not at all. Mine was still the best British throw. I just keep getting my feet in a muddle. I wish I knew what Ted was up to. Have you heard anything?"

"He came round. The night the lights fused. I couldn't believe Lotty and Dotty were so efficient they'd provided spare fuses."

"Never mind the fuses. What did Ted have to say?"

"The curator's job's still there if you want it. The building work starts in a couple of weeks and he's going to want an answer from you because if you can't do it then he needs to find someone who can. He didn't mention Australia though. Mind you, you hadn't just got a competition record then. I suppose he's leaving it up to you."

Liam thought back to the last words he had spoken to Ted Ellerby. "I don't know that I want anything to do with him. Did you hear what he called me?"

"A tart wasn't it?"

"A slut. And do you know the worst thing? He'd made me feel like one. Oh, not that we did anything physical ever unless you count a hug by the goldfish pond and winding up Adelaide, but he made me feel cheap and I didn't like that."

"Yes, but you had just turned down the first Ellerby premiere in ten years. I think you could allow him to be a bit upset. Let's face it, you're hardly known for the sweetness of your temper yourself."

"But I don't go around calling people sluts."

"You told me to fuck off."

Liam was shocked to hear the profanity from her lips and realised just how much his own language had refined since he had met the shy girl from Devon. "I wouldn't."

"Oh you did. And my mother heard you, if you want me to call in a witness." Julie's subconscious caught up with her conscious mind. "But why are we standing and whispering in the garden? Come on in and I'll make you a cup of tea or something. Lemon, I presume?"

"Lemon? Yesterday's flavour. I've got some elderflower here somewhere." Liam noticed the mug on the bench. "But you haven't drunk yours,"

"Can't honestly say I'm that fond of it really."

"But you've been drinking it every night since May. And now you tell me you don't like it? Why did you let me make it so often?"

Julie shrugged and felt rather silly.

Liam picked up the mug of cold tea and drank it in one go. "Come on, I'll make you some elderflower."

Julie soon found out she didn't like elderflower tea very much either but it seemed rude to say so as he had so politely made her some of this treat.

"What are you going to do about Ted?" she asked and had another go at swallowing the tea that tasted more of plums than elderflowers.

"You needn't drink that if you find it that disgusting. Better go and see him I suppose. Maybe tomorrow evening. I'd better do some work tomorrow or I won't have any money to get to Australia."

Julie thankfully abandoned the tea. "I should have thought it would take more than your wages for this summer to keep you out there for six months."

"True. Have to see if I can get a bank loan or something. I really want to go, you see, because, oh hell, I may as well tell you now. I've agreed with my coach that I'm going back into training so I've had to cancel Geneva."

The hope soared. "So you're staying with me and Brockleford?" Then a horrible thought crossed her mind. "Or will you have to move back to London?"

Liam didn't want to go into the complications that would cause. "It depends on Ted. OK so he says the curator job is still open, fine, but surely he can't be expecting me to go off to Australia for six months in that case." He looked at Julie across the table and wondered how anyone's eyes could get that big and not drop out. "So it looks as though I'll be here for the winter but spending most of it in London. I don't know where I'll be as long as I'm in training," he had to admit. "Can you see Ted standing for that?"

"Not really," she replied truthfully. "You'll have to talk it out with him. Stella's asked me if I want to go back to college to do some postgrad in marketing and management." She hadn't meant to break the news quite like that but that was it, she'd done it.

"Congratulations. I think. You going to go?"

"It makes sense really. It's only one day a week. I had to sign up in a hurry as it's August now. Sorry, I meant to ask you first."

Try as he might, Liam couldn't repress the sigh that bubbled up from somewhere inside. "You don't have to ask my permission for anything you want to do. I used to think about postgrad but let's face it, I only got into Cambridge because I can throw javelins, not because I'm academically gifted. So come September you'll be off to college and I'll be…what? A curator? One thing for sure, I won't be in Geneva and now it looks as though I won't be in Australia either."

"But you could still make the Olympics?"

"Oh, sure. Just means it'll be harder work."

"I have great faith in you. They're upgrading Debbie's job and calling me Publicity Manager. Impressed?"

"Now isn't that what I said they'd do all those months ago? Does that mean I'm going to be marrying an executive?"

Julie felt herself flush. "First I have to get my diploma. You know Ted might still sponsor you."

"That man called me a tart."

"A slut."

"Whatever. And while I don't mind too much being employed by him, accepting his charity is something different. I don't know that forgiveness can be bought with a bunch of yellow roses and a couple of silver trinkets."

"You wore the trinkets. In public."

"And I'll tell you why. Because the best throw I have ever done in my life was when I got that pole across the river and I was wearing them then. It wasn't the furthest distance I've ever thrown, it wasn't the first time I'd thrown a potentially lethal weapon but it was the first time there was a positive reason for doing so. And after I got foot-faulted on the first throw today I said to myself that I wasn't going to let it beat me. So I got myself into the frame of mind I was in when I threw that pole."

Julie felt there was a terrific compliment in there somewhere but he wasn't about to let it out overtly. "You mean you had this image of my head bobbing around somewhere near the distance lines?"

He leaned across the table and took her face in his hands. "I mean I told myself I would lose you if I didn't succeed."

She accepted the gentle kiss he gave her and felt her face going ever more scarlet. "That is the sweetest thing you have ever said to me."

"So will you make an honest man of me before I turn into a curator?"

"Is that what you want?" she parried.

"Do you?" he offered unhelpfully.

Julie told herself this was getting ridiculous It was gone one o'clock in the morning and they could spend the rest of the night going round in circles.

"No, but thank you for offering. My course starts in a couple of weeks and I really don't think I'll have time to think about it. Can't we stick with the elopement?"

Liam noticed that those huge eyes had dark shadows under them. "OK, we'll elope. But will you at least let me buy you a better ring that that thing I got in a junk shop?"

"I like this 'thing'."

"It's not even a real stone."

"You can't afford a better ring."

"True. But I thought I'd better offer. Go to bed, you're nearly asleep now."

They adjourned up the stairs and cuddled a bit more on the landing.

"Promise you'll make your peace with Ted?" Julie asked. "I think he's really very sorry for what he said."

"I'll talk to him. But one word about sluts, tarts, trollops or anything like that and he's blown it. Now, go to bed before I abduct you into mine."

Julie almost hoped he was serious. But only almost. "You wouldn't dare. Don't suppose you thought to buy that book while you were in London?"

"Not without you to explain the pictures to me."

"Good night," she said fondly and went into her room, firmly closing the door in the face of the man on the landing.

*   *   *

"Oh," was the best Stella could articulate. "Wasn't expecting you back today. Congratulations on your javelin throwing."

Liam came into her office but didn't sit down as she hadn't asked him to. "You did tell me I wouldn't get paid for the days I wasn't here. Which is fair enough really."

"Right then. Has Julie told you the festival is paying for her to do some postgrad?"

"Yes. I think she'll be good at it."

There wasn't a hint of envy in his voice and Stella relaxed a bit. "And what are your plans?"

"God knows. I'm dependent on Ted's mercy now, but the next part of my life will be taken up with some serious competitions and training finishing up at Atlanta. All I need to do is find myself a sponsor of some sort. Or try to get a bank loan which won't be easy."

"Talk to Ted," Stella advised. "So Geneva is off, is it?"

"I rang them from London. They were, shall we say, not happy."

Stella thought he had a lovely smile when he was being ironic. "Their loss." She decided this potential Olympian was going to need a bit of a shove in the right direction. "Right, guess what you're doing for today since you're back?"

"Tell me," he invited and the smile died.

"You and Nick are on duty at the Manor."

"But I haven't spoken to Ted since...."

"Since you had a row? Yes, I know. I think most of Brockleford knows. It was rather unsubtle the way the cello sonata turned into a work for the trombone. Sounded good though. Go on, get yourself tidied up a bit and get that hair tied back, but please don't plait it. It looked awful."

"It keeps it out of the way."

Stella sternly pointed a finger at him. "If you ever come in here with your hair like that I will fire you on the spot. No questions. Now get along to the Manor. That means Julie can get on with things here. Don't laugh, Debbie is teaching her her job."

*   *   *

Liam had seldom felt less like laughing than he did as he sat in Nick's car and was driven far too quickly for his liking towards the Manor. Nick wasn't too happy about the arrangement either. Liam McGuinness had sunk even further in his estimation since he had been on television and was about to become something of a local hero with all this lark about going to the Olympics. Nick Greenwood sometimes felt that life was just one big conspiracy.

"Here we are," he announced brutally. "I'll go and make the pre-tour coffee, you go and kick Ted out from wherever he is. Try the drawing room first. He's given up composing these last few days."

Liam sent up a silent prayer even though he called himself an atheist and padded along to the drawing room. Better to get it out of the way first, he thought to himself. Better to find Ted in the drawing room than to have to go and find the old man languishing in bed. He mentally rehearsed things in various forms as he walked along. Should he go for the coolly sarcastic? The aloof? There was no way he was going for the penitent. Maybe he should try the lightly comic? Maybe he should pretend he couldn't find Ted and ask Nick to go and have a look.

He pushed open the drawing room door and saw the lonely figure hunched over the piano. "Time to go. Tourist alert in twenty minutes. Nick's making the coffee."

"Come here a minute," Ted asked in a wobbly voice.

Liam wasn't too sure about that. "What's the matter? Got stuck?" He sounded artificially cheerful and, feeling guilty, he crossed the room and leaned over the older man. "Go on, put your arms round my neck and I'll show you how good I am at getting stuck people up. I've done it hundreds of times for my mother." What he wasn't used to was putting his mother on her feet and he lowered Ted with a bit of a bump. "Sorry."

Ted couldn't believe his luck. Not only had he got his arms round Liam's neck and the scent of his aftershave all up his nose, but this shy young man had manhandled him as gently as if he had been a baby.

"Your mother is a lucky woman."

Liam got the message, went scarlet and let go. "That's a funny way of putting it."

"Oh, now I've offended you again and you're screwing up your nose. Liam, I insulted you horribly and I apologise unreservedly. Will you forgive me? Come over here a minute." Ted closed his fingers round Liam's wrist and pulled the younger man across to the writing desk. In the desk was a white envelope which he handed across. "I know you called me an interfering old bastard, and you're right about that but I don't want you to waste your talent because we've had some silly quarrel. I had a word with your javelin coach and he put me in touch with some other people. There's a ticket to Australia in there, going out in a couple of weeks and coming back in March as recommended by your coach. I've been a bit selfish and added a return to London so you can join me, and Julie too I hope, for Christmas. And I've guaranteed your living expenses while you're at the training camp. But anything other than that you'll have to pay for." He laid his fingers on the other man's lips. "And don't you spit the word 'charity' at me in that high-handed way you have. This is the one time in your life when you have a chance to achieve your dream and I want to see it happen. There will be time enough to pay me back later. Remember what I said to you about taking charge of the memory?"

Liam didn't know what to say. It was as though he had played that old Halloween game of looking in a mirror and this time it had worked. Australia, training, competitions, and the Olympics. All he had ever wanted in his life. He bit at his lower lip. "I'm sorry I walked away from your premiere," he said thickly. "Did it go all right?"

"Perfectly. Wish I'd written the damn thing for the trombone in the first place. And I'm sorry I called you a slut." Ted decided that at the age of seventy four if he couldn't push his luck now and again he never would. "Any chance of another hug?"

"So long as you keep your hands outside my trousers this time."

Nick Greenwood opened the drawing room door to fetch the other two for coffee. "Christ!" he exclaimed under his breath and accidentally banged the door as he closed it so quickly.

Ted removed his face from Liam's hair. "That's your reputation gone."

"Again."

"Slut."

"Slut yourself. Where's my opera?"

*   *   *

"Well," Stella McGinty began rather formally. "This is by way of a double celebration. The festival is over for another year and we're saying 'a bientot' to one of our workers. 'Gone but not forgotten' is the phrase I believe. So first of all, a big thank you to all of you for all of your hard work these past few weeks and good luck and God bless to the one of us going off to Australia next week."

Sigs raised her mug of coffee. "Here's to you, Liam, sweetie. Think of us all shivering in the snow while you're basking in the summer of Australia. Only don't faint again will you?"

Liam had long realised he would never be free of the teasing. "Packed my hat."

"And then you're going to be a curator when you get back," Dotty marvelled. "I think that's awfully brave of you."

"Not for a few months," Liam had to admit. "In the meantime the builders are at work and you and Lotty are having to cope with it all."

"And we don't mind a bit," Lotty assured him.

"But when are you and Julie getting married?" Phyllis wanted to know and the others were all grateful for her lack of discretion. "Surely you're not going to let him go to gallivanting off to Australia without a ring on his finger are you, Julie?"

"I'm afraid I am. For one thing I need time to make my dress and all the rest of it and for another the church is all booked up until the other side of Easter."

"But you should get married in St Aethel's," Lotty cried in dismay. "Good heavens, St Michael's has only been going a hundred years or so and St Aethel's is so much nicer."

"St Who?" Julie asked and remembered her own thoughts on Brockleford church.

"St Aethelthryth Without," Lotty told her as though she were a complete idiot. "It always was the church for Brockleford until that ghastly Victorian monstrosity was built last century. You mean you've never been?"

"Never even heard of it," Julie admitted and dared not look at Liam.

"Shame on you," Lotty looked at Stella but Miss McGinty was still in charge of the Brockleford Festival.

"Take the pair of them tomorrow," she advised. "I want Liam to get the statistics done for me today as it's his last day here and I won't get anyone else who can manage the computer systems as well as he does."

"True," Dotty agreed sadly and was glad she and her sister were going to be working in the new archive at the Manor from now on and that didn't even have a computer in it so she wouldn't have to deal with printers any more.

Julie glared meaningfully at her fiancé but he wouldn't look at her. She knew he no longer considered himself a Catholic but he wouldn't commit himself to a Protestant wedding either. Maybe St Aethel would convince him otherwise.

*   *   *

"There it is," Lotty announced proudly.

Julie and Liam peered around the squirming mass of black Labrador that was sharing the car seat with them and couldn't see anything except a yew hedge and a brick wall. Lotty had driven them due west of Brockleford until the mountains of Wales were starting to emerge from their distant haze then she had stopped her white Fiat Panda and made her proclamation.

"Where?" Julie asked.

"On the other side of the wall. Off you go and don't hang about, I've got Dotty and Billy at home waiting for their lunches."

"Aren't you coming?" Liam wanted to know. This was all starting to get a bit serious for his liking. Before too long he would be meeting a crisis of faith that would alienate him once and for all from his family, or from his fiancée.

"I'd better stay and keep Lady company or she'll chew the car to bits. Go on, off you go. It'll probably be locked but you can see the outside."

The betrothed couple crossed the deserted lane and went through the rickety gate in the wall. St Aethelthryth Without was barely bigger than a shed. Four walls, thatched roof, no spire, no bell tower, just a few lopsided tombstones and a sad air of neglect.

"Is it still used?" Julie muttered to Liam and took hold of his hand.

"Must be or Lotty wouldn't have suggested it. Want to try the door?"

"Yes, please."

The church wasn't locked as, they decided, there was nothing worth stealing from it. The pews were dark with age and had little animals carved on their ends, the walls were plain white and there was no coloured glass in any of the windows. A bleak wooden cross was on the stone altar which didn't even have a cloth on it. The windows were tiny but in each recess there was an arrangement of roses and ivy that left a scent in the air.

"It's beautiful," Julie breathed. "Please say we can get married here."

"If that's what you want."

Julie regarded him sadly. "But it's not what you want?"

Liam looked round at the plain interior with its antiquity almost a tangible force bearing down on him and he lied through his teeth. "I could get married in a church like this. I don't consider myself a Catholic any more and if you start coming here once I've gone away then the vicar will get to know you. You know you can borrow the car any time you like."

Julie cuddled against him. She knew quite well when he was lying to her but she so wanted to get married in St Aethel's that she really didn't care. "I'll start coming next Sunday. The day after you go. And I'll book a date with the vicar then. How do you fancy a Christmas wedding if we can get one?"

"I'll be home for four days. What kind of a honeymoon are you planning on having? Make it in the spring when I'm back from Australia."

Julie sighed deeply. She had a rough idea of the crisis of faith that Liam was facing and knew the worst thing she could do would be to push him. "OK, spring. With daffodils and narcissi in the windows." She reached up and kissed the side of his neck. "We'd better go or Lady will have eaten the car after all." She looked down the church just once more as she reached to close the door and hoped spring wouldn't seem too long in the coming.

*   *   *

It rained that evening. A cold, autumnal rain that even two habitual bench-users wouldn't brave. The sitting room in Labrador Cottage was quiet that night. Julie had finished the tails of her peacocks and was diligently working her way up their bodies. Liam had his nose in a book although Julie had heard only one page turn in the last hour.

"Getting nervous about Australia?" she asked as she threaded brown and metallic threads together.

"Not really. Looking forward to it. But I'll miss all of you. No, I'll be honest, I'm terrified."

"What of?"

"I don't know. Making a fool of myself I suppose. I can't always pretend you're drowning somewhere near the hundred metre marker."

Julie thought that was incredibly flattering. "What would help? You've got those nice trinkets Ted gave you. I know! You can have an engagement ring."

Liam thought she had gone completely mad. "But men don't usually...."

"Go and make the tea if you're not going out for your run. My mind is quite made up. "You're unemployed as of now and I'm sure Stella will let me out for a morning so we can go shopping. I'll send you away with a souvenir."

"You are mad," Liam told he as he went out to the kitchen.

"And if you don't come willingly I'll invite Ted along too."

"Invite him anyway and I'll buy both of you lunch. I presume you want coffee?"

"Yes, please."

* * *

Ted Ellerby had never really enjoyed shopping but this was different. This was being in the company of two young people, touchingly fond of each other and out to buy an engagement ring. Only the ring wasn't for her. And no matter what Julie suggested Liam insisted he hated it. Ted had to admit the two were very considerate, They frequently checked to make sure he wasn't getting tired and had quite a spat before it was resolved Julie would pay for the mid-morning coffee and cakes.

Ted wearily stirred his coffee and wished the morning could last for ever and that he had the strength to see it through to the end. "So, we have trailed round everywhere in Chester and yet you, young Liam, say there isn't one engagement ring you like."

"Well, it's true. I think the whole idea's daft anyway."

"You were very taken with that silver ring in whichever shop it was."

"No I wasn't."

Julie began to think she was missing out on something. She hadn't noticed Liam being taken with anything.

"Yes you were. You quite distinctly pointed it out to me."

Liam's mind clicked. "That wasn't silver, that was platinum and way out of budget."

"Which one was that?" Julie demanded, feeling even more left out.

Liam flushed. "Oh, Art Deco number. Nothing to get excited about."

"Well, why don't we go back and have another look at it?"

"Because it's outside the budget."

"I never set a budget."

"No, but I did."

Ted could bite his tongue no longer. "Would a loan help?"

"Yes please. The festival owes me a pay packet so I can leave you a cheque which you can cash next week."

Ted thought that was so sweet. He had seen the cost of the ring, had a rough idea what Stella paid her summer helpers and knew that Liam McGuinness was damning himself to a pauper's life in Australia so his fiancée could have a proper engagement ring.

Julie felt as though her jaw must have dropped half way down her front. "What is going on?"

Liam leaned across to her as she was sitting opposite and kissed her nose. "Nothing. We'll go back for it in a minute. Right, I'm off to the loo."

"Me too," Ted announced. "Look after the bags please, Julie."

Before she had gathered her wits, Julie found herself alone at a table in the middle of a department store restaurant. There weren't even many bags to guard anyway. She had wondered whether she dared to suggest a bookshop for the long-threatened tome but her nerve failed her, especially as they had Ted with them. She poured herself another cup of coffee and dreamed of a spring wedding in St Aethelthryth Without. After ten minutes she began to think one of the men had eaten something that disagreed. After fifteen minutes she thought maybe they were both ill and there was only one toilet. After twenty minutes she was determined to strangle whichever one of them appeared first.

It was Liam who got the sharp edge of her tongue. "Where have you been?" she hissed under cover of the bawling baby at the other side of the restaurant.

"Errand of mercy." Liam sat in the chair beside her. "OK, take off the thing."

Julie defensively closed the fingers of her right hand over those of her left. "Not until you tell me why. You've got that look on your face that probably means you've had something tattooed while you were in the loo. What have you done with Ted anyway?"

"He's waiting for us in the toy department."
"Why?"
"Never mind 'why'. Hand over that thing."
"Why?"
"Do as you're told."
"No. Not without a reason."
"I'll get it anyway."
"You won't."

Ted Ellerby knew that if he looked at the toys any longer he would finish up by buying that rather cute lion so he left the department and headed back to the restaurant. He could tell from the atmosphere that something was amusing the customers but he never imagined it would be Liam and Julie, just about repressing their giggles as they wrestled over the ring on her finger. Neither was saying anything but they had got into quite a tangle and if it hadn't been so comical the manageress would have thrown the pair of them out as soon as they started. Ted gave up and went back for the lion. The giraffe next to it was rather charming too. And those two would be scuffling for ages yet.

*   *   *

It wasn't really surprising, the other customers thought, that the man should win the battle in the end. He'd got the girl on the floor, screwed up under the table and nearly breathless from laughing but he got the ring off her finger in the end then gallantly helped her to her feet.

Liam was quite aware that they had attracted an audience and he could sense that they were all really on Julie's side so he thought he'd better do this publicly. He guessed his face was probably all red from the tussle anyway so it couldn't get any worse. In front of several diners, the shy Liam McGuinness knelt in front of his girlfriend, took a small box from his pocket and let her catch a glimpse of the ring inside.

"Marry me in the spring?" he asked as endearingly as he could.

The entire restaurant held its collective breath.

"Don't do it!" shouted a recently divorced diner.

"Go on, love, he's asked you ever so nice," advised another.

"Yes please," Julie squeaked.

The baby started bawling again, everyone, except one, applauded and Liam got to his feet so he could put the ring on her finger. The manageress interrupted the cuddling.

"Here, have a pot of coffee on the house. And may I point out we have an excellent bridal department on the second floor. Congratulations."

"Thank you," Julie managed. She sat back at the table opposite Liam and wasn't too surprised when Ted slipped into the chair at Liam's side. "I suppose you knew all about this?" she asked without taking her eyes off the elegant ring she now wore.

"Completely. I'm afraid I was the accomplice in the purchasing. And I witnessed the whole shameful charade from the sidelines. Liam, you really should consider a career in acting. Here, this is for you. And one for you too." He solemnly awarded Julie the lion and Liam the giraffe much to their mutual surprise but they were too polite to ask why. "Just to say 'thank you' for a lovely morning out. Quite cheered me up. I think I'll go home and write something fiendish for an alto to sing on his return from Australia."

"Any alto in particular?" Liam asked and put the mock-ruby ring in a saucer on the table.

"No, not really," Ted assured him with a knowing grin

"What are you doing with that?" Julie interrupted and picked the ring out of the coffee dregs.

"Leaving it there."

"But you gave that to me in front of my mother."

"OK, so you can keep it. Sorry. It was only ever meant as a bit of a joke."

Julie looked at the fingers of his left hand, blunted at the tips after years of stopping cello strings but fortunately remarkably slender. She thought about it while she playfully picked his hand off the giraffe it was holding and she nibbled at the nails for a while.

"Better get you some lunch if you're that hungry," Liam remarked idly but let her get on with it as it was quite pleasant. His attention was distracted by Ted and he didn't pay Julie that much notice until he worked out what she was up to, by which time it was too late. He glared at the vastly amused faces of the other two and tried to wrench the ruby ring from his little finger. "You cow!" he told Julie sharply. "You can just get that off again now."

"Can't, sorry. You turned down every other ring I offered you so you can wear that one until the spring. Come on, it'll be lunch time before we're home at this rate and I, at least, have got a job to go to in the afternoon."

"And I have got compositions to write," Ted put in. He turned to the young man who had got his teeth into the offending ring by this time. "And what about you?"

Liam gulped a bit. "'I've swallowed the stone."

Julie grabbed his hand. The ring was bitten in two and the stone was gone. "You have eaten my engagement ring. Boy, are you in trouble now."

"Should I go home on the bus?" Ted asked.

"Don't you dare. I might need you as a witness," Liam pleaded as the merciless Julie towed him by the elbow from the restaurant.

*   *   *

For the first time Julie had to light a fire in the sitting room of Labrador Cottage. The finished peacocks had been framed and hung on the wall above the fireplace and she often looked at them and smiled to remember. She sat in front of the fire and tussled with her knitting while trying to stop the tiny black and white kitten getting the wool into more of a tangle than it was already. When the cottage was so quiet it was hard not to let the memories get her down but having the kitten around certainly helped. It was the middle of November. In about six weeks Liam would be back for Christmas and she was so looking forward to it six weeks might as well have been six years. She wasn't sorry to be disturbed by the rattling of the door knocker. She knew all the sounds by now and that tap meant it was Ted at the door. It didn't have the politeness of Phyllis' serenade or the verve of Dotty's desire to be let in and there were no dogs so it had to be Ted.

"Hullo, want some lemon tea? I think there's still some in the caddy."

"Too kind, but ordinary tea is fine. Had a letter recently?"

"Just this morning. You?"

"Likewise. I think our Antipodean correspondent must write in batches. He certainly seems to be working hard. And speaking of work, I finished the second act of the opera last night."

"Well done. How many acts to go?"

"Just one more. I think I'll show it to Anna when it's finished and ask her opinion of Liam's potential. I kept in that fiendish aria he reckoned couldn't be sung. Just to prove he can, you understand." Ted wandered on into the sitting room while Julie made tea in the kitchen. "What are you knitting?" he enquired on her return. "I'm afraid your little friend is making quite a bed in it."

"This is Dmitri, after Shostakovich. He's wonderful company even if he isn't ginger. And this is supposed to be a jumper for Liam but as I've no idea what size he is and as it's the first thing I've ever knitted in my life it could just as well turn out to be a dish cloth."

Ted admired the length of green knitting. "I'm sure it'll be very smart. He's going to need a sweater after coming here from the sunshine of Australia. How's the car?"

"Fine. Wasn't it just so sweet of him to say I could use it while he's away?"

"Very Liam." Ted took his cup of tea and sat wearily on the sofa. "It's on evenings like this I feel my age. Haven't seen so much of you lately. How's work?"

"I hate to sound ungrateful but it's a lot better now Debbie's finally left. She's a nice kid but she sends me up the wall."

"And the studying?"

"Great. I'm really enjoying it."

"So life is perfect?"

Julie glanced at the Art Deco diamond and jet ring she wore. "Well, almost. We should have been coming back from Italy today."

"And Liam should be working as a curator but there we are. If I'd littered my life with should-have-beens I'd have topped myself long ago. We can go to Italy another time. And I've just accepted a commission. The London Symphony Orchestra have asked me to write another symphony."

"Congratulations. What made you decide to do it?"

Ted smiled fondly at her. "It's done me no end of good to get back to writing again. And I've got you two to thank for that. Never wanted to write another note after I lost George but now, well, you two have given me something to look forward to again."

Julie thought that was so sweet of him. He was turning into quite the father figure these days. "So when do I get my oboe concerto?"

"Hm. Can I do my symphony first?"

Julie smiled. "Of course."

The two sat in a companionable silence for a while until a log falling in the grate roused Ted from his thoughts. "You still happy to come to the Manor for Christmas?"

"Looking forward to it."

"I believe you are. Your whole life is just waiting for that redheaded barbarian to come home again and put the sparkle back."

"Meaning I'm miserable?" came the unoffended riposte.

"As sin. In spite of the delightful Dmitri's company. Julie, I'd better go. I only dropped by really to make sure our correspondent isn't neglecting either of us."

"Come for supper tomorrow?"

"One of your legendary vindaloos?"

"If you like."

"Well, maybe something a little milder. Good luck with the knitting."

"And good luck with the third act and the symphony."

"Thank you. I wonder if Liam's still wearing his engagement ring?"

"He'd better be. Poor Liam, he really didn't want that ring, did he? Still, he shouldn't have eaten the other one." Julie had thought at the time that the discreet silver ring had looked very classy on the third finger of her intended's right hand but he had maintained he would have preferred a tattoo. "He'll probably come up with some pathetic excuse like it gave him blisters with his javelin or something."

"Probably. You know what he's like."

"True. See you tomorrow then." Julie escorted her guest to the front door and shivered slightly in the autumnal breeze as she watched him drive away in his car. She pulled a face at the crooked lion on the wall then went back to the sitting room where her knitting was waiting all tangled up with a slumbering ball of fur.

"Dish cloth," she said to it fondly, picked out the sleeping kitten and started sorting out the jumble of wool.

More Chronicles of Brockleford will be coming soon:

Brockleford Wedding
Someone is getting married in Brockleford, but it doesn't go without a hitch and the new member of staff at the Festival is causing quite a bit of trouble.

Brockleford Opera
The opera is finally finished and the staff of Brockleford Festival are all busy trying to make sure the premiere is ready and not a total disaster.

Brockleford Olympics
It's the summer of 1996 and while the Atlanta Olympics are in full swing the new teacher at the local school decides to do something for the village to celebrate.